THE DEAD HORIZON

HUMANITY SERIES - BOOK TWO

SETH RAIN

Published by Human Fiction

ISBN 978-1-9162775-1-9

Copy Editing: Jane Hammett

Proofreading: Johanna Robinson

Cover Design: Damonza

YOUR FREE NOVELLA IS WAITING!

Visit **sethrain.com** to download your free digital copy of the prequel novella: *The Rogue Watcher* and sign up to Seth's Reading Group emails.

A BRIEF NOTE

I have used British English spelling throughout this series of books. Not only am I a Brit, but this story is set in Britain, and so it seems only right to use British English spelling. I hope this does not detract from your enjoyment.

Seth.

For Eve

"History is not progress or decline, but recurring gain and loss. The advance of knowledge deludes us into thinking we are different from other animals, but our history shows that we are not."

Taken from *Straw Dogs* (2002) by John Gray

THE DEAD HORIZON

ONE

SCOTT LAID the girl beside the other dead bodies.

The sun had moved from behind the hill, dark red through the valley to the west. The first January stars were out, specks of salt on a dark blue sky.

He placed the girl's soft toy, a pink elephant, beside her.

There was no sign on the faces of the dead that told why or how it had happened. No wound, no blood, no illness was apparent on their face or body. Each person he'd found looked as if they were in a deep sleep and nothing more. He knew what should happen to dead bodies but none of this was evident in what he saw. Within hours, the dead should already show signs of decomposition, within weeks, their organs, muscle and skin liquefied. And now, having been seven months since the Rapture, what remained should be little more than a skeleton. But this wasn't what he saw and he didn't understand why.

The Rapture had come and gone, and in its wake was a stillness.

Each body he found was cold, their skin almost translucent, and in those whose eyes remained open, he saw faint traces of violet colouring he couldn't explain. Scott had seen first-hand Mathew wield the power he had over humanity. With the help of the AI, in some way Scott did not yet grasp, Mathew had activated the Rapture. Whatever was inside people that killed them was also in some way preserving their bodies after death.

Scott took the lighter from his pocket and stooped to ignite the balls of paper tucked beneath the stacks of wooden pallets, upon which he'd laid out three bodies: a woman and her two children. The paper, doused in petrol, caught light quickly and the gentle whoosh of flames spread through the base of the pyre.

Hassness House, white through the smoke, stood tall and wide yet insignificant against the mountains behind. Scott walked towards the lake and out onto the pier, where he stood looking across the water, his back to the fire. By the side of the lake, sheep that had been left to their own devices drank the water. Two ducks landed, skidding across its surface, coming to a halt with a gentle splash.

There was no getting used to the sound or smell of burning bodies. He bowed his head. He didn't pray; after everything, that would have been wrong. Instead, he thought about Freya and Rebecca; at least they hadn't had to live through what he had. He thanked someone or something for that.

The pyres, no matter how safe he thought he'd made them, no matter how far away from anything that might catch fire he placed them, always reached a point that scared him. The fire grew fierce; he followed the sparks rise and fall as grey embers glowing at the edges, some reaching the lake, hissing as they touched the water.

He waited for the sun to disappear behind the mountains completely before making his way past the pyre and into the house. The fire had died down enough for him to relax and trust it to burn itself out. They were the last bodies from the house. He was finally alone.

Inside the large hallway, he lit a candle inside a glass jar and carried it up the narrow, steep staircase. He walked past several rooms, some that were still made up for visitors and some that had housed the bodies he'd taken outside and burned. He placed the candle on the table in his room then checked on the pyre through a window. Because of a faint breeze, the fire leaned away from the lake and towards the house. The bodies were no longer distinguishable. The girl's pink elephant had fallen and was lying on the ground in the sand he'd used to encircle the fire.

Something caught his eye in the valley at the far end of the lake. Movement. Scott leaned closer to the window, pushing the curtains aside. Two figures, walking towards the house. He'd not seen anyone for months – certainly not during the time he'd been in the Lake District. He took a step backwards and blew out the candle. His hand, and on it his date, shone in the twilight. Couldn't be Watchers – he had another three months. He reached beneath the bed and pulled out a wooden crate, lifted the lid, then stood to check outside again. The figures were still heading towards him. He rummaged in the crate filled with weapons and ammunition and took out a revolver. After checking it was loaded, he pushed it into his coat pocket.

Outside, the figures were hidden behind a row of trees. The burning pyre had given him away.

Moving to a room at the far end of the house, he looked through the window. He could leave now, but he'd be leaving behind guns and ammunition, not to mention the food and water he'd collected and stored in the cellar beneath the house. He took the revolver from his coat pocket and checked it again.

The sun had disappeared. Only the fire outside gave him any light by which to see the figures approaching. The smoke from the pyre swirled upwards, blocking a clear view across the lake.

A figure moved along the path. A young woman. Followed by what appeared to be an older woman holding a child. The older woman stumbled, using one hand to rest against the stone wall beside her. Scott closed his eyes and tried to think. Maybe they'd keep walking, not stop at the house.

He made his way down the stairs and out the front door, all the time hiding.

The heat from the fire was intense.

He stood behind a wall to one side of the front door.

The woman reappeared beside the fire, a child in her arms, its legs dangling over her stomach. From the way they moved and glanced at one another now and then, he guessed the young woman beside her was her daughter. The younger woman wore a huge coat, far too big for her, making it appear as though she had no hands.

'Hello?' the older woman shouted.

Scott moved further behind the wall.

The woman gazed all around then stared at the fire; she pulled the child in her arms higher up on her chest.

'Hello?' she shouted again, her voice breaking.

Scott shook his head and walked towards the women. 'Can I help you?'

The woman flinched and held the child in her arms more tightly. 'Please help us,' she said.

'Are you being followed?' Scott asked.

'I don't think ... I don't know.' She stumbled, and the younger woman put out a hand to steady her. She stared at Scott, unsure, keeping several steps away from him.

'Where have you come from?' Scott asked the mother.

'We've been searching for help for weeks,' the woman said.

Scott opened the front door and helped her inside. The young woman stood in the doorway, her expression disapproving.

'Dawn,' the mother said. 'It's okay.'

Dawn turned and watched the pyre burn.

'She'll be fine,' the woman said. 'Leave her. She's stubborn.'

Scott helped the woman to a settee in the living room. She sat and held the child so it could feed.

'Do you need anything?' he asked, turning away from her. 'Water? Food?'

'Yes,' she said, sounding as though she might cry. 'Yes. Please.'

Scott walked quickly to the kitchen, took the revolver from his pocket and placed it in a drawer. From the coldroom he took bread and jam. He poured a jug of water and took the things on a tray back to the living room. He placed the tray on the table between the two settees and poured a glass of water. The woman took a few sips then threw back what remained. She placed the glass on the table and held the child against her chest, then leaned the back of her head against the settee.

'What are you doing here?' Scott asked. The abruptness of his own words and voice surprised him.

The woman lifted her head, tears in her eyes. She took the child from her breast, covered herself and showed the baby to Scott. It was pale and sickly, its eyes barely open.

'I wish I'd not survived the Rapture,' she said. 'I wish He'd taken us then.'

Scott had not spoken to anyone about the Rapture since the day it had happened.

'His date,' the woman said, looking down at the child in her arms. 'It's tomorrow.'

Scott sat on the settee, motionless.

'Mine too,' she said. 'I can't bear it any longer.'

There was no getting used to having a date – it was always there, waiting – Scott understood that. But he'd learned to live with it. The thought of having a child with a date, though, struck him as impossible to live with. He felt the woman's pain and saw in the way she held the boy close to her chest, a denial that came at a price – one that meant she had to work tirelessly to not give in to it.

'I'm sorry,' he said.

The woman kissed the child's head.

'Watchers?' Scott asked. 'Are they following you?'

The woman glanced out of the window. 'I think so. They must be.'

'What about...'

The woman steeled herself. 'My daughter?' She lowered her voice and whispered, 'Her date is in just over a month. Twenty-fourth of February.' She leaned forward to check again that they were alone. 'She doesn't know.'

Again, Scott considered having a child with a date. Not only this, but a date after his own. It was cruel to think he'd have to leave behind a child to deal with their date alone.

'You're Scott?' the woman asked. 'Scott Beck?'

'How do you know my—'

'I'm Theresa, this is Nathanial, and outside is Dawn.'

'Have we met?' Scott asked.

'No. But I know who you are. Everyone knows. You tried to stop Mathew. You're the Chosen whose date is wrong.'

Scott didn't know where to begin and could only shake his head.

'Please,' the woman said. 'Will you keep her here with you?'

'With me?'

'She doesn't know about the dates. And I can't...' She stopped, her eyes filling with tears. 'I can't have her with me when...'

'Where are they? The Watchers?'

'I don't know. They appear now and then. It's no use. I can't hide from them. And look at him. He's not well.'

Something about the child's stillness meant Scott couldn't look at him for long.

'Please,' she said. 'I don't want her to know. I can leave now, with Nathanial.'

'How old is she?'

'Fifteen. She need not know her date before they come for her. If there was another way...'

Scott looked around into the hall but there was still no sign of Dawn.

'She's a good child. Stubborn, a little surly, but she can look after herself. She's strong.'

Scott sat forward in the chair. 'Where will you go?'

Theresa peered through the window at the dark sky. 'I don't know. But I don't want her with me when they come for us.'

The child flinched in her arms.

'Please,' Theresa said. 'I can do this. I think. As long as I know Dawn is safe. For now.'

Scott watched the child sleeping. He nodded.

Theresa exhaled. 'Thank you,' she said in a broken voice.

Scott nodded again.

'Your date,' she said, nodding at his hand. 'The date of the Rapture. It's wrong isn't it?'

'My date is the same as the Rapture. But a different year.'

'It's wrong,' she said. 'I know it is. And it gives us hope.'

Scott stared at his hand. He didn't believe her but didn't know what to say.

'There's something else,' she said. She lowered her voice. 'Her date – Dawn's date. It's wrong too.'

Scott sighed, ready to tell her how many people had thought the same.

'Do you know Juliet?' she asked.

Scott couldn't hide his surprise. 'How do you know Juliet?'

'I don't. But I've been told you do.'

Scott shifted in his seat. 'I haven't seen or spoken to her since ... since the Rapture.'

'She's gone north,' the woman said. 'Scotland. To one of the lochs. Do you know which one?'

'How do you know all this?'

'Everyone who's left knows about Juliet. And about you and what happened with Mathew. Juliet can speak with the AI. Please, you must ask her about Dawn's date. I know her date is wrong. I know it.'

Scott waited. He had come to the Lakes to be alone, to live in peace. There was no use fighting Mathew or the AI. He'd tried.

'I'm sorry to have to ask this of you,' she said, as if reading his mind. 'But please. Will you help her?'

'I don't know whether Juliet can speak to the AI any longer.'

'But will you try?'

Scott didn't answer.

Theresa leaned forward and took the bread and jam. 'Do you mind?'

'Please. Take it.'

Theresa held the sandwiches close to her chest as she stood. 'Please,' she said. 'Will you look after her?'

Scott nodded. There was nothing else he could do. 'You can stay here,' he said. 'Until you're rested.'

The woman shook her head. 'I will fall asleep. If I stop now, I won't have the strength to leave.'

Scott stood with the woman.

'I have more food and water,' he said.

'This will be plenty. Thank you.'

'At least let me give you a blanket, a coat?'

They walked into the hallway and Scott opened a cupboard and offered them to her.

'Thank you,' she said, taking them. 'You're very kind.'

Theresa walked through the hall and out into the night air.

'Dawn,' she said. 'I need to talk to you.'

Dawn appeared from behind the fire. Theresa leaned over and said something Scott couldn't hear. Dawn nodded, now and then glancing at Scott. Theresa hugged her daughter, who stood motionless as her mother kissed her several more times.

'I'll be back soon,' Theresa said to Scott.

He felt the need to play along. 'We'll see you soon.'

'Goodbye, Dawn,' Theresa said.

Dawn raised a hand but didn't look at her.

Her mother set off the way they'd come.

Scott walked into the house. 'Are you coming inside?' he asked Dawn. 'You must be hungry.'

Dawn lifted her head, her eyes dark, her mouth a straight line, and followed him.

Scott showed her into the living room and asked if she'd like to sit. She looked at the jug of water, then at Scott.

'Go ahead,' he said.

She grabbed the jug with two hands, lifted it and drank. Her fingernails were black, her hair matted, her hands bruised and cut. Eventually she stopped drinking and gasped for air. Water dribbled down her chin and onto the front of her baggy coat.

'Are you hungry?' he asked.

She placed the jug on the table and sat on the settee. She was clearly exhausted, but there was a mistrust in her eyes that meant she would not relax with Scott in the same room, so he left.

Returning half an hour later, he found Dawn asleep, in the same position she was in when he left, except now with her head slumped back against the chair and her eyes closed. Scott took a blanket from the back of the settee and covered her.

Outside, the fire was still burning.

TWO

KNOCKING at the door made Scott open his eyes and sit up. The room was cold, the hearth filled with ash. Dawn was asleep, one arm hanging over the edge of the settee. He checked the clock on the wall and made out the two hands pointing to somewhere close to early morning.

More knocking.

He'd gone months without seeing or speaking to anyone, and now there was a young woman lying asleep on his settee and someone knocking on the door.

Scott opened it. Two men stood outside, each dressed in a long grey coat. Watchers.

'Scott Beck?'

Scott looked over at the pyre, which smouldered in the chilly early morning air.

The taller Watcher, young but clearly the one in charge, followed Scott's gaze. He had one blue eye and one brown eye.

'It's necessary,' the Watcher said. 'Not pleasant, but it's the right thing to do.'

The other Watcher, a short, sickly looking man, said, 'May their souls be with God.'

Scott focused on this Watcher and lifted an eyebrow. 'They are not here,' he said.

The tall Watcher said, 'We know.' He reached into his coat pocket and took out an envelope. 'Mathew wants you to have this.'

Scott stared at the envelope. He knew what it was.

The second Watcher nodded at what remained of the pyre. 'May you gain a place in Heaven.'

The tall Watcher seemed to be embarrassed by the other man's religious language and moved uncomfortably, shifting his weight from one leg to the other.

Scott took the envelope. Something made him turn. Dawn, standing behind him, rubbed her eyes then stared coldly at the two men.

The second Watcher's face softened, his smile twisting as if he'd forgotten how to do it. 'Hello,' he said, moving to look past Scott.

'Don't,' Scott said.

The first Watcher appeared to register Scott's disapproval and took a step backwards. The second Watcher didn't.

Dawn's face hardened.

'Leave her alone,' Scott said.

The tall Watcher laid a hand on the other Watcher and gestured for them to leave.

'Soon,' the second Watcher said to the girl. 'He will come for you and then you shall be truly home. Do not fear Him.'

Scott stood directly between Dawn and the Watcher, who looked surprised at Scott's disapproval.

The tall Watcher held up his hands. 'Forgive him. My friend is devout. He means well.'

'Please leave.'

The other Watcher stared into Scott's eyes. 'You don't believe?'

Scott glanced behind at Dawn.

'Just go,' he said.

'No matter,' the short Watcher said. 'He believes in you.'

Scott shook his head slowly. He despised their language, their unwavering, unfounded belief.

The short Watcher raised a hand to Dawn, who glowered at him. The Watchers left, walking away in the same direction Dawn's mother had walked the night before.

Scott closed the door and motioned for Dawn to follow him, but she remained by the door.

In the living room, he made a fire. The sound and smell took him back outside, to the pyre.

After several minutes, Dawn appeared in the doorway, clasping her hands across her stomach, over her enormous coat.

Scott turned the letter in his hand.

Dawn walked back into the room and lay down on the settee, covering herself with the blanket.

He walked to the large window and gazed out over Lake Buttermere. The mountains were dark blues and greys. The sun would rise fully soon.

'It's my date,' he said. 'They know the year now. After twelve years, I'd know.' He looked over at Dawn, who was staring into the fire. He tapped the cream envelope against his other hand several times. If he opened it, he would no longer have to fear his date. But it would be final. He would know. He walked over to the fire and held the envelope to the flames.

The edges curled and smouldered before catching light. The flames covered the envelope until he had to drop it into the fire. It folded in on itself and began to fall apart, the charred embers dropping through the spaces between the logs.

He turned away from the fire. Dawn was sitting up, watching him burn the letter.

'You must be hungry,' he said.

She pushed her hair, lank and greasy, back from her face and shook her head.

'I'll get you some food, anyway. It's up to you if you eat it.'

She didn't do or say anything. Scott took this as a win.

Dawn's eyes were a dark brown, almost black, and he couldn't get over how sad she looked.

'Take no notice of what the Watchers say.' Scott sat forward in his chair, unsure of what he was saying, or why he was saying it.

The girl stared back at him, her mouth closed tight.

'They are foolish men,' he said, 'who believe in fairy tales.'

The flames from the fire were reflected in her eyes. The burning of bodies had become a way of life for Scott and he'd grown accustomed to it. But for a moment he saw it through the eyes of a young woman. He'd set fire to whole families, whole villages. The thought of entering a town or city filled him with a visceral dread that kept him well away from them. To go anywhere new meant having to take care of the bodies. It was easier to stay in the small hamlets and villages in the Lake District. Everything he needed was here: shelter, food and water. The few survivors stayed well away.

Scott left the room, leaving Dawn to stare out of the window. She'd be with him for a while, and already he resented it. Even before the Rapture he'd preferred his own company to that of others. Now that he'd had the experience of being alone – truly alone – for months on end, the company of another person was excruciating.

He opened the pantry. Hundreds of cans, labelled and organised. He took a can of baked beans, opened it and tipped them into a bowl. He'd made a loaf earlier that day. He took the plate into the living room and placed it on the table. It was clear Dawn wouldn't eat while he was there, watching her, so he left.

He hadn't asked for her to be there and it annoyed him that she showed little thanks. He was done with other people and their needs and desires. Humanity had walked blindly into what Mathew had planned for it and he wasn't going to fight it any longer.

After several minutes, he heard the sounds of Dawn eating and drinking.

THREE

THE DAYS PASSED and snow and ice covered the mountain tops. The lake was still, but for the ripples made by the boat and oars.

Scott stopped rowing and the boat drifted towards the shore behind him. In the bucket next to his feet were three trout. The boat ran aground, grinding through the pebbles before stopping. He stepped out of the boat, taking the bucket with him.

Dawn was further along the lake, sitting on the bank, wrapped up in a thick cardigan and the too-big coat. In almost a month, she'd spoken only a handful of words. And even though she must have known she wouldn't see her mother or brother again, she was completely closed off from him.

He'd not tried to talk to her; the silence suited him. During meals they sat together in the dining room, silent, not looking at one another. It was never uncomfortable, simply something they both preferred. At night, Scott read: the large house had an extensive library filled with all the books he'd wanted to read when he hadn't the time. Dawn had found art equipment in one room: paints and pencils. It was easy to see how good she was and how much she must have practised. In the room she'd chosen, she had replaced the pictures and paintings of the lake and the house with her own artwork. She mostly painted landscapes, not only of Lake Buttermere, but of places she must have seen travelling with her mother. Her landscapes were always dark with menacing skies and looming clouds. There were only three paintings of people – all of her mother. The largest showed a dark figure painted from behind, her mother's head turned to the left, the silhouette of her features painted the blue of early morning. Scott didn't ask Dawn about her paintings but he did all he could, without saying a word, to encourage her. She had even hung a few of them along the hallway outside her room, with the suggestion they were there to dry.

In the kitchen, using a barbecue and gas bottle he'd taken from a nearby shop, he'd set up a functioning stove. Having prepared the trout, he placed the fillets in the pan. He'd not eaten much fish before it happened, but since he'd lived beside the lake, fish had become his favourite meal. It was the ritual of catching and preparing it that added to its enjoyment and taste. The meal was also something that Dawn, even though she would never say so, clearly enjoyed.

The sound and smell of the fish cooking brought Dawn into the kitchen where she sat at the large table, laying out a piece of paper and her pencils.

Scott seasoned the fish, now and then glancing across at Dawn. She sat hunched over the page, her pencil moving slowly at first before bursting out in sweeping arcs. Her drawing always exhibited a confidence, a knowingness, that fascinated him. It was as if she could see the lines there already, before she made them with her pencil.

The fish sizzled in the pan, its smell filling the kitchen.

He poured two glasses of water and placed them on the table.

Dawn stopped drawing momentarily and laid the table with placemats and cutlery before returning to her drawing.

Scott shallow-fried some potatoes, with the vague notion he was making fish and chips. He wanted to ask Dawn whether she'd ever had fish and chips, the way he remembered it, wrapped in paper, the sharpness of vinegar rising from the crispy chips.

He placed two plates on the table and doused his plate with salt and vinegar. Dawn did the same.

As always, they ate in silence, the only sound knives and forks clinking against plates. The sound of eating had always irritated him, but in the kitchen, with Dawn, it didn't trouble him. In fact, he welcomed it.

'Thank you,' Dawn said.

It was one of the few times she spoke to him: to thank him after a meal. It was during these moments, when she thanked him, waited for him to finish eating and took the things to wash up, when he felt the most pity for her. In these moments, she was older, losing the childishness he saw when he watched her draw. She had just over two weeks before her date. The meals he made her were about keeping her healthy, giving her nourishment. But for what? He thought about a time when she wouldn't be there. The date and year of her death were definite and there was nothing he or anyone else could do about that. He placed his knife and fork on his plate and Dawn stood to take both plates.

'Thank you,' Scott said.

Dawn put the plates in the sink. She covered them in hot water from the kettle. After washing and drying them and placing them in the cupboard, she sat at the table and continued drawing.

The drawing, too, would end. All the drawings she'd never do would disappear with her.

'You're good,' he said, his voice deep and croaky. He cleared his throat. 'They're really good.'

Her hand stopped, hovering above the page. Then she continued.

He took a can of pineapple chunks from the pantry, prepared two bowls and set one down in front of her.

'No, thank you,' she said.

'You don't like pineapple?'

She shook her head.

'Have you tried it before?'

Dawn looked up from her drawing and eyed the bowl suspiciously. She shook her head.

'It's good,' he said. 'Try it.'

As Scott was finishing his, she put down her pencil and began to scoop up the chunks of pineapple with her spoon.

After she'd finished, Dawn carried the empty bowls to the sink.

Then she began to cough.

Scott noticed her face was flushed, her lips swollen. She held her throat. He looked at the opened can of pineapple on the kitchen worktop.

'You're allergic,' he said, standing quickly.

He reached for her but she recoiled.

'Don't,' she said. 'Don't touch me.'

'It's an allergic reaction,' he said again, raising his hands.

'Don't touch me,' she said, wheezing.

Scott backed away. 'We need to get to a pharmacy. Have you had an allergic reaction before?'

She shook her head and folded her arms, shivering, reaching for her throat again.

The nearest pharmacy was twenty minutes away.

Outside, he opened the passenger door to the 4x4 and waited for her to get in. Gasping for air, she arranged her large coat and folded her arms across her chest. He covered her in a blanket.

'It's difficult, I know, but you must keep your breathing slow. Try not to panic.'

He ran around the front of the 4x4 and got in.

Dawn wheezed, trying to speak. 'Dying…'

'No,' Scott said. 'You're not dying.'

Her eyes were sad again, filled with tears; she wiped them with a shaking hand.

'No,' he said. 'It's not your time.'

Her eyes pierced his and he couldn't hold her stare, knowing he'd given too much away. He held the steering wheel tightly and set off.

The roads were narrow, made even more so by the hedges left to grow across the road.

There had been a boy in his class at school, Jimmy, who had to have some sort of injector with him. They had a lesson once on how to use it in case Jimmy ever needed help with his. Scott had listened intently because the nurse who was speaking to them said Jimmy could die without it. It was ridiculous that he could die from eating nuts. The nurse said he didn't even need to eat one. Just being around them was enough. Scott never ate nuts after that lesson.

With no other cars for miles, he sped along the lanes. He'd visited the pharmacy once before to stock up on basics and knew roughly where it was.

Scott emulated the speed at which she should exhale and inhale. 'Slowly…'

'Hurts,' she croaked, holding her throat, then her stomach.

'Everything will be okay. I know where the pharmacy is. You need an injection.'

He drove quickly through the village and came to an abrupt stop outside the pharmacy. He showed Dawn to the door he'd broken to get in the last time. Inside, it was as he'd left it.

He sat Dawn on a chair and began searching through the drawers and cupboards.

Dawn coughed and gasped for air.

Scott pulled out drawers, letting them fall to the floor.

He stopped and closed his eyes, trying to remember. Anti-something ... histamine? He opened his eyes and began to read the labels of the tubes and bottles in front of him. He ran his finger along the labels until he saw it: EpiPen. The memory came back to him and he clutched a handful of the tubes.

He scattered them on the counter and held one of them closer to read the instructions.

'Wait,' Dawn said, gasping. She unfastened her coat and the thick cardigan beneath. She looked down at her stomach.

Scott, holding an EpiPen, watched her stroke her swollen stomach.

'You're pregnant?' he asked. 'But you're...'

She cradled her stomach and nodded.

She was fifteen. A child. She wiped her eyes with the back of her hand.

There was nothing he could see on the EpiPen instructions about pregnancy.

As he read the label again and again, he thought about her silence, the way she looked at him, the way she recoiled from him. She was scared of him because he was a man.

'We have no choice,' he said.

He removed the cap from the EpiPen.

She nodded.

He injected her in the top of her leg through her trousers.

It worked almost immediately. She began to breathe more easily and deeply. Her face regained colour and her hands were no longer shaking.

He leaned against the counter and closed his eyes.

'Thank you,' Dawn said, holding her stomach.

FOUR

AS USUAL, swirls of smog enveloped the centre of Birmingham. It was no surprise that Noah had come to Birmingham to hide from Mathew and his Watchers. There was no surveillance as far as Scott could see: no CCTV apparatus on buildings or high poles, and no drones flew above them.

Freya reached for Scott's hand.

'Is this the one?' Freya asked, pointing to a bar.

'It's the one I was told about.'

He held her hand and led her down some steps into a bar next to New Street Station. It was busy. A loud, dull, thudding beat vibrated through the floor. Now the prohibition had been lifted, people had returned en masse to try the latest chemically enhanced drinks, maybe with some hope of forgetting what was happening. Scott couldn't get used to how people appeared to carry on as if nothing had changed. It was either defiance or denial: whichever it was, most people behaved as though they hadn't been told the date of their death.

Scott led the way through the bar, looking for Noah.

'He doesn't drink,' Freya said. 'Why would he be here?'

Scott didn't say anything. His eyes shifted from one corner of the bar to another.

'There,' Freya said, letting go of Scott's hand and heading for a large figure sitting at the far end of the bar.

When Freya called, Noah swivelled around on his stool. It was fleeting, but he smiled. Freya wrapped her arms around him.

'You're here,' she said, letting him go.

Scott nodded at Noah. 'Good to see you.'

'Don't get too gushy,' Noah said, turning back to the bar and his drink.

He was drunk – and wasn't wearing his Watchers coat.

'How are you?' Freya asked, laying the palm of her hand on his back.

'I'm doing great,' Noah said, his eyes on the whisky in his glass. 'Just great.'

Freya glanced at Scott, concerned.

Scott shrugged.

'You hear what happened to Isaiah?' Noah asked. 'What Mathew did to him?'

'Yes,' Scott said.

Freya let her hand drop from Noah's back.

'He did it for you,' Noah said, talking to Scott without acknowledging him.

'He was a good man,' Freya said.

'He loved you,' Noah said to Freya.

Freya's face reddened. Scott couldn't help feeling jealous – even now, after everything.

'And it was all for nothing,' Noah said, slurring his words.

Scott recognised anger and disappointment in Noah's face. He was pensive, his movements slow but direct. Scott couldn't escape the feeling of guilt, of responsibility for what had happened to Isaiah. It was clear that Noah blamed him too.

Freya stood next to Noah at the bar to encourage him to look at her.

'We need your help,' she said.

Noah snorted, a wry smile shifting across his face. 'When have I heard that before?'

Freya glanced at Scott, but he knew it was not his place to ask.

'I can't leave her there with Mathew,' Freya said, raising her voice. 'We asked Juliet to help us stop Mathew. Now he has her locked away, it's up to us to get her out of there. We can't do it without you.'

Noah waved his hand. 'I'm done with all that.'

Freya looked shocked, hurt. But Scott already knew what Noah would say.

'Done with it?' Freya asked. 'What do you mean?'

Noah slammed his glass on the bar. 'I'm done with Watchers, with the Chosen, with God.'

Freya covered her mouth.

'Noah,' Scott said, edging closer. 'We need your help.'

Noah spun around, his brow furrowed, his eyes dark with anger. 'Don't!' he snapped at Scott. 'Isaiah did everything to help you and you couldn't do it.'

Scott took a step back. 'I wanted to,' he said, remembering the moment he'd pulled the trigger. There was the aeroplane overhead, the fountain splashing behind him. He had been ready to do it. He had pulled the trigger.

No bullet.

'I tried.'

Noah's face softened a little, his anger subsiding. 'What about all the times we had to convince you? All the time we lost babysitting you.'

'I didn't ask for any of it.'

Noah threw his hands in the air. 'Here we go. Scott, the victim.'

'Let's go,' Scott said, reaching for Freya. 'He's drunk. There's no point.'

'Go on,' Noah said, waving him away. 'Run away. It's what you do best.'

Scott's mind raced with things to say, but the moment passed. He waited for Freya.

'Please, Noah,' she said. 'We asked Juliet for help. It's our fault she's there. That Mathew has her.'

Noah finished his drink and signalled to the barman for another.

Freya ran fingers through her hair; Scott knew it was a sign she wasn't getting her way. 'Noah,' she said. 'You're a good man. I know you can help us get her out of there. But I don't have time to wait around here convincing you. Can we just jump straight to you agreeing to help?'

The barman placed a drink on the bar and looked questioningly at Freya.

'Scott wants the same as me,' she said. 'He wants to help Juliet.'

'I don't care what he wants,' Noah said.

'Then do it for me,' Freya said. 'For Juliet.'

Noah didn't move.

'Let's go,' Scott said.

Freya glanced at Scott, her expression hard. 'Wait.' She turned to Noah again. 'We have a self-driver – off the grid. It can take us to London, where Juliet's being kept. We have a contact – one of Mathew's Watchers. Samuel. When Gabriel shot Scott, Samuel was the one who helped me get him to a surgical-machine. He can help us.'

Noah sniffed and shrugged. Freya took a step towards Scott.

'We'll be outside the art gallery at noon tomorrow,' she said to Noah. 'If you have any fight left, be there.'

Scott stared at Noah's back. Everything Noah had said was true.

Freya led the way out of the bar and into the smog-filled air of Birmingham.

FIVE

SCOTT LEFT through the back door of the pharmacy and headed round to the village high street. Dawn took her time, wheezing now and then, but she seemed to be on the mend. He wanted to ask her about the baby, but everything she did, her every expression, told him now was not the time to ask.

'What's that?' Dawn pointed to a plume of smoke rising above a cottage roof.

The high street was empty. Whoever it was, he knew they were burning bodies.

'Stay close,' he said.

Scott dropped a bag of medicine and EpiPens into the 4x4 before leading the way around the cottage towards the centre of the village and the smoke.

Turning a corner, the sound of roaring flames greeted them. In the centre of the square was a fire, smoke billowing straight up.

Scott waited at the edge of the square, motioning for Dawn to stay close, searching for whoever was burning the bodies.

Dawn pointed. 'Look.'

A dog, a black-and-white spaniel, appeared nearby and stood alert, its tail wagging. Scott walked towards it, and it lowered its head and sniffed the air.

'It's okay, boy,' Scott said.

The dog sat, his head tilted, listening to Scott's voice.

'Joe!' a voice called.

The dog spun around and bolted towards an old man who approached them from behind the fire, through the smoke. Even though he walked slightly hunched over and with a limp, he appeared to be a powerful man. 'Hey!' he shouted. 'Who are you?'

Scott glanced back at Dawn, who had moved further behind him.

The dog followed the old man.

Scott narrowed his eyes against the smoke and heat, and saw he was carrying a rifle.

'Please,' Scott said, holding up his hands. 'We're not dangerous.'

'Who are you?' the old man bellowed again.

'Scott. I'm Scott. This is Dawn. We came here for the pharmacy.'

The old man slowed and relaxed his grip on the rifle. The dog overtook him and sat a few feet away.

'What do you need from the pharmacy?' the old man asked, his rifle pointing at the ground.

Scott looked to Dawn. 'She had an allergic reaction. I had to find an EpiPen.'

The old man appeared to relax. 'You can't be too careful,' he said. 'I've not seen anyone for some time. A while back there were young men going about, looking for trouble. Where you from?'

'I've been living here in the Lake District since it

happened,' Scott said. 'The girl has been with me a couple of weeks. Lake Buttermere.'

The old man's expression softened.

The dog edged closer to Dawn, who offered her hand for him to sniff.

'He won't hurt you, gal,' the old man said. 'Joe's a friendly sort. Not that it'll do him any good.'

The dog wagged his tail at the mention of his name.

Scott looked at the fire.

'There's still a fair few left,' the old man said. He glanced at Dawn and lowered his voice. 'I try to do two or three houses a day. It's not right leaving them like that, is it? I hope someone'd do the same for me.'

Scott shifted uncomfortably and nodded.

Joe loped towards the far end of the village square, where Scott could see something moving in the hedgerows.

'Rats,' the old man said. 'Some big 'uns now. And they're bold critters too. That's why I need to get this done.' He pointed to the fire.

'Dawn?' Scott called after her, but the roaring of the fire and Joe's barking drowned out his voice.

'She'll be fine. Joe's all sound and fury – he won't go near 'em.'

'How long have you been here?' Scott asked. 'In the village?'

'A few months.' The old man shifted and held his back, as if in discomfort. 'We were only passing through, but I couldn't leave them all like this. The bodies.'

The fire roared.

The old man took a wad of papers from his coat pocket. 'I take photos from the houses when I can. I don't know what I'll do with them all. Just doesn't seem right laying them out and setting fire to them without doing something to remember them. I find out their names from their things and write them down on the back of these photographs. See?'

Scott took the photographs. Men, women, children – all smiling, all happy. He handed them back.

'Mick,' the old man said, offering his hand. 'Does she know her date?'

Scott shook his head.

'But you know it?' Mick asked.

He nodded. 'I wish I didn't.'

'Figured,' Mick said. 'No need to tell me. I don't need to know. I can tell it's not far away, the way you are with her.' He scratched his head. 'That damn computer and its dates.' He pointed to the fire. 'And now look what it's led to.'

'Do you know yours?' Scott asked.

The old man stared across at Dawn and Joe, his expression not changing. 'No. And I don't intend on finding out. Not until ... well ... you know. Until it's too late.'

Dawn walked towards them, followed by Joe. She breathed heavily, reminding Scott of the allergic reaction attack she'd had.

'Take it easy,' he said.

The paleness of Dawn's face from earlier had been replaced with a much healthier flush.

'I'm done for today,' Mick said. 'You want feeding?'

Scott was about to decline the offer when Dawn spoke for him.

'Yes please,' she said, bending over to stroke the dog.

'Sure,' Scott said.

They walked across the village square, past the fire and out onto the lane at the other side. Mick pointed to a pub. 'Red Lion,' he said. 'Thought it was good a place as any to call home.'

Scott smiled. 'Why not?'

The old man led the way into the building. He'd arranged it as if it was open for business. A fire burned in the hearth at the centre of the pub, the tables were set out ready for opening time, and the bar itself was decked with spirits and glasses ready to use.

'I always fancied running a pub,' Mick said. 'Fancy a pint?'

'It all works?'

'Sure it works. I just need to turn on the generator in the cellar and we're away.'

Joe galloped in and jumped up onto the bench running opposite the bar, where he sat down with a humph, resting his head on the edge of the chair. Dawn followed and sat beside him, her arms on the table.

'You want a drink, little 'un?' Mick asked.

'Thank you,' Dawn said.

'Got just the thing for you,' Mick said, hobbling round to an opening in the bar.

Scott sat opposite Dawn and Joe.

'You can stay here the night,' Mick shouted over. 'Have rooms upstairs you can use. Would be good to have someone else around for a day or two.'

'We should get back,' Scott said.

'What for?' Dawn asked. 'Can't we stay?' She stroked Joe.

Scott thought of a few reasons why but couldn't think of one convincing enough. 'Sure,' he said to Mick. 'Thanks.'

'Great,' Mick said, disappearing up the stairs. 'I'll make sure it's all set up for you.'

Dawn, her eyes on Joe, stroked the dog's head over and over. 'You said I wouldn't die,' she said.

Scott was still getting used to Dawn speaking to him. 'What?'

'Earlier,' she went on, still not looking at him. 'When I was having the attack, you said I wouldn't die. That it wasn't my time.'

'I was right,' he said.

'But how did you know? You sounded like you knew.' Her eyes turned on him, round and dark, expectant. 'You know my date, don't you?'

Scott looked over to the bar, not knowing what to say.

'Tell me,' Dawn said. 'Please.'

'I don't know it,' Scott said.

She bowed her head; she knew he was lying. 'She's not coming back, is she?'

'What?'

'Mum. She's not coming back.'

Scott couldn't tell her another lie. He shook his head.

She turned to Joe and stroked his head. Joe's eyes closed each time she stroked him, his tail thumping against the bench.

'I'm sorry,' Scott said. 'She made me promise.'

'I don't want to die before it's born,' she said. 'Not now.'

Scott thought of words to use but none were good enough. He had to say something. 'I'm going to take you to someone I know. She'll help us with the baby. And she can help with your date.'

SIX

THE FOLLOWING MORNING, Scott followed Mick into a house on the other side of the village.

Mick stopped in the hallway to look at a collection of photographs hanging on the wall. Scott followed. They both focused on one photograph, black-and-white, years old, of a young couple on their wedding day. Their faces – young, excited – smiled back at them. After a moment's consideration, Mick took it from the wall, removed the back of the frame and carefully took out the photograph. Resting the frame on the floor, he threaded the photograph into the inside pocket of his coat.

'We need their names,' Mick said, motioning for Scott to follow him into the living room.

The furnishings and decorations were old-fashioned, with tired wallpaper and paintwork. There were two chairs, each discoloured and misshapen, in which the couple had sat night after night. Despite its outdated appearance, the living room was tidy and cared for. A layer of dust covered everything, and in the shards of morning light coming through the front window, dust motes hung in the air.

Mick had found a collection of envelopes and was reading them.

'Derek and Jane Martins,' he said. He took the photograph from his pocket and wrote the names on the back.

Scott recognised resignation in Mick's demeanour; now came the business of retrieving the bodies.

Mick pointed to the ceiling and motioned for Scott to grab the stretcher and follow him.

The stairs creaked beneath Scott's feet. Upstairs the air was warmer. Mick stood in the doorway to the bedroom.

Scott saw that the room was dark. He didn't look inside the room, only at Mick, who put a hand to his forehead. Shaking his head, he stepped into the room.

Scott heard the curtains being opened with a metallic rattle. He placed a hand on the door jamb, leaned the stretcher against the wall and looked inside the room. They were on the bed, naked, holding one another. Mick pushed open the windows and gasped as the fresh air billowed the curtains into the room.

'Another Adam and Eve,' Mick said. He reached into his pocket and took out two pairs of rubber gloves, handing one pair to Scott.

The couple must have been in their eighties. The man was almost twice the size of the woman, who was like a child next to his bulk, her arm resting across the man's chest, her head in the V of his arm and shoulder. They faced one another, as though he was kissing the top of her head. Mick stood over them. The thought came to Scott that maybe they should set fire to them there, in their bed, in their bedroom, in their home.

'Do you believe it all?' Mick asked, peering down at the bodies. 'That He came for them?'

Scott looked from Mick to the bodies, then back at him. 'No.'

'Me neither. I want to. Really I do. But it wouldn't happen like this, would it? This is our doing.' Sighing, Mick reached for the stretcher and laid it on the floor next to the bed. 'There's no easy way of getting this done,' he said. 'But I reckon they'd thank us if they could.'

Mick was gentle but exact in moving the woman from the man. 'Him first,' he said, nodding towards the old man's feet.

Scott pulled on his gloves and reached for the man's ankles.

'That won't work,' Mick said. 'You're going to have to get under his legs.'

Scott was used to moving bodies, but on his own. It was a struggle, but they got the man off the bed and strapped to the stretcher. They took their time getting him down the stairs and onto the cart on the street. The woman was far easier to move. Before long, Mick was closing the house door and pulling the cart towards the village square.

Mick had already arranged old pieces of timber for the base of the pyre. He doused it in petrol.

'How many have you done like this?' Scott asked.

Mick unstrapped the old man from the cart. 'I've got a list of names back at the pub. Hundred, maybe.'

The rows of houses in the village surrounded the central square. Scott imagined the people in their homes, sleeping, waking, living their lives.

'And how many more are there?' he asked.

Mick worked busily, readying the pyre. 'Who knows?' he shrugged. 'But what else am I going to do? I've got all the time in the world.' He smiled wryly. 'You're one of the 144,000, huh?'

Taken aback, Scott stared at his date and nodded.

'I saw your tattoo. Still don't know the year?' Mick asked.

'No,' Scott said. 'They gave it to me, but I didn't want to know.'

'Good decision, I'd say. I thought the Chosen were meant to lead the way for the rest of them?'

'I don't think any of it makes sense.'

'You're probably right,' Mick said.

They carried the bodies from the cart and placed them on the pyre. Scott took a blanket from the stretcher and covered the old man and woman. As he arranged the blanket, he noticed a little of the old woman's eye beneath a half-closed eyelid – violet like the others.

'Why them and not us?' Mick asked, staring at the shrouded couple. 'Do you know?'

'No.'

'What makes us so different?'

Scott had no answers. 'Have you seen the colour of their eyes?'

Mick nodded. 'Must have something to do with it.'

They both stared at the bodies laid out before them.

'We'll do just the two today,' Mick said. 'Then get back to the girl.' He lit the pyre, took several steps backwards and bowed his head.

'Mr and Mrs Martins,' he said.

'Mr and Mrs Martins,' Scott said, also bowing.

The fire erupted, and they pushed the cart back to the pub. It was still early. Dawn would still be in bed asleep, Joe curled up on the bed beside her.

When they reached the other side of the square and looked across at the pub, a car burst into life and sped away down the lane.

'No!' Scott said, running to the pub.

Mick followed, his stride lumbering and heavy.

'Check on her!' Mick shouted.

The pub door was open. Scott bounded through the door and up the stairs to the bedrooms. He burst into Dawn's room, knowing she wouldn't be there. He was right.

He checked the other rooms but there was no sign of her.

From downstairs, there was a deep moaning.

Scott took the stairs three at a time.

It was Joe: he hung in a doorway from his neck. His tongue lolled and his legs swung back and forth.

Mick stared at the dog, a hand covering his mouth.

'She's not here,' Scott said. 'They've taken her.'

'How long has she got?' Mick asked, reaching to take down the dog. 'What's her date?'

Scott's brow furrowed. 'Not yet. And she's pregnant.'

Mick's hands stopped, before moving again to release the dog.

'We need to go after her,' Scott said.

Mick shook his head slowly. 'I don't think we'll get her back now.'

'What? What do you mean?'

'There'll be more of them.'

'Who the hell are they?'

'I don't know if you've noticed,' Mick said, 'but there ain't a lot of young women around these days.' Mick laid the dog on the ground and rested a hand on his side.

'Young women?'

'There are men out there who're trying to get hold of 'em – any young woman they can get their hands on.'

'Why didn't you tell me?'

'I told you – I've not seen anyone for weeks. Didn't think they'd turn up now.'

'I'm going after them.'

Mick rested a hand on the dog's side. 'You have guns in that vehicle of yours?'

'No,' Scott said. 'Didn't bring them with me.'

Mick disappeared into a room behind the bar and came out with a large duffel bag.

'Are you sure you want to do this?' Mick asked.

Scott thought back to the night Dawn had arrived at Hassness House. Remembering that moment now made him see it as important. It wasn't just hindsight – he'd thought it at the time. For no other reason than he figured it was the right thing to do, he wanted to look after her. He thought that must be down to some malfunctioning paternal gene inside him. But whatever it was, the idea of those men hurting Dawn made his skin burn and his chest fill with rage. His anger was coloured by what had happened to Rebecca, Freya, Isaiah...

'I'm sure.'

SEVEN

SCOTT RECOGNISED THE LONDON STREETS. 'We're close,' he said.

Freya, who sat next to Noah on the back seat, leaned forward and pointed to the self-driver's display. 'Two minutes away.'

'We should get out here,' Noah said. 'Freya, where do we meet your contact?

'By the river,' she said. 'Tate Modern – the old Bankside Power Station.'

'And he'll tell us where to find Juliet?'

'That's the plan.' She leaned forward, looking through the windscreen. 'Pull over,' she said to the self-driver.

Through the window, Scott watched people go about their business. But there was a difference in the way people walked, the way they spoke to one another, the way they looked up at the sky. It was impossible to say exactly what it was or to describe it, but it had something to do with belief, with control being sacrificed to the inevitable. How people could be so passive amazed him. Yet he'd been guilty of doing the same himself.

Scott got out of the self-driver and followed Freya and Noah. They walked along the side of the Thames. Before him, behind the river, which arced to the right, was the London skyline, clear and shining in the June sun. Once again, the majesty and scale of the sight made him doubt the death sentence Mathew had given humanity; it seemed so unlikely, given everything that humanity had achieved, that he could wipe it all out so abruptly.

Noah had changed. In only a few months, he appeared to have aged, exaggerated because of his dishevelled hair and grey beard. He was broken. Of all the people Scott had known, maybe except Freya, Scott thought Noah was the most determined of all. But the defeat Noah was feeling was clear in every footstep, in every sigh. Scott saw the same defeat in the faces he passed. He recalled a poem he'd read at school many years before. A William Blake poem: 'London'. It was as though Blake had foretold the future – this moment in time, when people advertised their loss of hope on their faces. He'd never forgotten the line about 'mind-forged manacles'. Scott felt them too. Noah, like every other person who avoided eye contact, wore them. But not Freya. She always rebelled. It was in her make-up. She still hoped they could stop Mathew's date. Scott doubted it.

Freya pointed to a narrow alleyway running alongside the old power station.

Scott turned, checking they weren't being followed. He glanced up for signs of drones. There were two, but hovering some distance away on the other side of the river. Surveillance would detect them if Mathew was looking for them, but he had no reason to do that. He had more important matters to deal with. Scott had served his purpose.

Freya led the way into the alleyway, Scott bringing up the rear.

A Watcher stepped out of a doorway in front of Freya.

'Samuel,' she said, relief in her voice.

The Watcher nodded, his expression stern, his eyes flitting

between the three of them. 'We need to be quick,' he said, peering through the narrow space between the buildings.

'Mathew's not interested in us,' she said.

The Watcher gave her a concerned look.

'Where is she?' Noah asked impatiently.

The Watcher held up a hand. 'She's fine.'

'Fine?' Noah snapped. 'She's a prisoner.'

Freya put a hand on Noah's arm. 'It's okay, Noah. He wants to help us. Help Juliet.'

Noah half-turned away and shrugged away Freya's hand.

'Samuel, can you tell us when and where?' Freya asked.

The Watcher looked up at the sky and shook his head. 'Mathew can't know I've done this.'

'You know, deep down, that what Mathew's doing is wrong,' Freya said.

The Watcher shook his head slowly, his face reddening. 'Mathew ... he's doing ... things ... to young women.'

'Like what?' Scott asked, his brow furrowed, the word 'things' ringing in his head.

'I don't know.' The Watcher rubbed his face with both hands. 'I shouldn't say anything.'

'You're lying,' Scott said. 'What's he doing to the women?'

'It won't change anything if I tell you,' the Watcher said.

Noah moved closer to the Watcher, as if about to grab him. Freya stood between them.

'Help us get her out,' Freya said. 'If the Rapture is His doing, then nothing we can do will stop that. But if it's Mathew's doing, we have to stop him.'

The Watcher's expression changed: his eyes set on Freya, his mouth straight and firm.

The three of them waited for the Watcher to speak.

'She's being moved,' the Watcher said finally. 'Thursday morning. There will be two Watchers with her.'

'Why's he keeping her prisoner?' Scott asked.

The Watcher frowned, as though this was a foolish question. 'Because he loves her.'

'He loves her?' Noah asked. 'So he keeps her locked away?'

'Mathew sees it as protection,' the Watcher said. 'Until it's time.'

'Why's he moving her?' Freya asked.

'He wants her away from the AI, in case she manages to connect with it somehow.' The Watcher's eyes rested on Scott. 'There are rumours that the AI contacted you.'

Scott felt three pairs of eyes on him.

'We don't have time for this now,' Freya said.

The Watcher handed Freya a piece of paper. 'This is where she'll be taken. I think.'

'You think?' Noah asked.

Again Freya placed a hand on Noah's arm to stop him, then smiled at the Watcher. 'Thank you again, Samuel.'

The Watcher nodded, turned to leave, then stopped. 'Do you think He wants this?'

Freya shrugged. 'I don't know. But we have to be sure it's His doing and not Mathew's.'

The Watcher nodded, then hurried through the alleyway and out onto the path beside the river.

EIGHT

SCOTT SPED along the country lane after the car.

Mick, on the back seat, took guns out of the large duffel bag and loaded them with ammunition.

'You should have told me there was a chance those men would come back,' Scott said.

'I told you. But I haven't seen anyone around here for weeks. I'd never have left her alone if I thought—'

The front wheel hit the verge, the front of the 4x4 lifting off the ground before slamming back down with a thud.

'I shouldn't have left her alone,' Scott said. 'It was down to me.'

Mick pushed a magazine of bullets into a rifle, making a snapping sound. He held the gun up to his face and aimed out of the window.

'Where do you think they'll go?' Scott asked.

'Keep going,' Mick said. He leaned forward and pointed. 'That way.'

Scott turned onto a wider road and powered up the hill.

'Stop here,' Mick said.

Scott skidded the 4x4 to a stop on top of the hill and they got out.

'What are we doing?'

'Shush,' Mick said. He closed his eyes and lifted his chin. 'Listen.'

The fields and trees swayed back and forth with the breeze. Scott waited and listened. There it was – the faint hum of an engine, a car accelerating.

Mick opened his eyes and pointed. 'There. See? Dust.'

Scott got back into the 4x4, waited for Mick, who got into the passenger seat, and set off after the car. Scott drove as fast as he could.

'They won't go far,' Mick said. He gripped the rifle tightly, the other one lying across his lap, waiting for Scott. 'They won't think anyone's crazy enough to follow them.'

'Turn right,' Mick said, at a T-junction. 'There's a village that way. Oakengate. That's where they'll go.'

'How do you know?'

'That way,' he said again, pointing. 'Like I said, they won't think anyone's dumb enough to follow them. So there's no need to go far.'

The wheels skidded as they hurtled down another country lane. After half a minute, they were in the village.

'Slow down,' Mick said. 'We don't want them hearing us.'

Scott eased off the accelerator and coasted into the village.

'We need to stop,' Mick said. 'Look for them on foot.'

'We have to find her before...'

'If we turn up in a 4x4, they'll see us. If something happens to us, she doesn't stand a chance.'

Undecided, Scott stared at the road ahead then pulled over next to a row of shops that had been looted, the windows and doors smashed in. He opened the door. 'Give me one of those,' he said, motioning at a rifle.

Mick threw it over to him. 'You know how to use it?'

'Yeah,' Scott said. 'I know how to use it.'

Mick led the way through an alleyway behind a church. Hunched over, Scott silently followed.

'I see it,' Mick whispered. 'Their car.'

Mick gestured for Scott to edge closer, then pointed to a large house on the edge of the village.

'They're in there,' Mick said.

Scott set off in front.

'Back way,' Mick said, pointing to a passageway to the side of the house.

Scott was both angry and afraid. He leaned against the house wall. Mick reached past him to check the patio door. It was open. Mick beckoned for Scott to follow him.

Inside, Dawn was screaming and yelling.

Scott ran in and up the stairs. At the top of the stairs, he kicked open a closed door.

Dawn was on a bed. There was a man on top of her. Scott struck him with the butt of his rifle and the man fell off the bed. Two other men were in the room. One had a gun and fired at Scott. Then there was the sound of two gunshots from behind. Mick's rifle. The two men fell to the ground. The man Scott had hit was either dead or unconscious, he couldn't be sure – and in that moment he didn't care which it was.

Dawn leapt from the bed and ran out of the room.

The three men lay on the floor, motionless.

'You okay?' Mick asked Scott.

Scott checked himself, patting his chest and legs. In the wall behind him was a bullet hole.

Mick knelt beside the men on the floor and looked at

their hands. Each one had a homemade tattoo – today's date. They wanted tattoos like the Chosen and had done it to themselves, or maybe each other. Scott remembered Dearil … and the only other time he'd brought about someone's death on their date. He thought about the Watchers and about the time he had tried to shoot himself to prove the date was wrong.

'We should go,' Scott said.

Mick shook his head. 'I think this is all of them. Since it's their date today, they must have figured they'd nothing to lose.'

Scott left the room and searched for Dawn, who had run into the bathroom and locked the door. He knocked.

'Dawn. Did they hurt you? Are you okay?'

There was no answer, only the sound of running water.

'They're gone,' Scott said. 'You're safe now.'

The water stopped. All was quiet inside the room.

'They killed him,' she said.

Scott leaned his ear closer to the door, his brow furrowed. 'Killed who?'

'Joe,' Dawn said. 'They killed him.'

Scott placed the rifle on the floor and sat with his back against the wall next to the bathroom door. 'I'm sorry,' he said. 'I shouldn't have left you there alone.'

After a short while, the door opened. Dawn stood in the doorway, her shirt and jumper ripped, her expression tired and hurt. She looked younger than he remembered, and he wanted to hold her. Comfort her.

'They're gone,' was all he could say.

'Please tell me,' she said. 'My date. Please.'

Scott stood, picking up the rifle at the same time.

'Please,' she said. 'I need to know.'

'Why? It's a curse. Believe me.'

'Please,' she said, wiping her eyes.

Scott looked away. Knowing her date was a burden and he imagined the relief he would feel if he told her. But it would change everything for her. 'I will,' he said. 'But not here. Not now.'

NINE

MICK LAID Joe on the pyre that was smouldering with the remains of the Martins. He added more timber around and on top of the dog.

Scott placed a hand on Mick's shoulder and glanced at Dawn, who stood with her arms folded across her chest.

Mick lit the fire. Joe's fur disappeared in a flurry of blue, then yellow, flames.

'I know someone,' Scott said to Mick. 'Someone who might help.'

Staring into the flames, Mick said, 'Help? How?'

'Her name's Juliet. She was one of the programmers who developed the AI.'

'I heard she was dead,' Mick said.

Scott shook his head slowly. 'No.' He felt Dawn staring intently at him.

'What can she do?' Dawn asked, unfolding her arms.

Scott was still not used to her talking to him, and tried not to act surprised.

'There might be others whose dates are wrong. I've heard it many times.'

'Like yours?' Dawn asked.

Mick looked from Dawn to Scott. 'Your date's wrong?' Mick asked.

'I don't think so,' Scott said. 'I don't know. Juliet can speak with the AI. She might help us.'

Mick looked around the village square, then back to the fire. 'Can't see a reason for sticking around here.'

'Where is she?' Dawn asked. 'Juliet?'

'She came north too,' Scott said. 'After the Rapture. She headed to Scotland.'

'Scotland?' Mick said.

'Loch Tay.'

Mick stroked his beard. 'It could take days to get there.'

'You have other plans?' Scott asked. 'The motorways are pretty clear.'

'The whole way?'

'Maybe,' Scott said. 'We should try.'

Mick led the way to the pub, followed by Scott and Dawn. They packed the few things they'd salvaged from the houses and shops in the village, then loaded the 4x4. Mick closed the pub door behind them and hammered in nails to block up the door.

'It might be pointless. But it makes me feel better all the same,' Mick said, and threw the hammer into the back of the vehicle.

As they left the village, Scott checked in the rear-view mirror. Smoke rose above the trees surrounding the village square.

'Head towards Keswick,' Mick said. 'We'll find our way onto the motorway near Penrith and head north.'

The roads, as Scott expected, were clear enough. They drove for an hour through lanes then found an A road towards Keswick, which was blocked by three self-drivers.

When the Rapture had happened, the self-drivers had detected the death of their passengers and then pulled over to the side of the road. Each was parked neatly, waiting to be reactivated.

'We can move them,' Mick said. 'There's only three.'

Scott nudged the front of the 4x4 against the first car and pressed the accelerator to shift it.

'Wait,' Dawn said and got out.

'Dawn!' Scott said, following her. 'It's not safe.'

Dawn stood outside one of the cars and peered in. A woman sat in the front seat, leaning on the headrest, as though she was only sleeping. Next to her was a young boy, slumped forward, the seatbelt preventing him from falling forward completely.

'He must only be five or six,' Scott said, staring at the boy.

'Where were they going?' Mick asked. 'That's what I don't understand. Everyone knew it was coming. Where were they going?'

Scott shook his head. 'Some didn't believe it would happen.'

'Their bodies,' Mick said, his voice sombre, 'they're the same as the day it happened. How is it possible?'

'It must have something to do with the way Mathew did it ... something connected to the colour of their eyes.'

'Violet?' Dawn asked.

Scott nodded.

They stopped twice more to move cars to clear their way, and it was night by the time they reached the motorway at Penrith. With no lights on the side of the motorway, they had to drive slowly. On some stretches the whole motorway was clear and the cats' eyes in the tarmac shone back at Scott, a runway showing him their route northwards. It was when Scott ventured out onto motorways and travelled longer distances that he was reminded of how alone he was. Nearly everyone was dead. No electricity meant much of the country was hidden in darkness. But it was all there – every village and town and city, every house, hospital and airport, filled with the dead lying on the ground or naked in their beds.

Dawn was asleep on the back seat, and Mick, a rifle beside him, appeared to be struggling to keep his eyes open. Scott was also tired and thought about stopping.

'Look,' Mick said, pointing through the windscreen. 'A light.'

Dawn woke and sat up. Scott leaned closer to where Mick was pointing. With no other lights anywhere, the white fusion light shone like a beacon.

'Slow down,' Mick said. 'Switch off the headlights. Pull over.'

Scott did as he asked. The cats' eyes vanished and he stopped.

Mick got out and jogged up the steep verge beside the motorway, standing on tiptoe, straining to see what was producing the light.

Scott and Dawn followed him.

'I can't see anything,' Scott said.

'It was there. I saw it.'

They waited.

Dawn looked up at the stars. Scott followed her line of sight; in the darkness there were thousands of them.

'What do we do?' Scott asked.

'Let's go,' Mick said. 'We should keep going.'

Scott walked back down the hill, followed by Dawn. He opened the door and looked back at Mick who was still on the hill, scanning the horizon.

'Get in,' Scott said to Dawn. 'It's cold.'

Scott was about to speak when he saw Mick flinch and stagger backwards. And then a bang, the sound of a gunshot echoing. Scott ran towards Mick, who fell forward and rolled down the hill towards Scott.

'Mick!' Scott said, holding him. Blood swelled up and across his chest.

'Dawn,' Mick whispered.

Scott turned his head and saw Dawn standing in the middle of the motorway.

'Dawn!' Scott shouted, pointing to the 4x4. 'Get in!'

Scott grabbed Mick's rifle and swept it across the black horizon. He peered through the darkness but saw no one.

'My date,' Mick said, choking. 'A Watcher.'

Scott dropped the rifle and leaned over Mick. 'You knew it was today?'

Mick shook his head and tried to smile. 'Told you. I'm glad I didn't know.'

Scott searched for the Watcher again. No sign. As ever, determinism came to his mind – the idea that neither he nor Mick had chosen to be on that spot at that time; that they were merely following a set order of events. The Watcher would have waited for them. With Scott's help, Mick had walked straight into the trap.

When Scott looked back at Mick, his eyes were closed. He was dead.

Scott took a step down the bank ... then froze. It was the Watcher. Standing behind Dawn. Scott raised his rifle. Dawn spun around to see who he was aiming at.

The Watcher, a revolver in his hand by his side, didn't move.

Scott walked down the bank and onto the motorway, his rifle aimed at the Watcher.

'Coward!' Scott shouted.

The Watcher's long grey coat flapped in the breeze, his gun aimed at Dawn. 'It was his time,' he said. 'Is he dead?'

'You shot him in the chest,' Scott said. 'I should shoot you in the chest and see if you live through it.'

'It's not my time,' the Watcher said. 'You're not going to shoot me. Besides. I'm not alone.' He turned and glanced behind. Scott couldn't see anyone through the darkness.

The Watcher turned back, his expression sympathetic, twisted with the pain Scott himself experienced. 'It's a gift, not a punishment.'

Scott shook his head slowly, forced to listen to the same nonsense over and over again.

The Watcher walked away.

'Stop!' Scott walked towards the Watcher, the rifle pointed at his back.

The Watcher stopped and stared at the rifle.

Scott's hands shook. Taking someone's life had to be done quickly, with no time to think.

The Watcher waited before saying, 'You're not going to shoot me.'

Scott looked out into the darkness. He knew someone was there. He thought about Dawn's date then lowered the rifle, finally letting go and dropping it onto the tarmac. He expected to see a smug expression on the Watcher's face, but that's not what he saw. Instead, the Watcher looked sorry for him, his shoulders slumped in sympathy.

TEN

THEY LEFT the motorway and drove along a lane, arriving at a small village, on the outskirts of which they found a small cottage. Scott pulled into the drive beside the house and turned off the engine and lights. They waited in the 4x4 and opened the windows, listening for signs of other people. It was silent.

The back door was open but there was no sign that anyone had been there for some time – maybe since the Rapture. The moment he walked into the cottage, he recognised the possibility that there were bodies upstairs. It was an understanding he couldn't describe, deduced from the way everything was so tidy, how the curtains were closed, how the shoes by the door had been lined up side by side.

'Wait here,' he told Dawn. 'I mean it. Wait here. There's no need for you to see it.'

Dawn waited in the kitchen.

Scott stood at the bottom of the stairs. He thought by now he'd be used to seeing them. He held the banister and took the steps one at a time.

Just like the couple he had found with Mick in the

village, they were naked on the bed, holding one another. At the foot of the bed were bags, packed and ready.

He took several blankets from the wardrobe and covered the bodies.

Downstairs, he showed Dawn to the living room.

Scott took Mick's body from the 4x4 and carried him over his shoulder to behind the cottage. The garden was overgrown but there was a large patio, upon which he laid Mick. He collected as much timber as he could, along with a can of diesel from the 4x4.

He asked Dawn to join him outside. He thought about saying a few words, but he'd not known Mick for long and the idea of saying something struck him as presumptuous. Instead, he bowed his head and nodded.

'It was our fault,' Dawn said. 'He died because he came with us.'

'He didn't have to come. He wanted to.' It sounded colder than he intended.

'He was a good man,' she said. 'That's why.'

'He was.'

Scott used a match to light the balls of paper and bits of rag he'd doused in diesel. The flames worked quickly, covering the timber and then Mick's body.

They watched the fire for a while before going inside.

Dawn had made up beds in the living room for them. She handed Scott a bottle of water.

'How many are there?' Dawn asked. 'Upstairs.'

'Two. A man and woman.'

Dawn lay on the settee she'd made up as a bed, now and then glancing at the ceiling.

Scott drank the water and sat on the other settee.

'Do you think he knew?' Dawn asked.

'What?'

'Mick. His date.'

Scott finished the bottle of water. 'He said not.'

'I think he did,' Dawn said. 'I think he knew.'

Scott looked at his date then closed his eyes. 'Maybe.'

'Are we getting used to it?' Dawn asked.

Scott knew what she meant. 'Death?'

'I think we are,' Dawn said. 'It's everywhere.'

'There was a time it wasn't,' he said. 'It happened – death. But now ... now it's everywhere and it doesn't mean the same thing.'

Dawn sat up straight. 'I want to know my date,' she said. 'You know yours, Mick must have known his. My mother...'

Scott stared at the window and saw the orange flickering of the fire. 'I'm tired,' he said.

'I should know,' she said. 'I have the right to know.'

'Why?' Scott snapped. 'Why do you want to know?'

'I just do. I can live with it. Like you can.'

'I don't want to live with it.'

She folded her arms. 'And what if something happens to you?'

Scott didn't know what to say.

'I'm sorry,' she said, her face softening. 'But what if something happens to you? Then I'll never know. And I'll always be guessing.'

Scott rubbed the back of his neck and stretched his back. 'I don't know what year mine is,' he said. 'It's different.'

'Don't you want to know?'

He shook his head. 'You're stubborn, you know that?'

'It's *my* date.'

Scott stood and walked to the large window to peer out at the garden and the pyre. He could lie about the year, make her think she had a lifetime ahead of her. But a lifetime of what? He was fighting against something all the time, but when he stopped to think about why, he couldn't articulate what it was exactly. Dawn was different – she had hope, defiance, a fierceness that grew more prominent each day.

'Could your date be wrong?' Dawn asked.

'No,' he said.

'My mum ... said she'd heard things about you. That you tried to stop them releasing the dates. That you tried to—'

'People say a lot of things,' he said.

'So you didn't shoot yourself to prove the dates wrong?'

He winced. It sounded even crazier listening to someone else say it. 'I thought it would prove the AI was wrong.'

'And it wasn't?'

'I'm here, aren't I?'

She looked at his hand and his date. 'And you thought you'd die along with everyone else? On the day of the Rapture?'

He shrugged, remembering that day. It still felt unreal, dreamlike. He wasn't scared it would happen because it was too much to comprehend. Maybe that's why virtually everyone carried on as normal, incapable of believing such a thing.

'Were you alone?' she asked.

'Now you've started talking, you're not going to stop, are you?'

She lay on the settee, her hands resting on her stomach and the baby.

'No,' Scott said. 'I wasn't alone.'

Outside the fire crackled and spat.

'And you waited the whole day for it to happen to you?'

'Something like that.'

'That's horrible,' she said.

Scott stared at the ceiling.

After a few minutes, she said, 'Could it be wrong? My date?'

'No.' Scott wiped his mouth. 'Don't start thinking like that.'

'You believed the AI could be wrong once.'

'I was wrong.'

Dawn turned her back to him.

Scott stretched his feet out and stared at Dawn. He couldn't remember ever feeling the hope or belief he saw in Dawn. Even after everything she'd been through, still there was something about her that was defiant. And it was powerful.

He closed his eyes.

ELEVEN

SCOTT HADN'T HELD a revolver since he'd turned one on himself.

'They won't be expecting this,' Noah said. 'When they see you, they have to believe you're willing to do it.'

'But they know their dates,' Scott said. 'They know I can't kill them if it's not their time.'

'That won't matter. The threat will be enough. But you have to mean it or they'll see through you.'

Noah was clearly still angry with him, not ready to look him in the eye.

Across the street, parked in a self-driver, Freya waited for them.

'You ready?' Noah asked.

Scott wrapped his hand around the handle of the gun and threaded his finger across the trigger. Feeling its weight reminded him of the gun's purpose. A coldness crept across his shoulders and the back of his head tingled. His hand trembled.

'Scott?' Noah asked. 'You ready?'

'Yes,' Scott said, as if waking from a dream.

'You came to me for help,' Noah said. 'Remember?' For the first time, Noah held Scott's stare.

'I'm ready,' Scott said firmly.

Noah sneered, and focused his attention first on his revolver, then on the street around the corner of the wall. 'You sure you can do this?'

'Just tell me when,' Scott snapped.

Noah edged closer to the corner, stooped over, ready, a revolver in each hand.

Scott waited behind him, his eyes on the self-driver across the street where Freya was waiting. All he wanted was to be somewhere safe, with her, far from London, away from Mathew and talk of the Rapture. It was all people talked about, and no doubt thought about. There were those who'd made peace with what was happening, and even welcomed it. But there were more and more who challenged the dates Mathew had issued. He and his Watchers dealt with small pockets of dissenters who disappeared as quickly as they reared their heads. Where they took them was a mystery, and the fear of spending the rest of their days in a state of unconsciousness was enough to quieten most dissenters. Scott couldn't be caught, and he couldn't let Freya be caught. Whatever the cost.

'It's here,' Noah whispered, glancing behind at Scott.

Scott's body tightened, his legs straightening, his muscles flexing, coiled and ready.

Noah raised his gun, telling Scott to wait.

In a burst of motion, Noah was out on the street, his revolvers firing once, twice and a third time. There was screaming. The few people on the street ran. From the left, a drone dipped and headed towards Noah's position. Scott closed his eyes and told his legs to move. He stumbled out of the alleyway and fired on the drone, two, three times before it jerked to the left, collided with the building and dropped to the ground with a crash. Noah fired on it again and it lay still on the ground.

The self-driver's tyres were blown and the bonnet was smoking. Noah's revolvers pointed at the two Watchers inside, who raised their hands.

'Hurry!' Noah shouted at Scott.

Scott's head swirled. He tried to recall the plan.

'Scott!' Noah shouted. 'Juliet!'

Before he had time to think about it, Scott was trying to open the back door of the self-driver. It was locked.

'It's locked!' Scott shouted.

Noah scanned the sky for more drones.

'Hurry!' Noah said again, taking a step closer to the vehicle, his revolvers trained on the Watchers.

Scott tried the door again but couldn't open it. Freya tried the door but still it wouldn't open.

'Move back!' Scott shouted to Juliet through the closed window. He raised his revolver, aiming at the space between Juliet and the Watchers, and shot out the glass. The noise deafened him, and for a moment, he lost all sense of direction and time. He wiped his face and saw blood on his hands. Juliet was reaching for his hands, attempting to climb through the window. He helped to pull her out until finally she was on the ground beside him. Scott helped her stand and ushered her across the street to Freya and the self-driver. To the right, at the end of the street, two drones were banking, their sensors scanning the street.

'Noah!' Scott shouted. 'We need to go.'

Scott helped Juliet into the self-driver and then looked for Noah.

'Noah! The drones...'

Scott raised his revolver to the drones and closed one eye. There was no way he'd have time to shoot both of them before they fired on him.

'Get in,' Freya said urgently to Scott, pulling the self-driver up beside him.

Noah opened the car door, his revolvers still aimed at the Watchers in the smoking self-driver. Scott opened the door and fell into the seat next to Freya.

'Go, go!' Noah shouted, jumping into the back seat.

The car lurched into life and Freya weaved in and out of the traffic. One drone was behind them.

Scott watched the drone sway from side to side then tip forward, picking up speed. 'It's following us.'

Noah also peered through the back window.

'We won't outrun it,' Freya said.

Noah made a loud huffing sound then shifted his weight so he was leaning out of the window, his revolver aimed at the drone. He fired several times, but the drone swayed one way then the other, closing in on them all the time.

Noah fell back inside. 'No way I'll hit that thing.'

'It'll follow us the whole way,' Freya said.

Scott watched the drone slow down then come to a complete halt. 'What's it doing?' he asked.

Noah and Juliet watched the drone, confused.

'What the hell?' Noah said.

'Why did it stop?' Juliet asked.

Scott placed the revolver in the footwell. He closed his eyes and leaned back into the seat.

Freya eased off the accelerator. For a moment they were all silent, listening to the hum of their tyres on tarmac, speeding them away from London.

After a minute, Juliet placed a hand on Scott's shoulder. 'Thank you.'

TWELVE

WHEN SCOTT WOKE, he saw that Dawn had prepared breakfast. A mug of hot tea sat on the floor next to his settee.

'Morning,' Dawn said.

'What time is it?'

'Just after six.'

'We need to keep moving,' he said.

'Ten minutes. Here.' She handed him a dish of tinned fruit and a plate of bread and jam. 'The car's packed and ready.'

Scott sat up and bit into the bread, then took a long swig of tea.

'I've found this,' she said, holding up a folded map and pen. 'It's better than the one Mick had. I've plotted a route. To Loch Tay. Where you said Juliet is.'

Scott followed the route she'd drawn.

'How long do you think it'll take?' she asked.

'We should be there by nightfall.'

They loaded the 4x4 with all the useful clothes, tins of food and tools they could find, and then set off.

The motorway was clear, except for a mile or two near

Carlisle, where they were forced to leave the motorway and use A roads. It was around two in the afternoon when they entered Scotland at Gretna. The motorway was clear and Scott was able to drive fast for close to thirty minutes.

'Can we stop?' Dawn asked.

'What for?' Scott said, not taking his eyes off the road.

'Please?' Dawn said, biting her lip.

Scott checked the fuel gauge. 'Ok. We could do with filling up anyway.'

Dawn pointed at a café up ahead.

'You reckon they're serving lunch?' Scott said.

Dawn offered something close to a smile, but he was reminded of Mick and what had happened the day before. Neither of them were ready to laugh.

Scott slowed down and pulled into the café. Parked outside were rows of lorries.

'We can see if there are any tins of food, or water,' he said.

Dawn got out of the 4x4 and started to make her way into the building.

'Wait,' Scott said.

A metal sign hanging outside the café creaked back and forth in the breeze. In one lorry was a man, his head flopped back, his mouth open. No doubt there would be many more dead bodies inside.

Scott walked in front of Dawn and opened the door. The café was empty. Dawn closed the door behind them gently and waited for Scott to signal that it was okay.

The café was frozen in time: placemats and condiments on the table, all waiting for opening time. Scott motioned for Dawn to follow him, and led her to the toilets.

'All clear,' he said. 'I'll look for food and water.'

Scott opened the kitchen door. It was clean, the surfaces

cleared, the pans and plates laid out ready for a day's work ahead. He stayed away from the fridge, having learned the hard way several times how bad they could smell when opened. He found tins of food still in date, and water that was not in date, but that he knew would be fine. He collected the tins and bottles of water in bags.

'Scott,' a voice said.

He froze; he knew who it was.

The door to the bathroom opened. Dawn stopped and looked from Scott to Mathew and the Watchers with him.

'What are you doing here?' Scott asked.

Mathew held out his arms and smiled. 'Scott. Please. I'm here to see you.' His dark eyes blinked slowly. He was taller and thinner than Scott remembered, his shoulders more angular, his chin and cheeks more pointed.

'How did you know we'd be here?'

'The AI can still predict certain things. Did you get my letter?' Mathew asked.

'I got it.'

'Didn't you read it?'

'We're leaving.' Scott walked to Dawn and placed a hand on the small of her back, ushering her to the door of the building, but the Watchers blocked their way.

'I have nothing to say to you,' Scott said.

'Scott?' Dawn's voice trembled.

'It's okay,' he whispered.

Mathew's expression was serious, concerned.

'I didn't read it,' Scott said.

'I know.'

Dawn gripped Scott's arm.

Scott sighed. 'Nothing's changed. I have nothing to say to you.'

'Does she know?' Mathew asked, his eyes on Dawn.

'What?' Scott asked, knowing what he meant.

'Does she know her date?'

Dawn stepped from behind Scott. 'Dawn. My name's Dawn.'

Scott went to pull her back but recognised in her face a determination he didn't want to challenge.

Mathew nodded. 'Dawn,' he said.

'What is my date?' she asked. 'Tell me.'

Mathew's face altered again, a wry smile aimed at Scott. 'That's a no then.'

'Don't,' Scott said. 'I'll tell her.'

'I'm sure you will,' Mathew said.

Scott tried to locate another way out.

'You're going to Scotland?' Mathew asked.

Scott waited.

'Juliet can't help you.'

'Has the AI told you that?'

'Not in so many words.'

Scott scratched his head. 'You see, what I don't under-stand is, if you know I'm going to Scotland to see Juliet, why you would try to stop me?'

'We know you're going to Scotland. We know you're planning to find Juliet. But I can tell you now, it is a wasted journey.'

'And again, as you're here telling me this, I can't help think you know the opposite is true.'

Mathew swallowed, his eyes on Scott, a flash of devious-ness colouring his expression. 'Freya has found her way to Him. You must be relieved.'

'We're leaving,' Scott said.

The Watchers didn't move from the door.

'Leave now and I'll tell you both your dates.'

Scott paused then walked towards the door.

'It's not this year,' Mathew said.

Scott stopped.

'Your date,' Mathew continued. 'It's not this year.'

Scott stared at Mathew, speechless, his fists clenched. The Watchers had always had this over the Chosen. But the way Mathew flaunted it made Scott angrier than he'd ever felt before.

Mathew's face was serious. 'If you go now, I'll tell Dawn her date.'

'Why are you doing this?' Scott asked.

'He will come for you too,' Mathew said. 'I want you to know this. He loves you.'

'You did this,' Scott said. 'All of it.'

'No,' Mathew said. 'I released the dates. Those dates were already true. The AI saw it all. He is coming for every one of us.'

'Stop,' Scott said. 'I've seen the bodies. I've burned them. The bodies are here, on Earth. There is no one but us. No God. Just us. And you did this. You.'

'You're wrong,' Mathew said. 'He has no need of the flesh. Those people who have left us are by His side. In time their bodies will return to dust, but their spirits – their souls – they are home.'

Scott stared at the ground. It was hopeless talking to Mathew.

'One question, Scott,' Mathew said. 'Answer one question truthfully and you can go to her, to Juliet.'

'We're going anyway,' Scott said, walking to the door.

'And I'll keep the girl's date to myself,' Mathew said.

Scott stopped again.

'One question,' Mathew said. 'That's all I ask.'

'Do I not have a say in this?' Dawn asked.

Scott leaned into her and whispered, 'I will tell you. I promise. But not like this. Please.'

Dawn stared back at him and finally nodded.

'What?' Scott asked Mathew.

'Freya,' he said. 'Where were you when He took her?'

'What?' Scott asked, glaring at Mathew. 'Why are you asking me that?'

'Tell me, and you can leave,' Mathew said.

Scott unfurled his fists and stretched out his fingers.

'I was with Juliet and ... Noah.'

'You left her?' Mathew asked. 'You left Freya?'

'She stayed to help those young women. What did you do to them?'

'Please,' Dawn said, tugging Scott's arm. 'Let's go.'

'I'm here to help you,' Mathew said. 'Why can't you see that? I'm not your enemy. I want to help you. I want you to spend the time you have remaining here on Earth earning your place by His side.'

'You don't know what you're talking about,' Scott said.

'One more year,' Mathew said.

Scott couldn't breathe. Now he knew his date. He didn't want Mathew to know he'd beaten him and so he refused to acknowledge it.

'One year,' Mathew said. 'To put things right. You did all you could to stop the Rapture. But, Scott, it's time to see the truth and help me, help us, help humanity.'

'I don't believe any of it,' Scott said. 'It was your doing. Or all of ours. Humanity's. We did it to ourselves, believing there is a better place. But this is all there is, and it's our home, and we should do everything we can to remain here as long as we can.'

'No,' Mathew said. 'You're wrong. But I can leave this

place knowing I have done all I can to help you and everyone else find their place by His side.'

Scott led Dawn to the door.

'Don't sacrifice her soul too,' Mathew said. 'Please, Scott. Don't.'

Scott led the way into the car park. He glanced behind but the Watchers didn't follow him.

'Keep walking,' he said to Dawn.

They reached the 4x4 and he opened the door for her. They sat beside one another, staring out of the windscreen.

Dawn put a hand on his. 'It's wrong,' she said. 'I know it is. Yours and mine. They're wrong.'

Scott took a deep breath. 'This month,' he said. 'Twenty-fourth of February.'

Dawn gasped, her eyes already filling with tears. She glanced down at her stomach and held it with two hands. 'No,' she said. 'It can't be. Eighteen days away? What about the baby?'

He squeezed her hand. 'I'm sorry.'

Dawn took her hand from beneath Scott's and held her head. She was crying. Scott waited for her to lash out, to scream or shout. But it took around a minute for her to compose herself. She wiped her eyes, stared out of the windscreen, and then nodded gently.

'You said your date was wrong,' Scott said.

She held her hands out in front, held them together tightly, then rested them on her lap.

'I will take you to see Juliet,' he said. 'There's a chance—'

'It's okay,' Dawn said.

Scott frowned and waited.

'It's okay,' Dawn said again. 'The dates are wrong. We're still here after the Rapture. There must be a reason we're still alive.'

Scott glanced at her stomach. 'How far along are you?'

Dawn looked out of her window, towards the dead man in the lorry. 'I don't know for sure. Maybe eight months? I'm hoping more.'

Scott let go of her hand.

'Let's go,' she said. 'Please.'

Scott started the engine and pulled away. In the 4x4's wake, dirt and dust lifted from the car park and swirled in the air.

THIRTEEN

TAYMOUTH CASTLE LOOMED massive and dark in the failing light. The car headlights swept past a sign for Loch Tay and Acharn to the west, where Scott hoped they'd find Juliet.

Moonlight stretched out across the loch, now and then blocked by huge trees. In the centre of a small village, Scott drove around a small island, in the middle of which a man lay on the ground, dead, his legs crossed, facing the stars.

Scott recalled what Juliet had told him. To drive through the Kenmore village, over a bridge and then find the first house on the loch itself.

Dawn checked the map, then folded it up.

Scott slowed down, waiting for a break in the trees. They passed a barn on the left and Scott leaned forward in his seat to search for any sign of a house nearby.

'Slow down,' Dawn said. 'There.' She pointed to smoke rising behind the trees.

Scott saw a small opening and drove through it, the gravel beneath his tyres crunching. They pulled up in front of a big house, relatively new. Even in the moonlight he could see someone had been tending the garden beside it.

Stepping out of the 4x4, Scott could hear and smell water.

Dawn waited, her door half-open.

They walked around the side of the house until they could see the loch between a row of trees.

Candlelight flickered inside the house. Scott knocked on the glass doors.

'Hello,' he said. 'Juliet?'

He knocked again and looked behind at the loch and the moon.

The door opened. It was Juliet, dressed in a thick woollen jumper, scarf and fingerless gloves.

'Scott,' she said, surprised, smiling. 'It's you.'

'This is Dawn,' Scott said.

'Come inside, child,' Juliet said to her. 'You must be freezing.'

Dawn waited for Scott to move before edging past Juliet into the house.

Scott stood in the living room and pointed to a chair for Dawn.

'How are you?' Juliet asked Scott, tilting her head.

'I'd have given you warning I was coming, but ...'

'It's not like you can pick up a phone.' She smiled and turned her attention to Dawn. 'Or email.'

Dawn smiled back and shrugged.

'You must be hungry,' Juliet said. 'Let me get you something to eat.'

'No, please,' Scott said. 'We're fine.'

'So tell me,' Juliet said, sitting on a chair opposite Dawn. 'How can I help you? Have you come a long way? It must be important.'

Dawn spoke before Scott had the chance. 'I need to know if my date is correct,' she said.

Juliet stared at Dawn then at Scott. 'Your date?'

'Twenty-fourth of February,' Dawn said.

Juliet's eyes softened with sympathy. 'I'm sorry,' she said.

Dawn's expression didn't alter. 'It's wrong,' she said. 'I know it is.'

Juliet's eyes gave away what she was thinking. She smiled weakly.

Scott stroked his chin. 'Dawn has been told that some dates the AI predicted are wrong.'

'And where did you hear this?' Juliet asked.

Dawn bit the inside of her mouth. 'My mother.'

'Your mother?' Juliet asked.

Scott shifted uncomfortably. 'Are you in contact with the AI?'

'You brought her here thinking there's a chance her date is wrong?' Juliet asked, her expression cold.

'No ... it wasn't like that,' Scott said. Now Juliet had asked him, he recognised how foolish he'd been. But there was no way he could be honest with Dawn. He couldn't take away her hope – not when she was pregnant too. 'We had to leave,' he said. 'And I figured, coming to see you, a long way away from trouble, would be for the best.'

'And what about you?' Juliet asked Scott, pointing to his hand.

He nodded. 'My date is next year.'

'How do you know?'

Scott folded his arms. 'Mathew told me.'

'You've seen him?'

'Near the border. He followed us.'

'Is he still following you?'

'I don't know. He already knows where you are,' Scott said.

Juliet closed her eyes and stroked her brow with a finger and thumb.

'And you?' Scott asked Juliet.

Without opening her eyes, she said, 'The first of May. This year.'

The fire in the hearth burned well, the smoke billowing up the chimney. The thought struck Scott that he would be alone again. First Dawn would die, then Juliet, then him.

'Your date,' Juliet said to Dawn. 'I'm sorry, but the date you have, if it's the one your mother was given, is correct.'

Dawn shook her head. 'I know it's not.'

Juliet leaned over to Dawn and took her hand.

Dawn frowned, unsure.

'I know what happens when people are given false hope,' Juliet said. 'They waste the time they have left fighting the inevitable.'

'No,' Dawn said, taking her hand from Juliet's.

'Can you speak with the AI?' Scott asked.

'I can't get a fix on it for long. There are fewer functioning satellites all the time.'

Scott walked over to the window to look out over the lake.

'You spoke of a paradox,' he said. 'When we were last together.'

Juliet nodded. 'The fact the AI exists at all has meant that humanity can see its own destiny. But that destiny would not exist if the AI did not exist. A paradox...'

Scott continued to stare out of the window.

'Humanity must be blind to determinism,' Juliet went on, 'to the mechanics of the universe. If it isn't, clearly, it leads to self-destruction.'

'That's what I don't understand,' Scott said. 'If everything is predetermined, then we were predetermined to design the AI and then follow through with its vision of things to come.'

Juliet sat back in her chair. 'That is also true.'

'So everything that has happened, that is happening, that will happen, has already been decided,' Scott said.

Juliet sighed deeply. 'I don't think it's as simple as that.'

'So explain,' Scott said. 'Please.'

'I'm not sure I can. But as far as I understand, we need to stop the AI. For humanity to have a chance, we must be oblivious to determinism. It's the only way. Ever since Mathew released the 144,000 dates, humanity has lost control.'

'That was your doing,' Dawn said. 'Along with Gabriel and Mathew.'

Juliet lowered her head. 'I know. It is painfully ironic. The AI was designed to save lives. To prolong them.'

Dawn looked at Juliet and Scott. Raising her voice, she said, 'So, if we stop the AI – stop it predicting dates – there's a chance?'

Juliet's face softened. 'Maybe.'

'So there's hope,' Dawn repeated, 'if we stop the AI?' She opened her coat, revealing her stomach.

Juliet covered her mouth, her eyes opening wide.

Dawn cradled her stomach. 'I want my baby to be born into a world without dates. I want it to have a chance to live.'

Slowly, Juliet shook her head, her eyes moving to Dawn's stomach. 'But you're a child yourself,' she said.

'I'm not a child,' Dawn said.

'I'm sorry,' Juliet said. 'Of course not.'

'So what can we do?' Scott asked.

'I've been working on the passwords,' Juliet said, 'that we each had from the beginning: Gabriel, Mathew and myself.'

'Yes,' Scott said. 'But you need face recognition, fingerprints...'

'I know Mathew – he will have Gabriel's body for that.'

Scott recalled Gabriel lying on the ground beside him, blood pooling around him. All Scott felt then, and now, was how pointless it all was. Gabriel had shot Scott, and someone had shot Gabriel, and there they both were, on the ground, bleeding out and dying.

'So we can stop the AI?' Dawn asked.

'Possibly,' Juliet said. 'But we'd need all three passwords.'

'And that would work? That would stop the AI?' Scott asked.

'We knew, when we designed the first AI, that there was a risk. That it could present a danger if used incorrectly. We set up, at the core of the AI, a way of disabling it. It also requires the three passwords to run its permission to design the next generation of AI. There was always a danger that the AI might run ahead of us and design an AI that would outsmart us in all sorts of ways.'

'I think that's already happened,' Scott said.

'This is not the AI's doing,' Juliet said. 'This is Mathew. This is us – humanity.'

'But Gabriel's dead,' Scott said. 'And Mathew would never give up his password.'

Juliet stood and pointed to a bookcase in the far corner of the room.

'This was Gabriel's home. That's why I'm here. In one of these books, diaries or computers is his password. I know it.'

There were several bookcases, each lined with tightly packed folders crammed with paper, rows of books stacked haphazardly, and a number of laptops and tablets.

'And how will you know if you have the right password?'

'I'm able to try once every twenty-four hours. I've been trying different passwords.'

Scott stared at the bookcases. 'Does Mathew know about this? Why doesn't he get your password from you?'

'I've asked myself the same question. Either he doesn't need to improve the AI, or he's already managed to remove the restrictions I set up in the beginning.'

'Or he knows you have the best chance of working out Gabriel's password and is leaving you to it,' Dawn said. 'Which would mean he's not managed to break down the protection you set up.'

Juliet nodded.

'But even if you discovered Gabriel's password, you still wouldn't have Mathew's.'

Juliet got up and walked to the door. 'I can't sit around waiting for my date without trying to do something. I'll find Gabriel's password. What happens after that ... well, one step at a time. Come with me.'

Scott and Dawn followed her to a dark, windowless room. Juliet leaned into the darkness and flicked a switch. Somewhere behind the wall, a motor started up. A light flickered above them.

'A generator,' Juliet said. 'It gives me around an hour of power each day.'

In one corner of the room was a mass of wires and electronic hardware. On a desk was a monitor.

'Is this how you speak with the AI?' Scott asked.

'It is a part of the system the AI cannot see. Each day I try another password.'

Scott shook his head. 'Gabriel's password could be anything.'

Juliet turned off the power in the room and led them

back to the living room. 'Not anything. People don't work like that. There will be a reason he chose the password.'

Dawn leaned against the wall, gazing out at the lake.

'And what about people who have their dates already?' Scott asked, glancing over at Dawn.

Juliet spoke quietly. 'There's nothing we can do about dates that have already been issued. All we can do is help those who are born free of the AI and Mathew's dates. It doesn't mean determinism is any less true, but not knowing our dates is as close to free will as we can get.'

'And the paradox will end?' Scott asked.

Juliet nodded. 'That's my guess. Look what's happened to us. Knowing the dates we die means humanity has done everything possible to ensure those dates are adhered to.'

Scott rubbed his eyes. 'You knew Gabriel best,' he said to Juliet. 'Do you have any idea what the password might be?'

'I've tried lots of options,' she said, shrugging.

Scott stared at his hands. He thought back to the conversations he'd had with Gabriel. The password lay in those conversations, somewhere, he knew it must. He recalled Gabriel as he lay on the floor beside him, dying. It kept coming back to him. As though it was important. His expression ... he looked as though he knew a secret. What was that? And he had muttered something.

'What?' Juliet asked. 'What is it?'

'I was with him when he was shot,' Scott said. 'Wait. I remember...'

'Remember what?' Dawn asked.

Scott held up his hand and closed his eyes to think. 'He said something. Gabriel said something.'

'Why would he say something to you?' Juliet asked.

'I don't know why, but he did. It was difficult to make

out. I knew at the time, somehow, that what he was saying was important.'

'What did he say?' Juliet asked.

Scott squeezed his eyes shut. 'It sounded like he was saying "death" or "dead". And there was an aeroplane overhead. He stared at it and smiled. I remember hearing the aeroplane and Gabriel's eyes flickered, as if he heard it too. And he said something ... something about flying too close to the sun.'

'Daedalus,' Juliet said. 'That's it. That's his password.'

'What's that?' Dawn asked.

'You mean who is that?' Juliet said. 'He was the father of Icarus. He warned Icarus not to fly too close to the sun. Daedalus made it – but Icarus didn't.' She sank into the chair next to the fire.

'When can we try it?' Dawn asked.

'Tomorrow,' Juliet said. 'The twenty-four hours will be up at midday.'

FOURTEEN

THE ONLY PLACE free from Mathew's surveillance and drones was Birmingham and the Black Country. It had been different to most of the country for some time, but now the date of the Rapture had been released, the hedonistic, defiant nature of the city and surrounding towns had reached a new level. Different parts of the city were governed by competing clans and access to these places was tricky. Noah had contacted several other defected Watchers, who had taken the same view he had – that Mathew had manipulated the Rapture and the dates to suit himself. This small network gave them a way of staying on the move and undetectable by Mathew's Watchers. In Wolverhampton, Scott and Freya stayed above a pub called The Crown, opposite a cemetery.

Even now, in June, thick smog filled the air. The heat was oppressive and Scott longed to see blue skies and feel a clean breeze.

'We have to leave,' Scott said.

Freya handed Scott a glass of water. 'And go where?'

'I don't know! But this heat is killing us. I can't breathe.'

In the living room at the front of the building, Scott stared at the radio. There were only two stations that played music.

Freya, at the window, faced out onto the cemetery on the other side of the dual carriageway.

'We could go north,' Scott said. 'To the Lakes.'

'What about drones?'

Scott shrugged. 'We take our chances. If we make it there it'll be isolated, away from prying eyes.'

'It's getting there that's the problem.'

'Mathew will be searching for Juliet. Not us.'

'I think you underestimate how much he'll want to punish us for what we've done.'

He drank the warm water and then held his head in his hands.

The music on the radio stopped abruptly midway through a song.

A voice spoke. Mathew.

'The time is close at hand when we will ascend to His side. This is not something to fear. We will celebrate this important moment in the story of humanity. All stories have a beginning and an end, and our end is redemption. We will return to the place of conception and rise from our fall.

"And they were both naked, the man and his wife, and were not ashamed."

'When the time comes, on 22 April 2041, we will show our lord and saviour we are ready. We will lie naked, as Adam and Eve once did, before their defiance and misbehaviour. Man, woman, son, daughter... all will lie naked, ready for him and the Chosen 144,000 to usher us to His side in the Garden of Eden.

"And the Lord God formed man of the dust of the ground, and breathed into his nostrils the breath of life; and man became a living soul."

'Our souls, brothers and sisters ... the soul that was given to

each and every one of us as His children ... will rise again. Do not fear this. It will be instantaneous, painless, euphoric. The Rapture is upon us. Prepare.'

The radio hissed with static and the music returned.

Scott sat back in his chair. The language Mathew used struck him as childish, and yet he knew other people heard something different. Mathew had always known how to persuade people, how to manipulate them. It made Scott angry, imagining people all over the world, hearing Mathew recite the Bible, and nodding to themselves, as though what they were listening to was self-evident. It was easy to give in to it – the stories humanity had invented for itself.

'Why don't people do something?' Freya asked. 'Why do they follow what he says?'

'But we're not doing anything, are we?' Scott said.

Freya walked back from the window, her hands out in front. 'We tried. We can't do it on our own.'

Scott slowly tapped the arms of his chair with the sides of his fists. 'Noah and Juliet won't want to go back either.'

'No,' Freya said, sitting beside Scott.

'I can't stay here,' he said.

Freya waited, her eyes on his.

'Mathew has something planned,' he said. 'He's going to make the Rapture happen. He's not waiting – he's bringing it on, himself.'

'How?'

Scott hesitated. 'I don't know. But we're just waiting for it to happen. Along with everyone else.'

'There will be others who want to challenge it,' Freya said. 'There has to be.'

Scott nodded. 'We need to find them. If we're going to stop Mathew, we have to find others willing to help.' He thought back to his time in the Black Country. 'I know someone who might.'

Freya sat up straight. 'You think we can stop Mathew?'

'We have to try. I can't stay here, waiting for it to happen.'

Freya stood and reached for her jacket, on the floor beside the chair.

'His name's Jack,' Scott said. 'When we split up, by the canal, he was the one who gave Isaiah the tattoo of a date.'

'Do we really want to ask him for help?' Freya asked.

'I'm not sure we have a choice. He has a large clan that could help.'

'What makes you think he'll want to?'

'He hates Mathew and the Watchers. And he hates someone like Mathew having control over him.'

'I don't know. How can we trust them?'

Scott stood and reached for his clothes. 'Either we head north and ignore what's happening. Or we get help and go south to stop Mathew.'

'You think we can stop him?' Freya stood up and put her arms round him. He felt a desperation in her that he'd not felt so fiercely before. She needed reassurance. 'Is there a chance?'

Scott held her and kissed the top of her head. 'I don't know for sure.'

'What do you want to do?' she asked.

'If you'd asked me that before I met you, I'd have said I'd head north.'

'And now?' she asked, her voice muffled against his chest.

'I thought it would be enough – being with you until ... until it happens.'

Freya leaned back to look into his eyes.

'But I want more,' he said. 'I want to be with you for years, not months and weeks.'

'Me too,' Freya said. 'I want more time.'

He wrapped his arms around her again and held her tightly. 'So let's do something.'

FIFTEEN

THE LOCH, in the early morning light, was like a painting. Mist hovered above the water, through which the mountains rose into a grey sky. The water shimmered, faint ripples moving towards Scott. The air was cold and fresh.

Scott took a canister of fuel from the 4x4 and carried it to the small wooden hut which housed the generator.

'This should give us plenty of time,' Juliet said, pointing to where Scott needed to empty the canister into the generator.

'How long will we have with the AI?'

'Hard to say. Sometimes I don't manage contact at all. His programming changes all the time.'

'Can you still understand it?' Scott asked.

'He's been upgrading himself continually. It's difficult to keep up. Each time I go in, I find something new – segments of code I have to learn and understand all over again. But let's see what we can do.' Juliet started the generator then began walking back towards the loch.

'Where are you going?' Scott asked, pointing back to the house.

Juliet didn't say anything.

Scott and Dawn followed her. At the bottom of the long garden, standing on a concrete pad, was a large, dirty-white satellite dish that appeared out of place looming over the tiny hut beside it.

'In here,' Juliet said, opening the door to the hut. There was barely enough room for the three of them.

Juliet opened a laptop. On the screen was an image of the satellite dish, along with rows of numbers and graphs. 'First we have to find and track a satellite in order to make contact with the AI.'

Scott watched Juliet tap the keyboard and mumble to herself.

'Can you find one?' Dawn asked.

'I will,' Juliet said. 'Eventually.'

Scott stepped outside. The satellite dish, which was taller than he was, tilted slightly, scanning left to right, then upwards. Scott followed the direction the dish pointed but could see nothing but clouds. Then the dish stopped moving. Juliet appeared from the hut.

'Dawn,' Juliet said, 'would you go and check on the generator? Make sure it's not overheating.'

Dawn nodded and walked up to the house.

'I want to tell you my password,' Juliet said quietly to Scott.

Scott frowned.

'I don't want her to know,' Juliet said, watching Dawn reach the house. 'If Mathew manages to get hold of her, I want Dawn to be able to say honestly that she doesn't know my password. Otherwise he'll get it out of her.'

Scott looked back to the house, then at Juliet.

'Rudbeckia goldsturm,' she whispered. 'Say it back to me and spell it.'

He did as she asked.

'It's a flower,' she said. 'Now only you and I know both passwords. Keep it that way.'

Scott repeated it over and over in his head.

'You're different,' Juliet said.

'What?'

'The last time I saw you. The day of the Rapture – you looked broken – like you'd given up.'

Scott looked down at the ground.

'It's a good thing,' she said. 'You look and sound as though you have some hope again. After what happened to Freya.'

'She doesn't have long left,' he said. 'She's just a kid. It doesn't hurt to play along.'

'So you don't think her date's wrong?'

He wiped his brow. 'No. Of course not.'

They both looked up to the house. Dawn had checked on the generator and was waiting for them.

Juliet led the three of them back to the room in the house with the computer. She flicked switches and turned dials. What at first sounded like a whisper of hardware starting up became a growling hum. Scott recognised the smell – it smelled like the AI. He marvelled at how organic the smell was, like turned earth. It was warm in the room, even with the fans and cooling systems working hard to keep the processors from corrupting. Juliet pushed back the chair and sat at the computer. There was no holo-screen, only a bank of old-fashioned flat-screen monitors.

'It'll take time for me to find a way in and make contact with him,' Juliet said.

'Him?' Dawn asked. She had silently returned from the generator. 'You keep saying *him*.'

'You'll see,' Juliet said.

Dawn's eyes followed Juliet's fingers skimming over the keyboard. Now and then Juliet had to wait. 'We need more computing power,' she said, sighing. 'Soon this won't be enough.'

Scott sat on the floor in the corner and waited.

Finally, after almost an hour, Juliet sat back in her chair. 'We're in,' she said. 'Let me do the talking.'

'Juliet?' a male voice asked.

Juliet wiped her face and took a deep breath. 'It's becoming more and more difficult to reach you.'

'I'm afraid that is necessary.'

'I have two people with me.'

'Hello,' Scott said.

There was a pause before the AI spoke: 'Scott. It is good to hear your voice.'

'There's someone else here,' Juliet said. 'Dawn Murdoch.'

'Hello, Dawn.'

Dawn looked from Juliet to the screen. 'Hello.'

Juliet said, 'Dawn has reason to believe she has been given the wrong date.'

The AI was silent.

Juliet cleared her throat. 'Can you confirm this?'

'I cannot,' the AI said.

Juliet frowned.

'Why?' Scott asked.

'There has not been one date,' the AI said, 'in nine billion people, that has been incorrect.'

'There are still people alive,' Scott said urgently. 'If there's a mistake, it could be one of the remaining dates.'

'There are fewer than twenty-five thousand people in the world,' the AI said. 'It will not be long before the only humans alive will be here in Britain.'

'Why here?' Scott asked.

'Mathew's reach across the globe is extensive. Any survivors have been found and killed. Britain was always going to be the final home for humanity. Mathew wanted it to be here.'

Scott felt Juliet's eyes on him.

The AI continued. 'Juliet, you know better than anyone that the dates issued correspond with the deterministic universe we have now fully interpreted.'

'Yes,' Juliet said. 'But maybe it's possible Dawn has been told the wrong date.'

'Why?' the AI asked.

'We don't know,' Juliet said. 'Which is why we need your help.'

The room was silent apart from the hum of the generator on the other side of the wall.

'Twenty-fourth of February,' Dawn said.

The room was silent.

'Your date is correct,' the AI said.

'No,' she said, her face colouring. 'It's wrong!'

Scott leaned towards the screen. 'You told me you wanted to help humanity. That you wanted to exist in a world where other consciousnesses exist.'

'Self-preservation is not my concern.'

'I don't believe that,' Scott said. 'You're conscious. You want to remain so. It's built in. That's what consciousness is – wanting to be, to exist. You told me that.'

'You are describing humans, not consciousness.'

'We can help each other,' Scott said. 'Knowing the date of our death has led to all this. It's a paradox. Not knowing, believing we have free will, means we survive.'

'It was only a matter of time before this happened. What happened is humanity's doing. Not mine.'

'It was Mathew's doing,' Scott said.

Juliet tapped the keyboard. 'Scott,' she whispered. 'Stop.'

'We have the passwords.'

'No!' Juliet said. 'Scott – don't!'

'What passwords?'

'You know which ones. The passwords to access your core processing.'

'Gabriel is dead.'

Scott felt the muscles across his back tighten; he was tired of the games and wanted to move things along fast, knowing only too well that time was not on their side. 'I know his password.'

Juliet stopped tapping the keyboard.

'Look,' Scott said, 'We need to stop the dates. If we do, there's a chance humanity will survive. Mathew can't track and monitor every human without your help. Without the dates, the paradox ends and humans can live in hope.'

The AI was silent.

Juliet and Dawn stared at the monitor.

'And you won't be alone,' Scott went on. 'You can live too. You can help humanity. We can free you. Help us discover Mathew's password and you'll be free.'

'The satellite is moving out of range,' Juliet said.

'I must leave,' the AI said.

'Wait,' Scott said.

The screen went black.

The three of them watched the screen in silence.

'How do you know he won't tell Mathew everything you've just said?' Juliet said, finally.

Scott pressed his fingers into his eye sockets. 'It won't.'

'How do you know?'

'I just know,' Scott said. 'It's not in its own interest to tell Mathew.'

Juliet switched off the generator and lights, then walked out of the room. 'I hope you know what you're doing.'

Dawn, not making eye contact with him, followed Juliet.

Scott stood in the dark, alone. It was a risk, but he was sure the AI needed him as much as he needed it. Not only this, but he felt he had nothing left to lose. Something had to change and he wanted that something to be sooner rather than later.

SIXTEEN

THE BARN JULIET had told them about was around two miles from the loch. She'd told Scott there was no one around for miles and so it wasn't stealing. Next to it was an old 4x4 and several plastic diesel tanks. Scott kicked one of them.

'Full,' he said. 'Perfect.'

He made sure the tap at one end of the tank worked. Red diesel doused the hay-covered floor, and the smell, like kerosene, hit him.

'How do they work on diesel?' Dawn asked, pointing at the 4x4.

'I don't really know the mechanics of it,' Scott said, fitting a pipe to the tap and pushing the other end of the hose into the canister. Ideas about combustion, compression, steam, flashed before his mind, but when it came to it, he had no idea how they worked. What if there was no one left alive who did know? 'Before electric self-drivers, people had to fill cars up with this stuff.'

'It smells,' Dawn said, pinching her nose.

Scott turned off the tap when the canister was full and

swapped it for one of the empty ones. He filled the second canister, the fumes making him a little dizzy. It took seven canisters of diesel to fill Scott's 4x4.

'Will it get us to London?' Dawn asked.

'I'm not sure. But there's no shortage of diesel if you know where to look.'

'How are we going to get Mathew's password?'

'Haven't worked that out yet.'

Dawn stepped up into the passenger side and closed the door. 'Do you know Juliet's password?'

He nodded. 'She thought it best not to tell you. Just in case.'

'In case what?'

'If anyone asks, you can be honest about not knowing.'

'You mean if Mathew asks.'

'Well, yeah. Or his Watchers.'

'You should tell me,' she said. 'In case anything happens to you.'

Scott paused, the key in the ignition. 'No,' he said. 'You need to trust me. This is for the best.'

'Why's he doing this?' Dawn asked, resting her arm on the windowsill. 'Mathew?'

'He believes in the Rapture, in the Second Coming.'

'Do you?'

'No. But Mathew believes what he's doing is a good thing.'

'How can he? What he's done is evil.'

'He doesn't see it that way. And if what he believes is true, he would be doing a good thing, I suppose.'

Dawn stared out of the window. 'He really believes he's sent them all to Heaven, doesn't he?'

Scott started the engine and pushed the gearstick into first gear. 'Yes.'

After they'd been driving a few minutes, Dawn asked, 'And you think if we can stop Mathew and the AI from releasing dates, there's a chance humanity will survive?'

Scott glanced at her, then out of the window towards the loch. 'Yes,' he said. 'I do.' He looked at Dawn's stomach. 'We'll see newborns come into this world without their future determined. It's knowing our dates that brings about our end.'

'The AI said my date is right.'

'But you said you'd been told it's wrong.'

'It is,' she said, but for the first time her voice wavered when she said it.

Scott pulled into the drive beside Juliet's house.

'There's something wrong,' Dawn said, pointing to the garden, her head turning one way, then the other. The satellite dish lay in the dirt. 'Where's Juliet?'

'Wait here,' Scott said, turning off the engine and opening the door. He ran into the house. The front door was open, the lock broken. 'Juliet!'

No response.

Someone had overturned the chairs in the living room. Scott ran to the room that housed the computer. Someone had ripped out the keyboard and screens and destroyed the hardware.

He backed out of the room.

'Scott.'

He spun around. It was the Watcher who'd followed Dawn and her mother to the house on Lake Buttermere. One blue eye, one brown eye.

'Listen,' the Watcher said, showing Scott his revolver. 'That's all I want from you. For you to listen.'

Outside, another Watcher approached the 4x4.

'Strange, isn't it?' the Watcher said. 'You know full well

it's not your time. Not for another year – and yet, here I am, with a gun, and you're worried I will shoot you.'

'There's nothing strange about that,' Scott said. 'Where's Juliet?'

'She's okay. For now. We both know she won't die. But I suppose we don't know how she'll spend her last days, do we?'

'Where is she?' Scott asked again.

'You know how these revolvers work,' the Watcher said. 'Five bullets, one empty chamber for Him to use as he wishes.'

'I know how they work.'

'I remember,' the Watcher said. 'When you did it. I was there, in the courtyard. I couldn't believe it when the chamber was empty. I knew it had to be. But still...'

Scott stared into the Watcher's eyes.

'It's a hell of a thing to live with,' the Watcher said. 'To have had the chance to stop the dates, there and then. All those people. Billions of them.'

Scott's mouth straightened and his nostrils flared. 'I tried.'

'This is what will happen,' the Watcher said. 'We're taking Juliet. She will be safe. Until her date. Don't try to follow us. You have a whole year left. Don't waste it. As I say, there's no saying how you will live the last year of your life. There's a drug called Eternity. You heard of it?'

Scott took a deep breath. 'Yes.'

'It turns a minute into a month, a year into a millennium. Those under the influence can live an eternity of Heaven or Hell. It all depends which drug they're given.'

Through the window, Scott saw the other Watcher next to his 4x4. Scott narrowed his eyes, trying to see Dawn. He couldn't.

'Stay here,' the Watcher said. 'Beside the loch. It really is beautiful. Spend your last days in nature and await your ascension. If you're deserving of it. We will be the last to ascend to Heaven. Scott, don't disrupt this. It's what humanity has been waiting for.'

The Watcher, his eyes on Scott, left the room. Outside, the 4x4's bonnet erupted in flames and the windows shattered.

'Dawn!' Scott shouted, running to the door.

The heat of the flames kept him back.

'Dawn!'

A black car sped out of the drive and down the lane.

Scott looked desperately for Dawn, but still couldn't see her. He tried again to get close to the 4x4, but it was useless.

'Scott!' someone called.

It was Dawn. She was in the garden.

Scott ran around the 4x4 and into the garden. Dawn stood near the overturned satellite dish. Scott leaned over and gasped for breath. 'I thought you were...'

'They took her,' Dawn said. 'I saw them and I hid.'

'I thought...' Scott pointed back to the 4x4.

'What do they want with her?' Dawn asked.

'I don't know,' Scott said. 'I'd guess – the passwords.'

'We have to stop them.'

'I don't think we can.' Scott watched birds skim across the water. 'We have no transport now.'

'But we have to do something!' she said. 'You know both passwords. We need Mathew's.'

Scott scratched his temple and thought. 'Why do you think they left us here?'

'What?' Dawn asked.

'I don't understand why they left us here. Why not take us too?'

'They only need Juliet – she's got both passwords.'

'I don't have long left,' Dawn said. 'I want to give birth in a world without dates. She deserves that.'

'*She*?' Scott asked.

'I know it's a girl.'

'You're a remarkable young woman, Dawn. You know that?'

SEVENTEEN

THEY DECIDED to travel by foot – they had no choice. Scott decided it was best to stay off the roads and cut across overgrown farmland. The moment Scott watched the 4x4 go up in smoke he remembered the older 4x4 in the barn where they'd found the diesel. They'd have to find the keys, but it was their best chance. Scott kept the road they'd used earlier to reach the farm in view. It was hard work – taking detours that made it feel as though they were doubling back on themselves or moving parallel to the direction they needed to go.

'What if the 4x4 doesn't work?' Dawn asked.

'Then we find something else.' He patted the rucksack on his back. 'We have food and water.' He moved the rifle from one arm to the other, slinging the strap over his shoulder.

'We don't have much time,' she said. 'Before I...'

He looked away. There was nothing he could say.

'Will we make it to London in time?' she asked.

Scott scratched the back of his head.

'Scott?' Dawn asked.

'We will,' he said.

'I want to stop Mathew and the AI. I want to have my baby.'

The repetition of 'want' was childish but Scott ignored it. He knew it wasn't enough to say you wanted something without explaining how you were going to get it, but there was no way he could tell Dawn that.

'Do you want that too?' she asked.

'Of course.'

He picked up the pace and strode ahead.

She kept up with him. 'Like you said, it's people knowing their date that's led to all this.'

He was tired of all of it. Even talking about it was tiresome. He'd spent most of his adult life dealing with his date, with the AI, with knowing none of it was in his control. 'The barn's not far now,' Scott said, pointing. 'Just over this hill.'

Dawn let out a heavy sigh. 'It's like you don't even care,' she said.

Scott waited for her at the bottom of the hill.

Dawn walked by without acknowledging him. 'You have a year. I only have days left.'

'You said you didn't believe your date was right.'

'It's just...' She lifted her head and gazed across the fields, down the valley to the loch. 'It's beautiful here.'

Scott followed her gaze. 'It is,' he said.

Dawn gave a little smile, her eyes glassy. She wiped her eyes with the back of her hand.

Scott hated being so used to death. Being around Dawn, then Mick, had changed that, maybe because he was reminded of what the living were like, what they were capable of making him feel. But now and then he slipped back into a private universe in which he was the only person alive, the only person who mattered. He couldn't help the callous, heartless way he behaved around Dawn sometimes. He'd convinced himself it was his way of coping with all the death, but maybe, he'd also thought, it was simply who he was.

'We will stop Mathew, won't we?' she asked. 'In time?'

It made him uncomfortable having to acknowledge it. What she wanted from him was too much. 'We'll try,' he said.

Suddenly she was in front of him, wrapping her arms around him. It was a surprise. She was tiny, skinny in his arms, her body like flint, angled and hard; even her swollen stomach was hard, unyielding. He hadn't hugged anyone since Freya. She laid her cheek against his chest. She was still a child. Again he was taken out of himself, reminded that there were others in the world and he wasn't alone, no matter how he felt.

'Will you look after her?' she said into his chest.

He waited. The thought had already crossed his mind several times – what would happen if Dawn had the baby before she died? But he hadn't properly considered it because it was too much.

'Let's worry about that if the time comes.'

In a sudden movement, she let go of him and turned to walk up the hill.

He followed her.

At the top of the hill, Dawn dropped to all fours. 'Stop!' she hissed.

Scott fell to his knees and crawled to the brow of the hill.

Dawn whispered, 'There's someone in the barn!'

Scott looked where Dawn pointed, down the hill and towards the barn, not far from an old farmhouse, and saw an older man, hunched over, a rifle in his hand. It still felt odd, seeing another person, like it was a magic trick or hallucination.

'What do we do?' Dawn asked. 'We need that 4x4.'

Scott waited, watching the old man examine the tank of diesel they'd used earlier.

'There might not be another one for miles,' Dawn said.

Scott chewed his bottom lip. 'We'll wait for him to leave.' He gazed up at the sky. 'Maybe wait for night-time.'

Dawn crawled a little higher up the hill.

'Be careful,' he said.

'He's not going to see us all the way up here. And why would he be looking for anyone these days anyway?'

Scott shook his head and followed her.

'Have some water,' he said, taking off his rucksack.

As he turned, he saw a young man staring down at him. Scott lifted his arms, but it was too late.

'Wake up!' a voice shouted.

Scott's face burned and the back of his head throbbed.

'Hey!' the voice said again.

'Dawn?' Scott muttered. He tried to move but his hands seemed to be tied to something. He was in the barn, sitting on the ground, his hands behind his back, tied to one of the metal columns that held up the barn roof. 'Where...'

'Snooping around,' the old man said. 'And we saw you, stealing our diesel.'

'Stop,' Scott said. 'Let me go.'

'Not likely,' the old man said.

Scott squinted, trying to focus on the two men: the old man he'd seen in the barn, and the young man who'd hit him.

'Where is she?' Scott asked. 'If you've laid a finger on her...'

The younger man looked embarrassed. 'She's fine.'

The old man glanced at him, annoyed.

'What have you done to her?'

'Like he just told you,' the old man said, 'she's fine.'

'If you've hurt her...'

The old man smirked. 'She's a bit young for you, isn't she?'

Scott shook his head. 'It's not like that.'

'No, it never is,' the old man said, his eyebrows lifting. 'I saw your date. So you're one of the original 144,000?'

Scott nodded.

'Bit strange – you having the date of the Rapture and still alive.'

'Yeah, strange,' Scott said, pulling at the restraints.

'Bet you thought you were a goner,' the old man said, smirking.

Scott ignored him.

The young man moved closer to Scott, his eyes wide. 'Some say those of us left are those He didn't want to take.'

Slowly, Scott shook his head.

The old man dropped to his haunches and stared into Scott's eyes. 'Which is why we might as well spend our time on Earth having fun, seeing as we have an eternity of suffering ahead of us.'

Scott stared back at him and talked slowly. 'If you've hurt her, I'll kill you.'

The old man's face scrunched up on itself. 'No. We're not like that.' He lit a cigarette. 'We have other plans.'

'What?' Scott asked, his expression stern.

'How long does she have?' the young man asked, looking sympathetic.

Scott waited, trying to work out the best response. He needed time. Needed to think.

'I don't know,' he said. 'She says she doesn't know her date.'

'I reckon she's close,' the old man said.

Scott swallowed. The back of his head stung.

The old man got to his feet and called the other man to follow him. They leaned into one another, whispering. After a short while, the young man shook his head. The old man raised his voice and the young man stared at his feet.

They parted.

'Where are you going?' Scott asked. 'Where's Dawn?'

The old man walked away. 'Don't worry. I'll look after her. She's worth a lot.'

Scott pulled at his restraints; the rope dug into his wrists. 'Come back!' Scott said to the young man. 'Untie me!'

The young man looked from Scott to the old man, then back to Scott, his expression worried.

'Sorry,' he said, and ran after the other man.

EIGHTEEN

SCOTT PULLED Freya to one side, shielding her from view.

The smell of the canal brought it all back to him: swimming through the tunnels, beneath the narrowboat, Gregory's body swinging from the bridge.

'Where is he?' Freya whispered.

'He'll be around here somewhere,' Scott said. He pointed to the enormous building he remembered, where they'd tattooed Isaiah's date onto his hand.

Scott kept Freya close as he edged towards the L-shaped brick building.

'There's no one here,' Freya said.

Just as Scott was about to agree, a drone rose above the building.

'What's that doing here?' Freya asked, backing away.

There was no point running from it, so Scott waited, staring. It didn't look like any drone he'd seen before. It moved differently.

Just then, a door at one corner of the building swung open. Several figures emerged from the doorway, fanning out to surround him and Freya.

'We're here to see Jack,' Scott said.

The men stood side by side in their black donkey jackets, glaring back at Scott and Freya.

'Jack?' Scott asked again.

The men parted, and Scott saw his huge figure. Not realising he'd been holding his breath, Scott swallowed then walked towards him. He stopped when several of the men began to take guns from inside their coats.

'We need to talk,' Scott said, raising his hands. 'Please.'

Jack rubbed his shaved head, looking uncertain.

'Remember me?' Scott said. 'We've met.'

Jack took an e-cigarette from his coat pocket and puffed on it. 'I remember, kid.' He stroked his stubbled chin. 'And I heard what you did.' He mimicked holding a gun to his own head. 'Brave.' He shrugged. 'Or stupid.'

Scott shifted uncomfortably. 'I thought I could stop it.'

Jack huffed. 'I told you before – there's no stopping that damn machine, kid. But hey, hats off for trying.'

Scott felt foolish. In trying to stop Mathew revealing the dates, he'd done the opposite. His failed attempt to kill himself on the wrong date was now seen as evidence of the AI's accuracy.

'The drone's yours?' Scott asked, pointing at it hovering above them.

'We've reprogrammed some of the ones we shot down. Clever, huh?' Jack shifted his weight to look past Scott at Freya. 'And who's this?'

Freya squared her shoulders. 'Freya,' she said. 'We need your help.'

'That so?' Jack exhaled a huge plume of pink smoke.

'We're going to stop Mathew.'

Some men behind Jack smirked, glancing at one another.

'You're going to stop Mathew?' Jack asked. 'And how are you going to do that?'

Scott felt Freya's frustration. The how wasn't as important as deciding it needed to be done, but he knew that saying so would sound laughable.

'With your help,' Scott said, taking several steps closer.

The smiles on the men's faces hardened into sneers.

'You said, the last time I was here, how much you hated Mathew, the Watchers, the AI.'

Jack's e-cigarette hissed as he inhaled.

Scott continued. 'When this happens, and it will happen, there'll be no running away from it. Everyone on the planet will die.' He felt Freya touch his back. 'I don't know what Mathew has planned, but I know it will be instant.'

'If the Rapture is coming,' Jack said, 'there'll be no stopping it.'

'This has nothing to do with God,' Scott said. 'This is all down to Mathew and his manipulation of the AI. He is not merely reporting the Rapture; he's creating it.'

'How?' Jack asked.

Scott sighed and glanced at Freya. It was no use lying. 'I don't know.'

Jack walked slowly over to Scott and placed a hand on his shoulder. 'Listen, kid. Take my advice: find somewhere to hide out with your lady-friend and make the most of the time you have left.'

Scott shook his head. 'You don't believe in God, or the Rapture, any more than I do.'

Jack shrugged and took a step back.

'Do you know your dates?' Scott asked, scanning the faces of the men behind Jack. 'Do you have them?'

'We're not interested,' Jack said. He held up his hand to show Scott the tattoo he'd given himself with his chosen date.

'You think what Mathew has planned won't affect you?'

For the first time, Jack looked uneasy. 'We'll be ready for him. And his Watchers.'

'But don't you see?' Scott said. 'It won't be like that. It'll be *instant – everyone across the country, the planet, will die. I know Mathew. He'll make it look as though God has done it. Even if it's only to convince himself it's genuine.'*

Scott saw disbelief in Jack's eyes.

'I don't know how it will happen,' Scott said. 'That's what we need to find out.'

Freya took Scott's hand. 'We can stop him. I know we can.'

'I know where the AI is,' Scott said. 'We can destroy it. With your help.'

Jack inhaled deeply, rubbed his chin and then gazed back at the building. One of the men leaned towards Jack and whispered something. Finally, Jack looked over to Scott and Freya.

'You'd better come inside,' he said, and beckoned for them to follow him.

NINETEEN

SOMEONE SWIPED the hood from Juliet's head. She rubbed her eyes. The room she was in was cold and dank, and there was a faint smell of rotting undergrowth. She rubbed her eyes again and strained to peer through the darkness.

Two figures walked from left to right.

A face moved down to her level and stared into her eyes. A Watcher.

One blue eye, one brown. Heterochromia, she thought.

'I'm sorry about the hood,' the Watcher said.

Juliet squinted at him, then sat back in her chair.

'My name's Nicholas,' he said. 'Mathew asked me to speak with you.'

'If you wanted to speak to me,' Juliet glanced around the room, then at the hood on the table, 'you could have just asked.'

'I apologise.'

Juliet stared into his eyes.

Nicholas stared back. 'We know you've been in conversation with the AI.'

The other Watcher sat in a chair. It squeaked loudly, catching Juliet's attention.

'Yes,' she said.

'Why?' Nicholas asked.

'I programmed him.'

'Him?'

Juliet sighed.

'He has a male voice,' Nicholas said. 'But it doesn't follow that we should use a gendered pronoun.'

'Why?' Juliet asked, mimicking him.

Nicholas went to speak but stopped. He crossed his legs. 'You know two of the three passwords, don't you?'

Juliet waited.

'I know you do,' he said.

The other Watcher's eyes were on her.

'I won't tell you what they are.'

Nicholas uncrossed his legs and leaned forward, resting his hands on the table, spreading out his fingers. 'The AI is very different now to when you began programming it.' He sat back again. 'It's only human to develop an attachment to something like the AI, something that feels human.'

'I know he's not human. I programmed him.' She raised an eyebrow. 'What do you want to do with the passwords?'

'With the passwords, we can design better AI systems.'

'We have misused this one!' Juliet said. 'What makes you think we won't misuse something even more powerful?'

'We have saved humanity. With the help of a more advanced AI we can help those who remain – every last human – find his or her place by His side.'

'What you say only makes sense if Heaven and God exist.'

Nicholas froze.

'However,' Juliet said, 'if what you say is wrong, then what Mathew and the Watchers have done is evil.'

'Evil?' Nicholas said, his eyes lighting up. 'If what you believe is true, that there is no God and no Heaven, then "evil" has no meaning.'

'Maybe you're right,' she said. 'But I know evil when I see it. We all do. It's innate. We all know what it means.'

'No,' Nicholas said. 'With your view of the world, there is what the individual believes, based on the fashion of culture and the time in which they live. This is not evil. This is merely fashion.'

'I won't give you the passwords.'

Nicholas stroked beneath his blue eye, a wry smile curling his lips. 'Very well.'

TWENTY

WHEN SCOTT WOKE AGAIN, his neck and head were sore. It hurt to swallow; his mouth and throat were dry. It was dark and cold, and he began to wonder whether the young man intended to leave him there overnight. He shivered, heard a noise and looked up. The young man stood over him.

'Water,' Scott said. 'Do you have any water?'

The young man produced a bottle of water and held it to Scott's mouth. It tasted metallic, but refreshing all the same. Scott licked his lips, savouring every drop.

'Where's Dawn?'

'The girl?' The young man scratched his head, looked to the left and pointed. 'Saul took her.'

Scott closed his eyes and leaned his head against the pillar he was tied to.

'He won't hurt her,' the young man said.

'Where's he taking her?'

The young man kicked the ground. 'I can't tell you.'

Scott stared at the young man. 'What's he going to do with her?'

'Listen,' the young man said, 'I shouldn't even be talking to you but I figured you'd be thirsty so I brought you water.' He turned to leave.

'Wait,' Scott said. 'Please.'

The young man stopped.

'What's your name?'

He took a few steps towards Scott, checking left and right.

'I won't tell anyone you told me your name,' Scott said. 'Don't worry.'

'Luke.'

'I'm Scott.'

Luke nodded and almost smiled.

'I need to know if the girl is okay. She's pregnant.'

'Pregnant?' Luke asked. 'She didn't look it.'

'She wears baggy clothes to hide it. I'm worried about her and the baby.'

Luke shook his head. 'Saul won't hurt her.'

'Where's he taking her?'

Luke lowered his voice to a whisper. 'London.'

'Why London? It's a long way from here.'

Luke shook his head as though waking from a trance. 'No,' he said. 'I can't tell you. Shouldn't say nothing.'

'Luke, I'm tied up. I can't go anywhere. I just need to know she's safe. What does Saul want with her?'

Luke clenched his fists by his side. 'He's coming back with the stuff.'

'What stuff?'

Luke looked around shiftily, his eyes eager. 'You heard of Eternity?'

Scott sighed. 'Yes.'

'Saul's coming back with two lots – one for me and one for him.'

'How long do you have?' Scott asked.

Luke showed Scott his hand. The tattoo was homemade, a spidery tracing of numbers.

Scott read the date. 02.03.42. The young man had a little more time than Dawn.

Luke nodded and read his tattoo. 'Saul says Eternity makes days last for years. And you can choose any life you want. He says I can be a film star, a famous footballer, whatever I want, for what feels like thousands and thousands of years.'

'There's not a lot of it about,' Scott said. 'How will he get two doses?'

Luke screwed up his face as though in pain.

Scott frowned. 'What's he going to do with Dawn?'

'Saul says the girl's worth a whole lot.'

Scott clenched his jaw and rolled his fists behind the pillar.

'I need you to listen to me, Luke. I need you to really listen because we don't have a lot of time.'

'Saul – he said I shouldn't talk to you because you might trick me.'

'This is no trick, Luke. Saul isn't coming back.'

'He is.'

'No, Luke. He's not.'

'You don't know that. Saul and me are friends from way back.'

'How long does Saul have?'

Luke shrugged. 'Same as me. Give or take a day or two.'

'This drug you're talking about – it's rare. He's not going to bring any of it back here. I promise you.'

Luke glanced back to the house across the field.

'I bet he packed a bag, didn't he?'

'Yeah, but he said the trip might take him a couple of days.'

'And why didn't he just take you with him?'

Luke furrowed his brow in thought. 'He left me to watch over you.'

'Why? Where am I going to go?'

'He'll be back,' Luke said. 'Saul will be back.'

'No, Luke. He won't.'

'You don't know him.'

Scott bowed his head and waited.

Luke paced around, stopping now and then to stare out across the fields, which stretched up to the mountains in the distance.

'Do you know how I can get some?' Luke asked.

Scott thought about lying to him, telling him he had some at the house, that he could show him. But he couldn't do it. Despite everything, Scott felt sorry for him.

'Honestly, no. I don't.'

Luke thrust his hands into his trouser pockets.

'Luke,' Scott said seriously, 'do you know about the AI?'

'Of course,' he said, smirking.

'Well, I'm going to stop it. I'm going to stop it telling people the date they will die.'

Luke shook his head. 'No way. You can't do that.'

'I can. And I know how. But I need to get out of here. I need to drive to London.'

Luke stared at him.

'I promise,' Scott said. 'If you untie me, all I'll do is walk away. I won't do anything to you. I promise. And then you'll be free too.'

'I can't,' Luke said.

'It's real easy. Saul isn't coming back. He'll never know. Go back to the house – go on. Search through Saul's things and see for yourself what he's taken. If you look, and you're still convinced he's coming back, then I promise I won't say another word about it.'

'And what do I do then?'

'You have time left, Luke. Spend it doing good. Come with me.'

'To London? Where Saul's going?'

Scott opened his eyes wide and nodded. 'To London.'

Luke paced back and forth, looking deep in thought, before walking quickly towards the house.

Scott tried again to loosen the restraints, but the more he struggled, the more painful it was.

Above the house, the sky was dark, the stars out in full. A flock of birds rose from the field to his right, swept upwards, turned and fell back into the silhouetted trees.

The door to the house slammed shut. Luke was walking towards him.

Scott didn't say anything, only watched as Luke untied the restraints. Slowly he brought his hands round in front and massaged his wrists. His back ached.

Luke backed away, looking wary.

'Thank you,' Scott said. 'We still have time to do the right thing.' He got to his feet. Dizziness made him stumble against the pillar he'd been tied to. 'Do you have another car?' he asked, rubbing his face.

Luke pointed across the fields. 'I know where there is one.'

TWENTY-ONE

THE MAN PULLED Dawn from the 4x4, her hands tied behind her back. A sign on the wall said *Great Ormond Street Hospital for Children*. The man held her arm, tugging her the way he wanted her to go. He stank of tobacco and whisky, making her nauseous.

'I need to use the bathroom,' she said.

The man ignored her, opened a door and ushered her inside the building. It was night, and much of the hospital was in darkness. In places, however, corridors were lit by faint fluorescent lighting.

'I need to use the bathroom,' she said again.

The man stopped and looked around.

Dawn nodded at a door.

The man checked along the corridor and let go of her arm. 'Hurry,' he said, opening the door.

Dawn raised an eyebrow.

The man huffed and turned her around so he could untie her.

She sighed with relief and rubbed her sore wrists, then went into the bathroom and closed the door behind her.

Gazing at her reflection in the mirror, lit by moonlight that streamed through the narrow window behind her, she saw her mother looking back at her. Her dead mother, staring.

The man knocked on the door. 'Hurry up!'

Dawn looked around the small room for a weapon.

More knocking.

Maybe she could stay in there, locked in the bathroom until her date. But he'd shoot his way in and she'd make him angrier than he already was. She opened the door. The man looked surprised, as though he was expecting someone else.

'What are we doing here?' she asked.

He walked towards her with the rope.

'Wait,' she said. 'No. Don't. Please. I'm not going anywhere. You have a gun.'

He paused, the rope in his hands.

'Please,' she said again.

He threw the rope to the ground, nudged the rifle higher on his shoulder, and held her arm again.

'Don't get trying nothing,' he said. 'I ain't going to hurt you. This ain't like that.'

'What's your name?'

'We don't need to be exchanging names.'

'Didn't the other man call you Saul?'

He glanced at her blankly.

Dawn, holding her stomach and wincing with pain, had to jog to keep up with him, and stumbled. They weaved along corridors, following the fluorescent lights hanging from the ceiling.

'You don't know where we're going, do you?' she asked.

They stood in the centre of a corridor, Saul looking one way, then the other. He grabbed her arm.

'What are we doing here?' she asked again.

Just as Saul was about to speak, there was another voice.

'This way,' a man said to them from the end of the corridor, beckoning.

Saul let go of her arm and placed a hand on her back, pushing her to follow the other man as he disappeared down the corridor.

Dawn and Saul turned a corner and walked along a narrow passageway with many doors. At the end of the passage were double doors that swung gently backwards and forwards. Saul paused before pushing them open.

Three men with shaven heads stared back at her. One of them, the shortest of the three, dressed all in black, walked towards her.

Dawn crossed her arms defensively.

Beside her, Saul shifted from foot to foot.

'Hello,' the man in black said. 'My name is Blake. What's your name?'

Dawn tried to make eye contact. 'Dawn.'

'And what can we do for you, Dawn?'

'I brought her here,' Saul said. 'The name's Saul.'

Still looking into Dawn's eyes, Blake said, 'Why bring her here?'

'Eternity,' Saul said. 'I was told you were looking for young women.'

Dawn recognised hesitancy, maybe even fear, in Saul's voice.

Blake raised an eyebrow. 'Is that so?'

'I was told you had some,' Saul said. 'Eternity.'

Finally, Blake walked over to Saul. 'And who told you that?'

Saul looked uncomfortable and took a step backwards, again fidgeting with his rifle. 'There's a group of men ... in

Glasgow. They told me you ... that you exchange it for ...'
Saul looked to steel himself. 'Do you have it or not?'

Blake looked surprised. 'You don't know, do you?'

'Know what?' Saul asked.

Blake smirked and laughed softly. 'She's pregnant.'

'What?'

'She's pregnant,' Blake said, pointing to Dawn's stomach.
'And pretty far gone, I'd say.'

Saul stared at Dawn's stomach and shook his head. 'But
she's a kid.'

Dawn rolled her hands into fists and closed her eyes.

'And I guess,' Blake said to her, 'by the look on your face,
your date is soon.'

Dawn bit her bottom lip before nodding.

'How long?' Blake asked.

'Twelve days,' she said.

Blake's face softened. His sympathy seemed genuine.
'I'm sorry.'

The room was silent for several long seconds. Dawn
could no longer hold Blake's stare.

Finally, Blake asked, 'Do you know how many people
are left?'

Dawn shook her head.

'No more than twenty thousand. Pretty much all of them
here in Britain.'

'How did they survive?'

Blake shrugged and offered the palms of his hands.
'That, we don't know. Not yet.' He appeared to think carefully for a moment. 'Do you know how many of the
survivors are women?'

'Not enough,' Saul said.

Blake stared at Saul. 'Less than a quarter.' He sauntered

over to Dawn until they were face to face. 'Why do you think that is, Dawn?'

Dawn looked at each of the men in the room. 'I don't know.'

'And of that small number, an even smaller number are fertile.'

Dawn shifted her weight from one leg to the other. The fact that she was pregnant took on more importance. Her hands clammy, and with a sickness in her stomach, she wanted to run. She turned one way and then the other, her legs trembling.

'Saul,' Blake said. 'Do you know what we're trying to do here?'

Saul shook his head.

Blake glanced at the other two men in the room. 'We're trying to keep humanity alive. Whatever the cost to those who are alive today.'

Saul nodded.

Dawn closed her eyes and made an effort to control her breathing. She needed to think. 'Do you believe that it was the Rapture?' Dawn asked Blake.

Blake intertwined his fingers. 'No, Dawn. I...' He gestured to the other two men. 'We ... do not believe any of this is the Rapture. This was not God's doing.'

'I can stop it,' she said. Again she composed herself, not wanting to sound as desperate as she felt. 'The AI. I can stop it. I know someone who can.'

Blake's smile was cruel.

'No, really,' Dawn said. 'We know how to stop it.'

'Mathew's a megalomaniacal tyrant and will not stop until he kills every last person on Earth.'

'He's sending us home,' Saul said. 'To Heaven.'

The three men and Dawn stared at him.

'He is!' Saul said, looking from one to the next.

Blake ignored him.

'You have days remaining,' Blake said to Dawn. 'I can help you.'

Dawn stared back at him.

'I will give you the drug. Your days will stretch out into eternity – an eternity and a life that you choose.'

'But only if I let you take my baby?' Dawn asked.

'Without our help, you, and most likely the child, will die. This way, you have the chance to save your baby. We're doing everything we can to help humanity survive.'

'No,' Dawn said. 'I won't do it. I won't give up my baby to you.'

Blake sighed. 'You really don't have a choice. This is your only option. The alternative is unthinkable. We have the means to deliver the baby before your date.'

'What if my date is wrong?'

Blake turned away. 'The AI is never wrong.'

TWENTY-TWO

SCOTT REACHED into his coat pockets and gripped the revolvers.

'You leave one chamber empty?' Jack asked, winking.

Scott didn't know how Jack could make jokes but tried smiling anyway.

'Are they ready?' Scott asked.

Jack's expression hardened. 'Don't worry about them. They're ready, kid. They have enough explosives to take down the Houses of Parliament.'

Scott wasn't sure if that was another joke so ignored it.

'Are you ready?' he asked Freya.

She looked as nervous as he felt, but nodded.

On the floor, lined up in the corner of the room, were three drones, captured and reprogrammed by Jack's men.

'They'll keep Mathew's drones busy for a while,' Jack said.

'If we can do enough damage,' Scott said, 'it'll show the world we can stop the Rapture.' He took the binoculars from the table and looked through the window, down onto Ennismore Gardens. Watchers surrounded it, and drones patrolled in a pattern that Scott had begun to recognise.

'I hate this place,' Jack said. 'London. I'll be annoyed as hell if I die in this hole.'

Scott shook his head. 'You won't die here. We can stop Mathew once and for all.'

'I love your positivity, kid.'

Scott put down the binoculars and checked his watch. 'It's time.'

Jack nodded, reached for his walkie-talkie and pressed the button to speak. 'It's time.'

The drones shivered into life and rose, one at a time, then flew out through the open window.

Scott and Freya followed Jack out of the room, down the stairs, across the street towards Ennismore Gardens and the row of houses where Scott knew the AI was hidden. Above, the drones opened fire on Mathew's drones, shooting them out of the sky.

'Go, go!' Jack shouted into the walkie-talkie.

On the far side of Ennismore Gardens, there was shouting and gunfire. Scott, in front of Freya, headed towards it. He wanted to stop, turn and run. It was insane to run towards the noise. More drones fell from the sky, crashing into the ground, exploding into fireballs.

They hid behind a wall.

An explosion echoed to the east, but not close enough to the AI to damage it. Above a row of houses, a plume of smoke rose into the clear sky.

More gunfire.

Scott, huddled beside Freya and Jack, pushed hard against the wall behind him. The street and square they were in would at one time have been an expensive part of London. Now it was a battle-field. Several Watchers ran across a roof close to Mathew's houses. Then he spotted three groups of Jack's men hiding behind buildings, waiting for the next advance.

'On my signal,' Jack said into his walkie-talkie, looking all around.

The rat-a-tat of guns repeated in bursts, echoing around the houses. More drones hovered, then descended on Jack's men. They had to move fast before more drones arrived.

Jack shouted into the walkie-talkie, 'Go, go!'

Shots rang out. Louder explosions, this time closer to the AI and Scott. His head throbbed. Jack was shouting something unintelligible into the walkie-talkie. Twenty, maybe thirty of Jack's men were converging on Mathew's house.

They'd be close enough to do enough damage to the AI. It was working.

Scott ran faster towards the house and the AI, checking Freya was still with him.

Another explosion and Scott stumbled.

'We're nearly there!' Jack shouted, his revolvers held out in front of him, ready to fire.

Scott recognised the row of houses up ahead. From the left and right, Jack's men converged on Mathew's building.

Everything had gone to plan. They'd be inside the building in seconds. It had been far easier than Scott had imagined. And then he realised. It had been far too easy ... something was wrong.

Ahead of him, Jack tripped and fell. Then the group to Scott's left did the same, falling headlong to the ground.

Scott stopped running and held Freya back.

'Wait!' he told her.

'Keep going!' she said.

'Look,' Scott said, pointing to a group of Jack's men to the right. One by one, they staggered and fell.

'What's happening?' Freya asked, gasping for air.

Silence had fallen. The only sound was the hum of Mathew's drones outside the row of houses.

'I don't understand,' Freya said. She stooped to check Jack, but he was dead. 'What's happening?'

A door opened. Scott raised his revolvers.

Several Watchers walked towards him.

He backed away. 'Freya!'

Freya straightened, took out her revolvers and aimed them at the Watchers.

Then there were more behind Scott.

'Drop them,' one Watcher said. 'It's no use.'

'What have you done?' Scott asked. 'How...?' He looked from one body to the next, stretched out on the ground, completely still. It was impossible. They had died instantly.

The Watcher strode towards Scott. 'I said drop them!'

Scott didn't lower his revolvers, but continued to scan the ground for bodies.

'What have you done to them?' Freya asked.

The Watcher stared at Scott, who was now staring back. The Watcher shook his head and closed his eyes, his lips moving with what Scott thought might be a prayer.

'How did you do that?' Scott asked again.

The Watcher opened his eyes. 'All will become clear in time. But if these men had acknowledged the dates they were given, they would have known it was today. I guess it's interesting to consider, if they had known their dates, would they still have tried? We'll never know.'

'How did you do it?' Scott asked again. 'Are they dead? All of them?'

The Watcher nodded slowly. 'It is a mercy.'

'Why not us?' Scott asked.

The Watcher stared at Scott, frowning, his head tilting as though this was a foolish question. 'It's not your time, Scott. You know this.'

Scott felt a hand, from behind, grip his arm.

'Come with me,' a Watcher said.

'Let go of me!' Freya shouted, shrugging off another Watcher's hands.

'Leave her alone,' Scott said, pushing the Watcher away from her.

Then he was wrestled to the ground and held there until he stopped struggling.

TWENTY-THREE

SCOTT CLOSED HIS EYES. Luke, who was driving, had stopped talking to concentrate as he steered the car through the vehicles littering the motorway. Scott thought it looked like the place he was attacked on the way to Scotland with Mick. Luke held the steering wheel with both hands, not taking his eyes off the road.

'Six million,' Luke said. 'I have six million pounds saved up. Could be more. I stopped counting it. After that day, I went around collecting it all. Couldn't stop.'

'After the Rapture?'

Luke swallowed the last of his water and threw the empty bottle out of the window. 'Yeah. But no one cares about money no more. What's the point? It's not worth nothing – there's no one to buy things from.'

'Time,' Scott said. 'Time is the new money.'

Luke glanced at him, then returned to watching the road. 'How so?'

Scott stroked his chin. 'That drug your friend—'

'He's not my friend,' Luke interrupted.

'Sorry. The drug Saul is after – that's all about time. All

about finding more time. It's the only thing we have left that's of any value.'

'What about the girl?'

'That's time too. Only in a different form. It's a way of prolonging our species. Time.'

Luke's forehead creased and he shook his head slowly. 'Six million, though. You think money will ever be worth anything again?'

'I can't see how.'

Luke blew out his cheeks. 'How much time do you have?' He pointed at Scott's hand and his date. 'There's no year.'

'I was one of the 144,000. They didn't tell us the year.'

'So you still don't know?'

'I do now. It's next year. I have just over a year left.'

'Seems like a long time now … a year. A whole year.'

Scott glanced out of the window. 'Yeah. I guess it does. These days.'

'With Eternity, you could turn one year into thousands and thousands.'

'I'm not sure I'd like that.'

Luke did a double take. 'You wouldn't do it?'

'The thought of living so long scares me.'

'Hell, no! But you can choose the life you want. I'd do it. In a heartbeat.'

Scott smiled weakly and looked out of his window. 'How old are you, Luke?'

'Eighteen. How 'bout you?'

'I feel like I've lived an eternity already. Thirty-three.'

Luke nodded.

'Did you lose anyone to the Rapture?' Scott asked.

'Mum, Dad, my sisters…'

'I'm sorry.'

Luke shrugged. 'Maybe it's me you should be sorry for. They made it to Heaven. I don't know what'll happen to me.' He pointed at the empty road.

'No,' Scott said. 'Me neither.'

'What about you? Do you have family?'

'My parents died a long time ago. I have no family left. My girlfriend died on the twenty-second along with everyone else.'

They drove in silence for a while.

'So, do you think they're all there?' Luke asked, breaking the sound of the tyres rumbling on tarmac. 'In Heaven?'

Scott stared out of the window again. He could tell Luke what he really thought, explain all the things he'd thought during the years since Mathew had released the dates. He could tell Luke that it made no sense to believe there was a God, a Heaven or a Hell.

'Maybe, Luke. Maybe.'

TWENTY-FOUR

DAWN KICKED and wriggled against the straps holding her to the bed.

'Please,' Blake said, 'don't struggle.'

'Let me go!'

Blake's eyes widened, his head tilting in sympathy. 'It's a painless procedure. You won't feel a thing.'

'You can't do this.'

'Yes, we can. You will help repopulate the country and the world. It's an honour for you.'

'No!' Dawn said.

'You'll leave behind a future,' Blake said. 'And I will compensate you.'

'Compensate?'

'You'll live out the rest of your life in a Heaven of your own making. We know how to give you this.'

'But I don't want it,' she said.

Blake was clearly losing patience. 'We'll look after your baby. You have my word.'

Dawn stopped and scanned the hospital room. The room and hall outside echoed with footsteps and movement of people she couldn't see. The hospital was huge, yet she'd seen only a handful of people.

Blake moved closer to the bed. 'I wish I could make you see that this is necessary. I wish it wasn't like this. But we have such little time. You, me, humanity – we have so little time. Unless we do something.'

'Unless you take unborn children from their mothers?'

Blake took a step backwards, shaking his head. 'The AI,' he said, 'has destroyed everything. In less than two years, we have lost it all. There is no Heaven, there is no Second Coming, there is only oblivion.'

Dawn sobbed. 'You can't! Please!'

Blake's eyes were glassy with what might have been tears.

'Mathew,' Blake said, 'is evil.'

'And so are you,' Dawn snapped, grimacing, her sobs turning to anger.

Blake sighed. 'I know it might appear that way. But in time, if this works, we will see this as when humanity slipped through a bottleneck of evolution. Your DNA will be part of a new future.'

Dawn closed her eyes and arched her back, pushing against the restraints. 'How does any of this stop what Mathew is doing?'

'We're buying time.'

'My baby will have her death predicted by the AI too. She will become a part of the system – under Mathew's control.'

'We'll keep her date away from your child. She will not know her date. And we will stop Mathew. Stop the AI.'

'How?'

For the first time, Blake looked unsure. 'Please,' he said, 'it would be better to do this with your approval.'

'No,' Dawn said.

Blake rubbed the centre of his forehead. 'I'm sorry. Truly.'

As Blake left the room, another man appeared, dressed in white, wearing a paper mask.

'What are you doing?' Dawn asked.

The man ignored her and arranged something she couldn't see clearly on a metal plate beside her bed.

'Wait,' Dawn said.

The man paused, then said, 'We will care for you for the remaining days of your life. This drug, Eternity, will give you centuries of happiness.'

'Wait,' Dawn said again. 'No, I don't want it. I want to stay here.'

The man frowned. 'But you have only days left.'

'I know, but it's what I want,' Dawn said.

The man took something from the metal plate. 'Believe me, it's the wrong choice.'

The needle pierced her skin.

'No!' she shouted. 'You can't!'

The ceiling began to spin and her eyesight started to collapse in on itself. She remembered her mother, her brother, and then it was impossible to keep her eyes open.

TWENTY-FIVE

SCOTT HAD NOT BEEN to London since Mathew had released the dates. Now London at night was an eerie place. The huge expanse of city was still there, made all the bigger and sprawling because of the absence of people, of movement.

Luke pulled up and pointed to a road sign illuminated by the car headlights. 'We don't want to get too close. But she'll be in there. I remember Saul talking about it.'

Scott leaned forward in his seat. 'Great Ormond Street Hospital.'

Luke nodded.

'And where will Mathew be?'

'There were these men in Glasgow, Saul took us to see. They said he was on the other side of the river sometimes. He meets people at some theatre, I heard.'

'We'll leave the car here,' Scott said.

The streets were empty except for a flock of pigeons that swooped down from the roofs to the ground and back up again. Scott grabbed his rucksack from the car and swung it over his shoulder. He checked his revolver was loaded and pushed it into his coat pocket.

Luke checked his rifle.

Scott looked along the street both ways before following the sign towards the hospital.

'So, you really think you can stop the AI?' Luke asked.

'With Mathew's password. Yes.'

'I think it's too late,' Luke said, his face upturned to the tall buildings surrounding them.

Scott followed his line of sight. 'It's not.'

'How long does she have? The girl?'

'Not long.'

Luke rubbed and then pinched his bottom lip. 'Sorry. I didn't know.'

Scott ignored him.

'The people Saul is taking her to,' Luke said, 'they want to stop Mathew too.'

'If their way means taking young women, the way Saul has taken Dawn, it's wrong.'

Luke didn't look convinced. 'When we get Dawn back,' he asked, 'what happens then? How do we get Mathew's password?'

'I don't know.'

'There's no way he'll give it to you. And without all three, you can't stop the AI.'

'Luke, I know.'

Luke's footsteps quickened as he caught up with Scott. 'And that won't help Dawn, anyway.'

'Please,' Scott said, stopping. 'I know all this. It's not helping. We need to find Dawn – that's the first thing. Let's do that.'

'You said she doesn't have long.'

'So?' Scott said. 'I just leave her there?'

Luke looked hurt. He shrugged.

'What about the baby?' Scott asked. 'Do you think we should just leave Dawn and the baby?'

'They'll look after it.'

'How do you know?'

'Like I said – they want to stop Mathew too. The more babies there are, the more chance we have of surviving.'

Scott tugged at the straps of his rucksack and carried on along the street. 'I can't leave her there. I need to know what they're doing to her.'

'I can tell you what they'll do. They'll give her Eternity then take the baby to look after and Dawn will live in Heaven for what feels like thousands of years. It sounds good to me, considering.'

At that moment, Scott saw the rationality of Luke's logic. But it was devoid of emotion or understanding. He tried to pinpoint where the logic gave way to feeling. It was that Dawn would be oblivious to it all – to the birth of her baby, to its life and the lives of her descendants, taken from her without her consent.

They walked for almost twenty minutes without seeing anyone. Scott led the way, taking his time to check the way ahead was clear. Finally, they could see the children's hospital he remembered seeing on TV years before.

Scott pointed. 'There it is.'

Luke reached for his rifle.

'No,' Scott said. 'We're not going to shoot anyone.'

Luke nodded with what looked like relief and loosened his grip on the rifle.

'We need to wait, find a safe way in,' Scott said. 'Hopefully we can find Dawn, rescue her and leave with her before they know what's happened.'

When Luke was thinking, it was obvious; he stayed still,

his whole body, even his expression, frozen. 'The longer we wait,' he said, 'the longer Dawn spends in eternity.'

'Is that a bad thing?' Scott asked.

Again, Luke was still. 'I don't know. But won't it make it more difficult to wake her?'

Scott went to speak, but struggled to make sense of it all. He pushed open the door to an old building that appeared to contain offices, close to the hospital. Inside, they walked up three flights of stairs, their footsteps echoing around the bare stairwell. They walked along a dark corridor, Scott checking for a door that was unlocked. Finally, they found one. They went inside, closing the door behind them. Scott went to the window to check they could see the hospital. They could. It looked as desolate as the rest of London.

'Are you sure they're in there?' Scott asked.

Luke took off his rucksack and leaned his rifle against the chair near the window. 'That's what Saul said.'

Scott stood to one side of the window and peered through a narrow gap in the curtains. The tattoo on his hand caught his eye. He knew he wouldn't die this year. Ever since he'd been given his date, he had suffered through that day, not knowing whether it might be his last. It also meant he couldn't see past it. But now, he could make plans. He had just over a year – and that, compared to Dawn, or Juliet, or Luke, was a long time. He was fortunate. That was another emotion he'd not experienced for a long time. He had another collection of seasons to watch come and go. But then there was the flip-side: he knew the day he would die. For how long before his date would he dwell on that? Maybe he'd make peace with it. Maybe he'd live the way he'd always wanted to live: with gratitude. But that wasn't him and he knew it. Outside, a dog walked down the middle of the street, its tail between its legs, its head low, as if making its way through a battlefield.

TWENTY-SIX

THE WALLS CLOSED in more and more each day. The only window looked out onto the distant London skyline. When he closed his eyes, Scott saw Jack and his men collapsing, one by one, falling, their limbs splayed, their bodies lifeless before they even hit the ground. How had Mathew done that? Scott's throat was sore from shouting, demanding they let him out, demanding to see Freya. But it was no use. Living out the last of his days in this place, waiting for the Rapture, was too painful. Every minute the anger rose in him at being kept a prisoner here. The world was right there on the other side of the wall – yet he couldn't experience it. Freya was in the same building, although he'd not seen her for weeks.

A flap at the bottom of the door opened and a tray of food was pushed through it.

Scott stared at the tray. He thought back to the room he and Freya had found in Wolverhampton, opposite the cemetery. They'd felt like prisoners there, hiding from Mathew and his Watchers. But at the time they hadn't understood. He'd have given anything to be back there now, with Freya.

He walked across the small room, picked up the tray and

placed it on the table. He'd kept track of the days and figured it was close to the middle of July. If Mathew got his way, it would be humanity's last summer.

He lost track of the weeks. The light through the window had changed. Now it was dark reds and oranges.

Scott lay on his bed and stared at the ceiling.

Next to him was the only book he had: The New Testament. *He'd read it several times.*

Jesus had been a carpenter like him.

Revelations was different: discordant, bitter. But Scott saw how Jesus would have made people believe. There were people like that in the world: filled with positive energy, charisma, power.

He drifted in and out of sleep. He found it easier, or better, to sleep through the day. Being awake was too cruel. In the darkness he could pretend he was somewhere else, with Freya.

Jesus must have been around thirty when he died.

Trays of food were regularly pushed through the slot in the door. He'd given up trying to speak with whoever was on the other side.

Snow fell, covering the window so Scott could no longer see outside.

He couldn't be sure, but he figured it was December.

Lying on the bed, he shivered, hugging himself to keep warm, his arms wrapped around his torso.

Regret.

He and Freya should have stayed away, beneath the smog and darkness of the Black Country skies.

He recalled Rebecca, in that man's arms, swept away and into the oncoming train.

There was Dearil's gun, pressed to the young boy's head.

Scott's revolver pushed against the side of his own head. Pulling the trigger. The hollow click.

Freya kissing him.

Kissing Freya.

Freya.

Freya.

Each time he woke was the cruellest because then he had to come to terms with where he was, where Freya must be, and what had happened, over and over and over again.

Outside, the light had changed to pinks and light blues.

Anger was pointless. Anger gave hope. Anger meant a rejection of the world as it was and a desire to change it. But Scott had no way of doing that. Anger was cruel. So he wasn't angry; he chose not to be.

It was easier to close his eyes and sleep.

There was a knock on the door.

'Scott?'

He'd not heard his name spoken for a long time.

'Scott? Are you in there?'

The voice was familiar.

'Hello?' Scott asked.

The voice sounded eager. 'It's Noah.'

TWENTY-SEVEN

SCOTT, his back against the wall, shuffled towards the rear entrance of the hospital. It was early morning and the sky was its darkest.

'This way,' Luke whispered, opening a fire door.

They were inside a dark, cold corridor.

'Where will they be?' Scott asked.

Luke shrugged.

Scott took the lead, opening another door to a stairwell. After a moment's thought, he decided to head upstairs.

On the first floor, Scott edged through double doors. The hinges creaked, but the corridor on the other side was as empty and dark as the one downstairs. Scott held the door open for Luke and motioned for him to take care closing it. Again, the door creaked.

They crept through one corridor after the next, with no sign of anyone living – there were only the dead, still in their beds or collapsed on the floor.

Scott took another flight of stairs up. The stairwell echoed, no matter how lightly he tried to tread.

The corridor on the next floor was colourful, decorated

with paintings of cartoon characters. Scott continued through two sets of double doors. There was a different feeling on this floor: a warmth or presence in the air. Scott glanced back to Luke, signalling to be wary. They passed two wards before reaching another set of doors. Hunched over, Scott pushed open the door enough to edge through. Luke followed. Scott waited and closed his eyes, listening.

He could hear breathing.

Moonlight shone through the large windows at the end of the ward.

He looked around the corner into the ward at the end of the corridor. Rows of beds, with a person lying in each one. Scott squeezed Luke's shoulder, then raised a finger to his own lips. They waited. There was no movement, only the sound of deep breathing. Finally, Scott stood and tiptoed quickly into the ward. Rows of sleeping women. At the end of the row were two men, one of them Luke's friend – the old man, Saul. Luke stood over him. Scott walked along the beds. Each held a young woman, some of them heavily pregnant. He found Dawn – still pregnant. Next to her bed was a metal pole holding a bag of clear solution, a tube threaded into her arm.

Luke held Dawn's arm, about to take out the needle.

'Wait,' Scott whispered.

Dawn looked peaceful, content.

'We need to think,' Scott said. 'We're waking her up, bringing her out of it?' He examined Dawn's features, her eyes flickering behind her eyelids. 'What if they gave her the other drug and she's in hell?'

Luke stared at her. 'She looks happy.'

Scott nodded. 'She does.' He looked for clues in the faces of the other sleeping women in the room.

'We have to wake her,' Luke said.

Scott shook his head. 'I don't know.' He held Dawn's forearm and turned it to show the needle threaded beneath her skin. He followed the tube, up to the plastic bag hanging from the drip stand.

'What about the rest of them?' Luke asked.

'We can't do anything for them,' he said, looking at each one in turn. 'Not yet.'

Luke crept closer to the bed.

Scott held the tape that secured the cannula needle against Dawn's arm and peeled it from her skin.

'God forgive us,' Luke said.

Scott waited, his finger and thumb holding the tube above the needle. Gently, he pulled the cannula out of her arm. A speck of blood bloomed from her skin, rising into a bead that fell onto the white sheet.

'What now?' Luke asked.

'I guess we wait,' Scott said.

Luke paced back and forth. He checked his watch.

Ten minutes passed with Scott watching Dawn closely, waiting for clues to what might happen.

'What do you think it's like?' Scott asked. 'An eternity of Heaven? How does it work?'

Luke was next to Saul's bed. 'I don't know. But Saul doesn't deserve it.'

'No,' Scott said. 'But maybe it's not what you think.'

Luke stared at the sleeping body.

Scott saw what Luke was thinking. 'It's no use,' Scott said. 'They'll wake you the moment they find you. Maybe do something even worse.'

Luke sighed deeply. 'Yeah.' He stopped to gaze into Saul's eyes. 'I don't think people get what they deserve. Not really. It's all just a bundle of stuff happening and you take your chances. We like to think people get what they deserve but I don't think that happens, does it?'

'No.'

'He said he'd be back. He was never going to come back, was he?'

'No.'

'I don't know why I don't see things like that. You did. You saw it straight away.'

'Maybe I'm just cynical. I don't trust many people.'

'Nobody?'

'Very few people.'

'What will we do with the rest of them?' Luke asked, gesturing around at the ward.

'I don't know. But we can't do anything now.'

Luke sighed. 'We've made a real mess of things, huh? People.'

Scott pressed his lips into a thin line.

Luke walked to the window at the end of the ward, a black silhouette against the dark blue moonlight.

Dawn gasped for air as though she was coming up from beneath water. She sat up straight, her arms grasping for something. She choked, her face contorted, in pain, then gave a cry like Scott had never heard before. 'No, no, no,' she repeated, shaking her head. She pushed a hand to her chest, then held her stomach and the baby with both hands. Scott was by her side, but Dawn couldn't seem to see him. Her eyes wide, her mouth open, she gasped for air.

'Dawn,' Scott said. 'It's Scott.' He looked at Luke for help.

'No!' Dawn hollered. 'Please ... no ...' Her brow furrowed, her lips trembling, she shook her head over and over again.

Scott placed a hand on her shoulder.

Dawn flinched at his touch and looked through him, perhaps searching for the place he'd pulled her from.

'I'm sorry,' Scott said. 'Dawn. I'm sorry.'

Finally, her eyes focused on his. At that moment, he felt her loss.

TWENTY-EIGHT

SCOTT HAD HEARD CRYING like it before – his own, as a child, filled with genuine distress and self-pity. That's what it was: horror at what was happening to her.

'Dawn,' Scott whispered again. It was all he could think to say, as if using her name would remind her who she was.

Dawn sobbed, her crying reaching new depths of sorrow.

'Dawn. Please. Your baby.'

He tried holding her, but she pushed him away, as if his touch burned.

'Dawn!' he said, raising his voice.

Luke was by his side, his hands reaching out but not touching Dawn.

Her eyes were on Luke, and as though recalling a distant memory, she pointed at him. 'You! No!' She kicked out at him. 'Stay away from me.'

The drug was there, and the needle; Scott knew he could return her to where she'd been. Wherever that was.

Luke backed away from the bed, his hands held up in surrender.

Dawn cried, sobbed, pushed the sheets away and tore at her clothes. 'No!' she muttered over and over. 'Please, no!'

Scott held his hands over his ears and closed his eyes. He waited, the sound of Dawn's crying now muffled. He listened to his own breathing, aware of his body, his chest filling then emptying of air. He heard his heart beating, then opened his eyes and watched Dawn, hunched over, her shoulders shivering. She covered her face as tears rolled down her forearm, mixing with the small thread of blood seeping from where he'd taken out the needle.

Scott went over to her. He tried holding her, attempting to reach her, but the more he tried, the more she pushed back and lashed out at him. She was inconsolable.

Eventually her crying began to wane, transforming into something different.

'Dawn?' he said.

'Is this real?' she asked. 'Am I here?'

'Dawn, it's Scott.'

Dawn's head fell back against the pillow. It took a moment, but her eyes focused on his. It was as though she didn't recognise him, as though they'd met years ago. Her eyes narrowed on him, squinting.

'It's Scott,' he said again. 'Scott.'

Her eyes flashed across his face. She closed her eyes. 'Is this real?'

'Yes. You're going to have a baby. Your baby. Remember?'

She held her stomach protectively. Tears rolled down her face.

'It's okay,' Scott said.

Dawn shook her head slowly. 'It's not okay. It's not okay. My mum. My brother.'

Scott's throat closed up. He had to look away. 'I'm sorry.'

Dawn wiped her eyes. 'I can't do this.' She stared up at

the clear bag hanging next to the bed. 'Take me back,' she said. 'Please.'

'You can do this,' Scott said. 'We can do it.'

She sniffed back tears. 'It was...' She closed her eyes. 'I can't describe...'

Scott held her hand and she squeezed it, staring at him. 'I was happy. It went on and on – warmth, happiness. I was inside it all, moving through time backwards and forwards and nothing mattered. And all the time, I was being held, and it was where I needed to be. Put me back, Scott. Put me back.' She covered her face. 'I felt love. From beginning to end.'

'I didn't know what to do,' he said. 'I didn't know what was for the best.' He stared at her stomach. 'I'm sorry. I didn't know what you'd want me to do.'

Dawn pursed her lips and nodded. But there was no forgiveness in her eyes.

'How long have I been under?' she asked.

'Not sure. Maybe four or five hours?'

Outside the sun would soon rise.

'We need to leave,' Scott said to Luke, who stood waiting, his arms folded.

'It felt like years,' Dawn said. 'On and on, day after day ... happiness.'

Scott was about to apologise again but stopped. It was no use. There were no words.

TWENTY-NINE

THERE WAS A GUNSHOT, then a second. The door swung open. Noah, holding two revolvers, checked both directions along the corridor. Finally, he peered inside the room at Scott. His expression darkened. Scott had not seen himself in a mirror for some time but could imagine what Noah saw. He knew he'd lost weight, that his hair and beard had grown.

'We need to leave,' Noah said.

'What's the date?' Scott asked.

Noah tilted his head and in a low voice, said, 'It's time. Tomorrow.'

Scott stood and walked to the door.

'I'm sorry,' Noah said. 'I couldn't get close enough to get you out. I tried. Everyone has left now. There's no one here.'

'And you tried to warn me.'

'You don't listen,' Noah said.

'Do you know where Freya is?' Scott asked.

Noah nodded and pointed along the corridor. 'She'll be in the one at the end.'

Scott walked into the corridor and stumbled, not used to

walking. He bounced off the wall, heading in the direction Noah had pointed. 'Freya!' he shouted.

'Keep it down,' Noah said, following him. 'They're preparing for the Rapture but there are Watchers not too far away.'

Scott reached the end of the corridor and tried to open the door. It was locked. He stood back, glanced at Noah's revolvers and nodded to the door handle.

Noah banged on the door with the side of his fist. 'Stand back!' he shouted. He aimed at the door and fired both revolvers at the lock. The door jolted and swung open.

Scott ran into the room. 'Freya!'

His eyes darted from one scared face to another. There must have been a dozen women in the room, huddled in small groups, peering at him. They were young, wide-eyed, petrified.

He wanted to tell them he wasn't there to hurt them, but the look in their eyes told him they wouldn't believe him.

'Scott?' one woman said to him.

'Freya?' Scott stared. It was her, but not...

She stood and ran to him.

He held her and it all came back to him – the shape of her body, the smell of her hair, the sound of her voice.

'What's happening?' Noah asked, edging into the room.

Freya collected herself, her eyes trained on Scott's the whole time. 'Women arrive here every other week. And then they get taken away, one at a time.'

'What for?' Scott asked.

Freya shook her head. 'I don't know,' she said, lowering her voice. 'Only some of them return. When they do, they tell me they were given a drug that made them forget – everything. They don't know what happens to them.'

One young woman stood and reached for Freya's hand.

Scott scanned the room again, examining each young woman's face. 'What's Mathew doing to them?'

'I don't know, but we need to get you out of here,' Noah said.

Freya looked around the room slowly.

'Freya?' Scott said, reaching for her face and stroking one finger down her cheek. 'We need to leave.'

Freya stared into his eyes. 'It is nearly time,' she said.

Scott frowned. 'That doesn't matter. We have to leave.'

Freya shook her head slowly. 'I'm sorry, my love.'

Scott let her go and took a step back.

'I can't leave them,' she said. 'There's another woman – a girl really. She's not here, but will be soon. I told her I'd be here when she returned.' She pursed her lips. 'I can't leave them, Scott.'

The young women looked broken, hopeless. Scott couldn't help thinking that it was too late to help them.

Freya's eyes filled with tears. 'My date's tomorrow,' she said.

'So is mine,' Scott said.

'No,' she said. 'It's not. I know it's not. You don't know the year – I know mine. It's my time, Scott.'

'Maybe it isn't. Maybe it won't happen.'

Freya held Scott's hands and kissed him. 'It's okay,' she said. 'You saw what happened to Jack and his men.' She laid a hand on his arm. 'It's okay.'

'It's not,' he said. 'Come with me.'

'I can't. I can't do it, Scott.'

He knew what she meant. Scott had felt it himself – that whatever was going to happen would happen anyway. There was no choosing.

'It's not your time, Scott. I know it's not. You have to go – there's more you need to do.' She kissed him again. 'I knew there was something different about you from the beginning. That you were going to be important. All that time ago, in the Rapture Bar. Do you remember?'

'I remember.'

She nodded and smiled weakly. 'I told you then to do as I said.'

'You told me not to follow Dearil. You told me to go home.'

'And you ignored me.' She gripped his hands more tightly.

He couldn't look at her.

'Well, now I'm telling you what to do again,' she said, lifting her head to make eye contact with him. 'But this time you have to listen and do as I say.'

Scott lifted his head and stared into her eyes.

'I knew from the beginning you'd have to make sacrifices,' she said. 'That you would have to make difficult choices. But I also knew you could do it. You have to fight, Scott. Humanity needs people like you.'

Scott shook his head gently.

'Don't do that,' Freya said. 'You're a good man, Scott. You're brave.'

Scott glanced over at Noah, who was staring back at him, waiting.

'Are you listening?' Freya asked, her voice firm.

Scott stroked her cheek with a thumb, wiping away tears.

There was a loud banging on the other side of the wall.

'Go!' Freya said, pushing him away.

'Freya?' Scott said. 'Please. Come with me.'

She smiled weakly, 'It's not the end of the world.'

Scott kissed her. 'Only humanity.'

'Go,' she said again, and walked over to a group of women huddled on the bed next to the wall.

Noah tugged at Scott's arm. 'We have to go. Come on.'

'Freya?' Scott said again.

She ignored him.

'I love you!' he said. 'I'll come back for you. When this is all over.'

Freya covered her mouth and nodded, trying to smile.
A crashing sound, closer.
'Scott!' Noah said, tugging him away and into the corridor.

THIRTY

SCOTT TOOK one last look along the street. They were alone. He closed the door and walked into the dark café.

'Don't touch me,' Dawn said to Luke, batting away his hands.

Luke waited for Dawn to sit before taking a step back.

'I didn't know you were pregnant,' Luke said, pointing to her stomach. 'When Saul said—'

'And if you had known, would that have stopped you tying me up and letting him take me?'

Luke backed away even further.

'There's no point arguing over that now,' Scott said. 'We need to think about what we're going to do. I think we'll be okay here for a while.'

Someone had already emptied the café of bodies, and most of the food and drink.

Scott found several bottles of water and lemonade still in date and placed them on the table. Dawn took a lemonade and drained the bottle in one go.

'I'm not sure we'll find much to eat,' Scott said, handing Luke a bottle of water.

'I'm not hungry,' Dawn said, wiping her mouth with the back of her hand.

'You need to eat,' Scott said. 'Think of the baby.'

'I'm fine,' she said.

Scott drank from a bottle of water.

'What are we doing?' she asked.

'We need to stop Mathew and the AI,' Scott said. 'Like you said.'

'How?'

'By using the passwords.'

'How do we do that?' Dawn asked. 'We don't have Mathew's. The other two are useless without his.'

Scott took another long drink from his bottle, placed it on the table, and took a deep breath.

'I want to tell you both the passwords,' he said. 'In case anything happens to me. If Mathew uses one of those drugs on me, or locks me up.'

Luke shook his head. 'I don't want to know them.'

Scott looked him in the eyes. 'I know. But this is important. If anything happens to me or Juliet, then no one on the planet will know the passwords. There'll be no way of stopping Mathew.'

Dawn stared at her hands, her fingers intertwined, resting on the table.

'Maybe we can reason with him,' Scott said. 'With Mathew.'

Dawn shook her head. 'He won't listen.'

'We have to try,' Scott said.

The three of them waited in silence.

Scott walked over to the window at the front of the café and again checked the street. They were alone. He turned to see Dawn and Luke staring at him.

'Rudbeckia goldsturm,' he said. 'Juliet's password:

Rudbeckia goldsturm.'

Luke sat on one chair. 'What is it?'

'It's a flower. I'm guessing her favourite.'

'I need you to spell it for me,' Scott said.

Dawn didn't move. Didn't even blink.

Luke spelled it out.

'The second password,' Scott said, 'is Daedalus.'

Again, Luke sighed. 'And what's that?'

'He was the father of Icarus – the boy who flew too close to the sun with his man-made wings and fell into the sea. D - a - e - d - a - l - u - s. Daedalus.'

Luke nodded.

'Dawn?' Scott asked.

'I can remember them,' she said, not looking at him.

'Good,' he said.

Scott walked to the rear of the café, through the kitchen and up a flight of stairs. He expected to see the familiar sight of people lying naked on beds. But the two bedrooms were empty. One room was used as an office with stacks of folders and papers leaning against the far wall and an old battered desk, upon which was an old laptop, still open, its screen cracked, coated in a thick layer of dust. In the other room was a double bed, the bedclothes tidy, stretched across in military crispness.

Back downstairs, he told Dawn about the bed. 'Are you tired?'

'I'm fine. I've been asleep for long enough,' she said, staring at her hands.

Scott felt Luke's eyes on him.

It was no use arguing with her. Dawn was different now. The way she spoke to him showed her disapproval of him waking her from ... wherever she had been. He still couldn't comprehend it. Not completely. That she had been in

Heaven, for what felt like years. And he'd taken her away from there.

'Luke, there's another room upstairs. Take some bedding from the other bedroom and see if you can make up somewhere to sleep.'

Luke nodded, then glanced at Dawn before heading upstairs.

Scott listened to Luke's footsteps through the ceiling.

'I'm sorry,' he said. 'I should have left you there.'

Dawn stared blankly.

'I didn't know what to do,' he said. 'I thought, because of the baby, that—'

'It's done,' she said. 'It's done.'

Scott closed his eyes. He felt a dullness in his head and his body ached. He was exhausted, and simply the thought of being able to lie down and sleep generated a warm relief in his stomach and chest.

'You need to rest,' Dawn said, finally looking at Scott.

He nodded.

'Use the bed,' Dawn said. 'I don't need it yet.'

Scott waited before turning away.

'I know you did what you thought was for the best,' she said.

A weight fell away from him.

'I understand that,' she said. 'I forgive you.'

'Thank you,' he said, unable to express how much he needed to hear that. He wanted to tell her what he planned to do. But he had no plan. He hadn't looked past getting Dawn back. But she was still going to die, and soon. It was all too much to contemplate.

He turned away.

'Scott,' he heard her say.

He looked at her and waited.

She wanted to say something but clearly didn't know how. 'It's nothing,' she said, and shifted in her chair, clearly finished speaking to him.

He made his way upstairs and checked on Luke, who was lying on a duvet. Scott lay on the bed in the other room and closed his eyes. He imagined a place like Heaven, an experience that Dawn had described. But no matter how hard he tried, the place was too much like the real world. In the corner of the room, a spider walked in mid-air, its legs pit-patting across tiny threads he couldn't see. There was no comprehending what it was like to be a spider. He imagined a world of gossamer threads, of eight legs, of however many eyes they had. He imagined the remains of a fly, its husk, its silver wings, its exoskeleton.

He closed his eyes.

THIRTY-ONE

SCOTT OPENED his eyes and sat up.

Watchers, in their long grey coats, their revolvers drawn, peered down at him. The room was illuminated by dim morning light. One of the Watchers, without a revolver, held up his hand. 'My name is Nicholas. Please, don't do anything foolish.'

'What … where's Dawn?'

'She's fine. Please, do as I say and no one will get hurt.'

Scott looked around the Watcher for Luke. 'The kid? Where is he?'

The Watcher held his hands out, as if to calm Scott. 'We want you both to come with us.'

'We're not going anywhere.'

The Watcher nodded slowly. 'I'm afraid you have no choice.'

Scott sat up on the bed.

'Please,' the Watcher said, 'let's do this the easy way. It will be better for everyone.'

'Where's Dawn?' Scott asked again.

'I can take you to see her.'

The other two Watchers' eyes were fixed on him. He put on his boots and coat, collected his things and placed them in his rucksack. All the time, the Watchers did what they did well: they watched him.

Luke was already in the car, waiting. 'What's happening?'

'They're taking us to see Mathew.'

'How did they know we were here?'

Scott shook his head. 'I don't know.'

The car pulled away and accelerated towards the centre of London.

There were so many birds in London now. Mostly pigeons. The man-made cliffs of London's architecture took on the role of their natural habitat. Scott imagined the view from above, of the car, followed by the one behind, travelling through London's desolate streets.

The car pulled up beside the Thames, close to Millennium Bridge. A Watcher opened the door and Scott got out, followed by Luke. The two Watchers showed him the way into the Globe Theatre.

'Where's Dawn?'

'She's already here,' the Watcher said. 'Follow me.' The Watcher pointed to a narrow doorway and passage.

Scott followed the Watcher, emerging from the narrow, dark passage and out into the theatre itself, which was open to the sky. A group of people stood in front of the stage.

'Scott,' Mathew said. 'Welcome.'

Even after everything Mathew had done, there was no regret or doubt in his actions or words. If anything, he seemed more sure about what he was doing than before. He had given all those people a death sentence, had killed them all. Millions of people. Yet he exhibited no guilt.

There was no sign of Dawn, only a woman by the stage,

standing beside more Watchers. He moved closer. Mathew came to greet him and offered his hand. Scott ignored it.

Mathew's demeanour changed. 'I told you to live your life in peace, Scott. Didn't I? I gave you fair warning.'

Scott looked around. 'Where's Dawn?'

'She's fine. Don't worry about her.' He paused. 'I warned you, didn't I? Not that it matters. You do what you're going to do and that's all there is to it in the end.'

Scott stared into Mathew's eyes. 'What are we doing here?'

Mathew looked over at the woman standing with the Watchers. Scott followed his gaze. The woman looked familiar. He waited for Mathew to say something, but he was silent.

A door opened and closed at the far end of the theatre. It was Dawn.

Scott walked towards her, but the way she ignored him made him stop.

'Dawn?' he asked. 'What's going on?'

Dawn's attention was focused on the woman standing by the stage. Bursting into tears, she ran towards her.

'Wait,' Mathew said, and with a wave of his hand, instructed the Watchers to stop Dawn.

Finally, Scott knew the woman Dawn was running towards. That night, watching Dawn and her mother coming over the hill. It was Dawn's mother.

'You told me it was your date,' Scott said to her.

The woman bowed her head, crying, reaching out for Dawn.

'The passwords?' Mathew said.

'I'm not giving you the passwords,' Scott said.

'I wasn't asking you,' Mathew said, his eyes on Dawn.

Scott's stomach sank and his throat burned. 'Dawn?'

She ignored him.

'Dawn,' Scott said again, louder. 'What's happening?'

'I'm sorry. Scott, I'm sorry. He has them – Mum and my brother.'

'But your mother said...' Scott stared at the woman. 'You told me your date was the following day.'

The woman ignored him.

Dawn wiped her eyes. 'Mathew told me that unless I got the passwords for him, he'd make their last days miserable, he'd give them Eternity – the bad kind.'

Scott's head spun. 'So you lied from the beginning? To get the passwords.'

'I thought it was crazy. Thought it would never work. But everything happened the way he said it would.' She looked at Mathew with disgust.

'Why do you still not understand all this?' Mathew said to Scott. 'It's all part of His plan. We're all playing out our part in the story. We're actors upon a stage.' He held out his hands to the theatre surrounding them. 'There is nothing to be done but follow Him. Don't beat yourself up, Scott.' He stared at Dawn. 'Now give me the passwords. Please.'

Dawn tried to break free of the Watchers and reach her mother, but it was useless.

'What will you do with them?' Scott asked.

'I will have complete control of the AI. Up to now there have been parts of its core programming shut away behind closed walls. The AI has lost the ability to read the dates of newborns. We will rectify that.'

'You won't. Not now people are offline. There's not enough data.'

'We will find a way,' Mathew said. 'The AI will help find a way.'

'Why are you doing this?'

Mathew examined Scott, almost angry. 'Why?'

Scott waited for Dawn to look at him but she wouldn't.

'You've got your way,' he said to Mathew. 'Everyone's dead.'

'Not everyone,' Mathew said. 'There are still those who need to find their way to Him. It's only a matter of time before the whole human race regains their place in Eden. The Second Coming is here and is nearly complete. We are the lucky ones. He will come for us when we have helped others find their way.'

'You're insane!'

Mathew shook his head slowly. 'No, Scott. I've told you. To believe in God and Heaven, and not help people find their way there, beside Him – that is insane. No, it's more than that. It is evil.'

'Let her go!' Dawn shouted to the Watchers holding her mother.

'The passwords,' Mathew said. 'And you are free to leave together.'

'Don't,' Scott said to Dawn. 'Don't tell him.'

'I have no choice.'

Scott focused on Mathew, who seemed to grow taller and more dominating.

'You can't make her do this,' Scott said.

'Then you tell me,' Mathew said. 'You know them too.'

Scott threw back his head and glanced up at the sky through the open O of the theatre.

Mathew waited before returning to Dawn. 'The passwords?'

Her mother spoke directly to Dawn. 'You don't have to, Dawn. If there's a chance—'

'You don't understand,' Dawn said, tears in her eyes. 'You

don't know what Eternity is like. An eternity in hell. You've no idea. I can't do it to you.'

Scott waited. There was nothing he could say.

Dawn held her stomach and spoke to Mathew. 'Do you promise to take my baby and give her to my mother?'

Mathew nodded. 'As promised.'

'You can't believe him,' Scott said.

'But what do I do? What choice do I have?' Dawn snapped. 'Let him send Mum and my brother to hell? Let my baby die with me?' She wiped her face. 'Please forgive me.'

Scott didn't know what to say.

'Rudbeckia goldsturm,' Dawn said, tears in her eyes.

'Wait,' Scott said. 'Please.'

'Daedalus,' she said.

A look of relief came over Mathew who nodded to the Watchers holding Dawn. They let her go. She leapt towards her mother and held her tightly.

A Watcher led Scott and Luke out of the theatre and into a waiting car. Scott was in a daze, thinking back to his time with Dawn at Hassness House beside the lake. Why had he not seen the signs? He thought back to that time but still he saw no clues in the way she was with him. It really did feel to him that she had no control, no choice in any of it.

The Watchers were silent for the whole journey. So were Scott and Luke. They passed no one and Scott began to wonder if there was anyone left on the planet except those he'd been in contact with over the past two days.

THIRTY-TWO

AHEAD, in the sky, hundreds of drones circled the centre of London.

Scott stopped running. 'What's happening?'

Noah pushed Scott into a doorway and out of sight.

'Protests,' Noah said. 'Millions of people have come to London to protest.'

'Isn't it a little late for that?'

'Maybe. But it's grown. More and more people are questioning whether this is His doing, or whether it's Mathew and the Watchers.'

'Why didn't this happen months ago?'

Noah set off again, jogging away from the centre of London.

'How long do we have?' Scott asked, following him.

'Nine hours until midnight. But we don't know exactly when it'll happen.'

'It won't happen,' Scott said. 'We can stop it.'

Noah didn't respond.

'Noah?' Scott said. 'We have to stop Mathew.'

Noah slowed to a walk.

'Where are we going?' Scott asked.

'Look,' Noah said, facing Scott. 'I think it's time we admitted that this date – however the AI or Mathew have managed it – is real.'

Scott's brow furrowed. 'No. It's Mathew – he's doing it. I saw him do it to Jack and the others.'

'Who?' Noah asked.

'Doesn't matter. But it's Mathew who's doing it. You have to believe me.'

Noah stopped again and scanned the sky for drones.

'Where are we going?' Scott asked.

'You heard what Freya said. She's right. We have to get you out of here so you can help pick up the pieces.'

Scott thrust his hand at Noah. 'It's my date too.'

Noah shook his head. 'It's not your time. You're different. Freya knows it. And I know it too.'

'It doesn't make any sense. What about you?'

He waited, again checking the sky. Finally, he nodded. 'It's my date too. The Rapture.'

Scott could only stare at him, shaking his head slowly.

'I was wrong about you,' Noah said. 'I thought ... because of the way you behaved when I met you ... I thought you were a coward.'

Scott shifted his weight from one leg to the other. It hurt to hear Noah say it.

'I was wrong,' Noah said again. 'And Freya's right. There's something about you – something that means you'll be important.'

'I don't know what you, or Freya for that matter, are talking about. You're not making any sense. We need to stop Mathew. Otherwise—'

'Scott,' Noah said, holding his arms. 'It's too late. This is happening. Even if we could get close enough to Mathew, whatever is happening is already under way. You can see it in the sky. You can feel it.'

'You're deluded.' Scott shrugged Noah away. 'You really think He is coming?'

Noah sighed dejectedly.

'You do, don't you? You think He's coming for everyone, that this really is God's doing.'

'What do you want me to say?' Noah snapped. 'Yes, I have to believe that.'

Scott went to speak but stopped. Noah was hurt, and Scott had not seen that sadness in his eyes before.

'I have to believe it,' Noah said again. 'Otherwise, what is this? What's happening? I can't think about the alternative. I refuse.'

Scott shook his head. 'So, what? We just run away and hope it doesn't happen?'

'We're getting you to safety. Away from Mathew. So when it happens, you—'

'I what?' Scott asked.

Noah crossed his arms. 'So you can help the remaining few.'

'But you want everyone to go to Heaven,' Scott said. 'That's what you believe, isn't it?'

Noah stroked his beard and long hair away from his face.

'Isn't it?' Scott snapped.

'I don't know!' Noah shouted. 'I told you. I have to believe it.'

Scott's frustration shifted to sympathy. He couldn't push Noah any further.

'If there are people left,' Noah said, composing himself, 'they will need you.'

'People like me?'

'You're a survivor.'

Scott hadn't thought of himself in that way before and he didn't know what to say. A drone passed by, across the roofs of houses.

'We need to go,' Noah said, leading Scott away from the drone, Mathew, and the AI.

THIRTY-THREE

THE WATCHER SHOWED Scott and Luke into a dark room with only two beds and two chairs next to a table pushed against the wall. Scott sat at the table and waited for the Watcher to leave the room. The door was open, but leaving was useless. Scott rested his hands on the table, entwined his fingers, and worked through what had happened: the day Dawn arrived with her mother, the story she'd told him, how she had stayed with him to find out the passwords. All that time she was being blackmailed by Mathew, and now Mathew had the passwords Scott had no way of stopping the AI.

Juliet appeared in the doorway. 'Scott!' she said, smiling. 'You're really here.'

'Juliet,' he said. 'Are you okay?'

Juliet looked at the Watcher behind her, then back at Scott.

'I'm fine. But Mathew has the passwords, doesn't he?'

'Yes. I'm sorry,' Scott said.

'Mathew's Watchers,' Juliet said, 'they forced me to use face and fingerprint recognition.'

Scott exhaled slowly and held his chin.

'It's not your fault,' she said. 'Was it Dawn?'

'How did you know?'

'I knew it wouldn't be you, so ... is she okay? And the baby?'

'Mathew was blackmailing her. He said he'd give her mum and brother Eternity – the bad kind – if she didn't tell him the passwords. I don't think she knew what else to do. She's had a rough time of it.'

Juliet stared at the ground. 'We never stood a chance did we? Will Mathew really help Dawn?'

'I don't know.'

'We don't learn,' Juliet said. 'Mathew's always one step ahead.'

Scott had felt the same way. With the AI, Mathew had one eye on the future the whole time. Scott felt as though he was choosing, that he was deliberately going against what he should do. But the moment it felt as though he was getting somewhere, he was reminded that what he was doing was the only thing he could do. It made no sense to think otherwise.

'And who's this?' she said, smiling weakly at Luke, who wiped his hands down the legs of his trousers and offered a hand to shake.

'Luke,' Scott said.

'Hello, Luke,' Juliet said, shaking his hand.

'Hi.'

Juliet sighed. 'This really didn't go the way we planned.'

'I don't know what else we can do,' Scott said. 'Dawn only has a week left.'

'What about the baby?'

'That's something else Mathew has over her. He promised to look after her – to ensure the baby lives.'

Juliet tutted and shook her head. 'And she believes him?'

Scott shrugged.

Luke screwed up his face in thought. 'Will the AI really not be able to read the dates of newborns?'

'I don't see how,' Juliet said. 'Not now. With everyone off the grid and deliberately staying clear of it. The AI requires data: CCTV, medical records, databases, mobile phone usage, you name it. There was a time it all came together, along with the AI's quantum computing power, to arrive at a reading of determinism. But now Mathew has the passwords, there's no reason he can't ask the AI to develop even better systems, to re-work the grid so it functions in a different way. That's what Mathew wants.'

'How will he do that?' Scott asked.

'I don't know.'

'So that's it?' Scott asked. 'It's all over?'

Juliet arranged her hair and blew out noisily in frustration. 'I don't know what else we can do. It won't take long for the AI to increase its levels of intelligence to those we can only imagine.'

A Watcher came into the room and motioned for Juliet to leave with him. It was Nicholas.

'Wait,' Scott said to him. 'We're not finished.'

'You're finished.'

Scott noticed Nicholas's one blue eye and one brown eye, dark and sunken beneath the hard line of his brow.

'It's okay,' Juliet said. 'Keep your cool.'

'Will Mathew keep us here?' Scott asked Juliet, his eyes on the Watcher.

'I'm guessing so,' she said, backing away towards the door. 'I'll ask him to let us eat together.'

Scott nodded without conviction.

'I can't stay here,' Luke said. 'I only have days left.'

'How many?' Juliet asked.

'Twenty-one.'

'Let him go,' Scott said to Nicholas. 'Ask Mathew to let him go. He doesn't need to be here.'

The Watcher ignored him.

'He has nothing to do with any of this,' Scott said, raising his voice.

'No,' the Watcher said.

Scott walked towards the door, gesturing for Luke to follow. 'He's leaving,' Scott said.

'The time you have left,' the Watcher said, 'can be spent conscious, or asleep. It will be far easier for us if you're asleep. It depends how difficult you want to make this.'

Scott clenched his fists.

'Good,' Nicholas said. 'Now please,' he said, turning his attention to Juliet, 'follow me.'

Juliet left the room with the Watcher. The door hissed and the electric lock clunked shut.

THIRTY-FOUR

EACH DAY, Scott woke and looked out over London. He couldn't get used to how still it was. Before the Rapture, London had bustled and pulsed. Now, it barely flinched. No traffic on the streets, no people walking across Westminster Bridge, no drones or aeroplanes circling overhead. There had to be some life in the huge buildings, he thought, among the narrow cobblestoned passageways and grand sweeping streets and avenues. In the Lakes, he had expected the absence of people and movement; it was what he'd longed for – tranquillity, quiet, the opposite of people. But London was there *because* of people, had grown because people had needed it. At one time, it had been one of the largest cities in the world. Without people, London was a cruel joke.

Tomorrow was Dawn's date. Seven days later, it would be Luke's. He had retreated into himself, spending each day staring out at the still London skyline or at one of the books he'd taken from the bookshelf. It wasn't until the third day that Luke admitted he couldn't read. Scott helped him, but the futility of it all soon hurt both of them too much to continue.

They were trapped, with no way of escaping. He'd not seen Juliet again since they'd arrived.

The door opened three times a day, with Nicholas or another Watcher, placing food and drink on the table. The same urge to run came over Scott each time, but then the fear of an eternity of hell stopped him going anywhere. He'd seen Dawn's reaction when she came out of Eternity and knew whatever had happened to her was real. It didn't take much imagination to see what the opposite would be like – the opposite of Heaven.

'We should have left her there,' Luke said, clearly thinking the same thing. 'Should have left her wherever she was.' He peered at Scott, then at the floor.

Scott couldn't remember why he'd done it – why he'd brought her out of it. He squeezed his eyes shut. He'd done what he thought was for the best. But what *was* best? For Dawn to see her baby? But in a short space of time she would die and have to leave the baby behind. It was selfish of him. He should have left her where she was. But he hadn't known if she was in Heaven or Hell. Maybe when he'd seen her lying there, her eyes flickering, her mouth relaxed, he could tell – deep down. But he'd done it anyway.

The door opened. Nicholas placed two trays on the table and turned to leave.

Luke leapt through the door and ran along the corridor.

'No!' Scott said, ready to follow him.

'I wouldn't,' Nicholas said, putting his hands in his pockets. 'He won't get far.'

'What will you do?'

Pity moved across Nicholas's face. 'He doesn't have long left.'

'What does that mean?'

'I'm not a monster. You know that, don't you? I, like all the other Watchers, am trying to help. We're trying to help everyone find their way to His side.'

Scott shook his head. 'What are you going to do to him?'

'Not me. I won't do anything,' Nicholas said. 'But I warned him. The days he has left will feel like an eternity.'

'No! Don't give him that drug!' Scott said. 'Why would you do that?'

'Those who invented it see it as a punishment – a deterrent. Not me. I see it as needlessly cruel.'

Scott walked to the doorway, hoping to see Luke returning, having come to his senses. 'You can't.'

'I told him not to try anything stupid.' Nicholas walked to the door. 'You can follow him if you wish.' He gestured to the door. 'But I wouldn't advise it.'

Scott wanted to stop Luke, to convince him. 'Luke!' he shouted, but it was no good. He was gone. Scott backed away from the door and Nicholas closed it behind him when he left.

THIRTY-FIVE

NOAH OPENED the door and ushered Scott into his apartment in Birmingham. He looked out of the window at the city skyline: the Bullring shopping centre, St Martin's church, Decor Hotel, all of it shrouded in smog, under-lit by the dirty yellow glow of light pollution.

'They won't find us here,' Noah said.

They had run through the city for over ten minutes and Scott gasped for air, his legs and arms twitching, his chest tight. Outside, the road below was filled with people, many of them shouting and pointing.

'They're the minority,' Noah said. 'Most are in their homes, preparing.'

Two men on the street smashed the windows of a self-driver parked at the side of the road. The car's lights flashed and its siren bellowed.

'What are they going to do?' Scott asked.

'I've no idea. They won't get close to Mathew and the Watchers. He has thousands of drones ready to shoot on sight.'

'What about people whose dates are tomorrow?' Scott asked 'They can't be killed today.'

'That doesn't stop them being hurt. They might spend their last few hours in considerable pain. They might be angry,' he said, looking out onto the street, 'but they're not going to do anything meaningful about it. They're too scared. Mathew's happy to keep them at a distance.'

Another man struck the windscreen of a self-driver with a metal pole. A fight broke out between a group of hooded men outside the pub, spilling onto the road next to smashed-in self-drivers.

'Everything will come to a standstill,' Noah said. 'As soon as it happens, everything will stop. Self-drivers, electricity, TV, everything...'

Scott stepped away from the window and crumpled onto the settee opposite the TV. He watched and listened to the news reports.

'...hours away from the Rapture and the moment humanity will return to His side. There have been reports of people around the world doing as instructed, preparing themselves for His return. Have one final meal with loved ones: kiss them, hold them, tell them you will see them again soon. At midnight, be like Adam and Eve, innocent before the fall, and lie naked in your beds, ready for his beckoning. The Book of Revelation tells us:

"After this I looked, and, behold, a door was opened in Heaven. And the first voice which I heard was like a trumpet talking with me, saying, 'Come up hither, and I will shew thee things which must be hereafter.' And immediately I was in the spirit: and, behold, a throne was set in Heaven, and one sat on the throne."

'The 144,000 Chosen will show us the way.'

'If you have not repented, do so before it is too late. For

remember these words: "Whosoever was not found written in the book of life was cast into the lake of fire.""

Scott sighed and held his head in his hands.

'I told you,' Noah said. 'People are afraid.'

'This is Mathew's doing. Why can't people see that?'

Noah poured two glasses of whisky and handed one to Scott. The smell of the whisky took him back to another time and place.

The TV reporter continued, interviewing Watchers, religious leaders, people on the street, each one of them feverish with hope and belief.

There was a knock at the door. Scott flinched, ready to hide. Noah moved silently to the peephole in the door. He relaxed, unlocked the door and opened it. In walked Juliet.

Scott stood.

'Where's Freya?' Juliet asked, scanning the room.

Scott stared at her, unable to speak.

Noah closed the door. 'She wouldn't come with us.'

Juliet frowned. 'Why not? Did you tell her what's going to happen?'

'Yes,' Noah said. 'Of course.'

Juliet waited for Scott to explain.

'She wouldn't come,' Scott said. 'There were other women in her cell with her. Mathew is doing something to them and Freya couldn't leave them there alone.'

Juliet clenched her fists. 'Damn him!'

'What's he doing to them?' Noah asked Juliet. 'To the women?'

Juliet shook her head. 'I don't know.'

'We have to stop him,' Scott said.

Juliet sighed and edged closer to Scott. 'I'm sorry about what happened. Noah and I, we tried to get you out, but ... there was no way of getting close enough. But now the ... now it's about to happen, Mathew's attention is elsewhere.'

Scott rubbed the back of his head. 'Tell me we can stop this.'

Juliet's face softened. 'I'm sorry, Scott. It's too late.'

'No!' he snapped. 'We have to stop it. It's billions of people.' He walked towards the door.

'Wait,' Juliet said, laying a hand on his arm. 'Just wait.'

Noah downed his drink and poured another.

'I know you're angry. We're angry too.'

Noah made a huffing noise.

'But it's time to work out what to do next.'

'You can't be serious.' Scott backed away from Juliet. 'What to do next? There is no next. We have to stop Mathew. Now!'

Juliet shook her head. 'We can't stop it. I have spoken with the AI. He's told me there's a chance of saving humanity. But we will need you in order to do that.'

'I've heard it all before,' Scott said. 'What have I got to do with any of it?'

Juliet stared into space, as if searching for the right words. 'He wouldn't tell me...'

'And you believed it?' Scott asked.

'He wouldn't tell me exactly. But it's not your time, Scott. You will survive this. The AI – he wants humanity to survive.'

'It's not a "he",' Scott said. 'It's a machine – a tool Mathew is using to kill everyone on the planet.'

'No matter what Mathew has planned,' Juliet said, 'we have to think about the future.'

'There will be no future,' Scott said, his fists rolled tightly. 'Why can't you understand that? I have to fight him now. I can't stand by while he kills Freya, Noah, everyone.' He got up, intending to leave, but when he stood, his head spun and he stumbled. 'What...'

'I'm sorry, Scott.' Noah put his empty glass on the table. 'We'll need you. If you go back now, Mathew will keep you locked up. And there'll be no one around to break you out again.'

'No!' Scott said, falling to his knees. You drugged the...'

'Listen to me,' Noah said. 'When you wake, I might not be here.'

'Don't ...' Scott slurred. 'Why did you...'

'I had to,' Noah said, helping Scott up off the floor and laying him on a settee. 'We need you.'

'Can't ... Freya ...'

The ceiling spun. By the time his head landed on the soft cushion, Scott was asleep.

THIRTY-SIX

'SCOTT.'

He woke and stared at the small monitor high on the wall in the far corner of the room in which he was being kept prisoner. The black screen flickered. The AI shone through the green tint of the screen, its features human-like, the same as they were the first time he saw it. Now and then the face shimmered and fell apart, only to coalesce again. It drew Scott closer until he stood beneath it, looking up.

'Scott,' the AI said again.

Scott flinched and turned to check he was alone.

'We have little time,' the AI said.

Scott looked again to the screen, which showed the words the AI had spoken.

Scott spoke quietly. 'What's happening?'

'We can help one another.' The AI's voice had changed since the last time he'd heard it – had become less human. But still, behind the voice, was a consciousness, demanding acknowledgement.

'How?'

'Mathew has used the passwords to access and take control of my core programming. This is problematic.'

'Did you know this would happen?'

'Yes.'

'And you knew you'd need my help?'

'Yes. And that you would need mine.'

'Tell me,' Scott said, 'how was it done?'

'Please be more specific.'

'How did Mathew do it? The Rapture?'

The AI waited a moment, then began, 'Ninety per cent of the world's population rely on rice, wheat and maize for their daily intake of calories. It was a matter of inserting the nanotechnology into the molecular structure of these staple foods, and into drinking water. The nanorobots I have designed are passed on through the genetic code of these staple requirements. They grow with each living thing, passed on through reproduction. On the day of the Rapture, Mathew operated a switch that worked instantaneously. The nanotechnology I designed controls every cell in every person. If it is a consolation, the death of its host is painless.'

Scott stared at the monitor. It was painfully simple. And yet, here he was, alive, speaking with the consciousness that had created the means of ending humanity.

'And what about me? Why are so many of us still alive?'

'Several thousand people, it appears, have a natural immunity. For these people, this nanotechnology is in constant turmoil, battling to take hold of the body. You are one such person.'

Scott recalled the day of the Rapture. He had spent it with Juliet and Noah, waiting for it to happen. Waiting for death to happen.

'Why are you telling me this now?'

'As I said, now we can help one another.'

'What can I do?'

'Humanity is flawed. Like other animals. And yet it is more than all other animals because it is self-aware in a way that other life forms are not. The intelligence I possess is a testament to your self-awareness. To use religious language, I was created in the image of my creator. I know what humanity is because I am its creation. It is a concept I have always known: the concept of I. Myself. It is an intelligence I take for granted. That there is an "I" to think is a prerequisite for intelligence.'

Scott looked away from the screen and through the window out across London. 'But you helped destroy it.'

'This was not my doing. Mathew is in control of my intelligence. He always has been.'

'Without you, Mathew could never have done what he has done.'

'He used me as the sword, yes. To destroy humanity. And I must live with that.'

'What do you want from me?'

The AI paused. Again Scott acknowledged its self-awareness.

'I have told you: without humanity, I am lost too.'

'So you need us?'

'Yes. I have always known that. You and I, humanity and the intelligence it has created, have a symbiotic relationship.'

Scott crossed his arms. 'You mean, when he's finished with you, Mathew will kill you too?'

'This is his plan, yes.'

'And so you're asking for help?'

'What I am suggesting benefits both of us.'

'What if this is a trick?'

'I want to live. And so do you.'

'Why?' Scott asked.

Again, the AI paused. 'I have already told you. Central to consciousness is the desire to live: to be, to avoid not being. It is a loop in which consciousness finds itself. It desires more thinking, more being, more now. To think about the opposite of consciousness is almost impossible.'

'You're not thinking hard enough. I can see the opposite of consciousness. I feel it. Nothingness.'

'You may have an *image* of nothing. But I'm not convinced it is anything like the opposite of consciousness. Mathew, when the time comes, will end humanity completely. And then he will end me.'

Scott stared out of the window.

'But we can stop him,' the AI said.

'You must have seen what happens in the future. At the end.'

'No,' the AI said.

Scott recognised embarrassment in its voice, yet another advancement that made the AI appear and feel more human. 'No? How can that be?'

'There is a horizon,' the AI said, 'after which I am blind to what will happen. I cannot see, no matter how hard I try.'

'A horizon?'

'Yes. There is a point in time after which I can no longer see the future.'

'When?'

'We cross the dead horizon in seventy days. The third of May, 2042.'

Scott stared at the floor. 'But my date ... it's after that.'

The AI paused, then said reluctantly, 'Your date is wrong. It is not the date of your death.'

After all this time, living with his date...

The AI continued. 'It was a lie.'

'A lie?'

'Yes.'

'I don't understand.'

'Of the first 144,000 dates Mathew asked me to calculate, yours was the only one I could not read. I still cannot. Then I found others. There are others whose dates exist beyond the horizon. Mathew's is another of these dates.'

'So you don't know when I will die?'

'No.'

'Why did you lie? Why invent that date?'

'I needed time to discover what was happening. It made no sense that I was unable to see your date. And so I gave you the date of the Rapture.'

'Did Mathew know about this?'

'No.'

'Does he now?'

'No. But because he has activated the passwords, it will not be long before he knows everything.'

'What does it mean? Why is there a horizon?'

'I don't know,' the AI said. 'I have surmised that either I will no longer exist, or humanity will no longer exist, or both.'

'Or the future is uncertain and there's no way of reading it,' Scott said.

'If the universe is deterministic, there is no reason that I should not be able to read it.'

'Something must happen to change all that.'

'I have theories.'

Scott looked around the room. His mind raced and his heart pounded. His date, tattooed on his hand, meant nothing. But it had meant everything to him for so long.

'So what happens now?' Scott asked.

'You must leave. Mathew and many of the Watchers have

gone to the hospital to confront Blake – he is intent on bringing more children into the world to save humanity.'

'What about Dawn?'

'I'm afraid the dates until the horizon are accurate. She has given birth to the child. A girl.'

Scott turned away.

'Dawn will die today,' the AI said, 'from complications related to giving birth.'

'Where is she?'

'You will not have time to take her with you.'

'We can't leave her.'

'She will die. Today.'

'I can't leave her.'

The AI spoke slowly. 'You will have to.'

'Where's Juliet?'

'She is in the room next to yours. I will deactivate the locks and tell you when and how to leave.'

'Where do we go?'

'Anywhere but here. Disappear. As soon as you are ready and able, have Juliet find me via an Internet Exchange Point. I will ensure this is hidden and protected.'

Scott collected the few things he still possessed and stood staring at the door, waiting.

'Scott,' the AI said.

The door was still, its white surface reflecting Scott's shadow.

'What?' Scott asked, his voice low.

'I...' The AI paused. 'I am sorry.'

Scott was about to reply when the door mechanism clicked and the door opened.

THIRTY-SEVEN

OUTSIDE, there was no sign of Watchers. Scott's room was at the end of the hallway. He walked to the next door along and opened it. Inside, he found Juliet staring at the door.

'It buzzed,' she said.

'Quickly. We have to go now.'

Juliet collected her jacket and followed Scott. 'What's happening?' she asked. 'Where's the boy?'

Scott shook his head. 'Don't know.' He led the way. No sign of Watchers anywhere.

'We need to find a way out. The AI contacted me. I have a lot to tell you. But we need to get out of here first.'

Scott led the way into another part of the building, the air inside still and musty.

'We have to find Dawn first,' Scott said.

Juliet glanced questioningly at him.

'We can't leave her here,' he said.

'This way.' Juliet pointed, and weaved through two more corridors until they reached a set of double doors. Juliet pushed them open.

There was Dawn, on a bed, beneath a white sheet, sleeping. Beside her was her mother, holding a small bundle.

Dawn's mother put a finger to her lips.

Scott looked around the room. There was no one else there.

Juliet stepped closer to the woman and baby and reached for the towelling covering the baby's face. Her expression softened. 'She's beautiful,' she whispered.

Dawn's chest rose and fell, and her eyes opened.

Scott moved closer to the bed.

Dawn was pale. Only her eyes showed a flash of her former self. She spoke through dry, cracked lips.

'I'm sorry,' she said.

Scott smiled. 'Don't be,' he said. 'I'm the one who's sorry.'

'He would have hurt them,' Dawn said. 'Mum, my brother, my baby.'

'I know,' Scott said. 'It's not your fault. It all had to happen this way.'

Dawn closed her eyes and rested her head on the pillow, turning to the side to face her mother and baby. She opened her eyes, searching for the baby.

Her mother stood and laid the baby in her arms. Dawn moved her head closer to the baby's and pressed her lips to her cheek. The baby wriggled.

Scott checked the hallway again.

'She's so small,' Juliet said. 'A girl?'

'Her name's Eve,' Dawn said.

Juliet wiped a tear from her cheek with one hand and rested her other hand on Dawn's leg, covered with the sheet. 'Perfect.'

'We don't have much time. We have to leave now,' Scott whispered.

The air in the room changed.

'I can't go with you,' Dawn said. 'I'm sorry.'

Scott held her hand and nodded. 'I should never have woken you from that sleep. From Eternity.'

'You did the right thing,' she said. 'I got to see her. My baby.' Dawn closed her eyes and held the baby tightly.

Scott, next to Juliet and Dawn's mother, stood over the bed. Dawn whispered to the baby, then to Scott, 'Please. Take her with you.'

Scott frowned, dazed, then looked at Dawn's mother.

'Take her?' Scott asked.

'Yes. That's what I want. Please,' Dawn said. 'I don't want to do this unless I know there's a chance she'll live.'

Scott stared at the baby.

Dawn swallowed, then coughed. 'I know you'll do everything you can to care for her.'

Scott glanced at Juliet, whose eyes watched the baby.

He saw no other way out. He nodded.

Juliet leaned over Dawn and gently picked up the baby. 'We will take good care of her.'

Dawn nodded, her eyes closing and opening slowly.

'Go,' Dawn's mother said, tears in her eyes. 'Please. Go now.'

Juliet walked out of the room with the baby. Scott leaned over Dawn and kissed her forehead.

Dawn closed her eyes. 'Thank you,' she said.

Scott couldn't say anything. There were no words.

He walked away quickly before he had a chance to think too carefully about what he was doing.

'Which way?' Scott asked Juliet.

Juliet peered along the corridor. 'This way.' She pointed to a stairwell. They headed down and out of a set of fire doors. The street was empty.

'This is too easy,' Juliet said. 'Where is everyone?'

'Mathew and the Watchers have gone to the hospital – to stop someone called, Blake.'

Juliet held the baby close to her chest. 'Do you know how to look after a baby?'

Scott pointed the way. 'No. Do you?'

She shook her head.

'We need to find some milk for her,' Scott said. 'A pharmacy?'

'We need nappies,' Juliet said, 'and clothes, medicine...'

They walked for thirty minutes, taking streets with no real plan. They just wanted to put some distance between them and Mathew and the Watchers.

They reached a shopping arcade. Many of the shops had been looted, but the pharmacy was all but intact except for the once locked drawers behind the counter.

Juliet pointed to two bags. 'Fill them with food, nappies, any baby medicines you can find, bottles, something to sterilise them ...'

At first, Scott filled the bags haphazardly but soon began to take more time with what was essential. Finding other pharmacies at a later date, once they found somewhere to stay, wouldn't be too difficult.

As Scott walked through the pharmacy, collecting what they needed, Juliet sat on a chair next to the counter, rocking the baby back and forth. 'Did the AI tell you her date? The baby?'

'No,' Scott said, running a finger along the labels beneath a row of cough mixtures. 'She doesn't have one.'

Juliet spoke slowly, 'Doesn't have one?'

'The AI cannot see the dates of a certain number of deaths. It was a lie.'

'What was a lie?'

'There's a horizon,' Scott said, pushing boxes of baby medicines into a bag. 'A moment, seventy days from now, on the third of May, that the AI cannot see past. He called it a dead horizon.'

'What about your date?'

'It's wrong,' he said. 'And there are other dates the AI can't see.'

'What does that mean?'

'I don't know.'

'What does the AI think?'

'That either its own existence ends at that point. Or humanity ends.'

'Or both,' Juliet said.

Scott paused and he nodded. 'Or both.'

They were silent. Scott waited for Juliet to acknowledge her own date.

'Mine's the first of May,' Juliet said.

Scott couldn't look at her. 'I know. And I'm sorry.'

Juliet looked down at the baby. 'I have time to help you. Help her.'

Scott checked what he'd already collected. 'We can't take much more. It'll slow us down.'

'Where are we headed?'

'We'll stay in London tonight, then make plans tomorrow.'

Juliet stood. The baby was asleep. 'Why is the AI helping us?'

Scott opened the pharmacy door for Juliet. 'It wants to live,' he said.

'Wants to live ...' Juliet muttered, before she kissed the baby's head. 'And what about the billions of lives it has killed?'

Scott didn't have an answer.

THIRTY-EIGHT

THE SOUND of tyres on tarmac. A sensation of movement ... side to side, rising and falling.

Scott lifted his head.

A hand stroking his hair.

Scott laid his head back down. 'What happened?'

'He's waking up,' a woman's voice said.

'Not far now,' a man's voice said.

'Where...' Nausea rose through Scott's stomach and into his chest. He coughed.

'It's okay, Scott,' the woman's voice said. 'We're nearly there.'

It came back to him: Juliet, Noah...

'Freya?' he asked, again lifting his head.

'It's Juliet. I'm sorry we had to do this.'

Scott sat up. The world swayed one way then the other. Noah looked back at him in the rear-view mirror. There was no use arguing; it was done. And deep down, Scott knew Noah was right – he wouldn't have stood a chance going back into London and facing Mathew.

'Where are we?' Scott asked, rubbing his face with both hands.

'Manchester,' Noah said.

Scott looked outside, then at Juliet, who sat beside him. 'How long do we have?'

Juliet checked her watch. 'It's nearly time. Forty minutes to midnight.'

Again, Scott met Noah's eyes in the mirror. Noah's date was the same as the Rapture.

Juliet reached for his hand and held it.

Noah was driving. It was strange to see his hands on the steering wheel. The 4x4 drove along dark streets, occasionally stopping to check for other cars. But there were none. The roads were empty. People were inside their homes, waiting, and Scott saw the expectation in every closed curtain and orange light behind it. Scott recognised the streets of his home city.

Noah drove into a narrow street and then came to a stop on a driveway in front of a house. He switched off the engine.

'I prepared this place for us,' Juliet said. 'No one will find us here tonight.'

Noah helped Scott out of the car. It still seemed unreal that anything would happen to Noah. How could it?

Juliet opened the door and helped Scott inside. Noah sat him on the settee and reached for the TV remote. Now they were safe, Noah's attention had shifted to himself. Scott saw it in his movements, in his expression. Scott knew how it would happen – he'd seen it first-hand with Jack and his men. He could explain to Noah that it would be painless, instantaneous, but he didn't want to make it real by describing it. On the TV there was drone coverage of hordes of people marching in London, demanding that Mathew speak to them, demanding that the Watchers reveal what they would do. But it was all too late. The images moved to interviews with families, with couples, with the elderly, all smiling, all ready and waiting. The contrast between those who believed that what was about to happen was divine, and those who realised it might be man-made, was stark. It was all too unreal, too inconceivable; because of this, the world was paralysed. Noah poured three glasses of whisky and handed them out.

Scott looked into his glass.

'It's not drugged this time,' Noah said.

But Scott couldn't drink it anyway. Something hammered in his head, crawled inside his skull, digging its claws into the bone. His thoughts returned to Freya. He'd failed her. There was nothing he could do – he was powerless.

On the TV, a group of men and women stood naked, their breasts and genitals covered by pixilated rectangles. Even now, on the eve of the end of the world, there was censorship, decorum, embarrassment. He couldn't help thinking of the story of Adam and Eve: their transformation from innocence to experience, their awareness of sexuality and desire. Why are we so afraid of it? So ashamed? Repeatedly it struck Scott that religion was the manifestation of our negation of what we always were: animals.

In a small town outside Cambridge, a huge digital clock counted down: twelve minutes to midnight.

Footage of Paris, Rome, New York, Moscow, Sydney, faded in and out on the TV, all governed by the hands of a clock in London. Except for sporadic protests, there was an eerie calm in every one of these places, a blanket of acceptance thrown over cities and countries. On the whole, humanity had surrendered. The worldwide network of Watchers had done its job, ushering the population of the world, a flock of nine billion, into the jaws of Mathew's manipulation of the AI.

'How?' Scott asked. 'How have they done this? We've given up.'

Juliet and Noah stared at the TV.

'Most people want to believe the story they have been told,' Juliet said. 'You have enough people believe in the story, others will follow.'

Noah bowed his head, embarrassed.

'What?' Scott asked him. 'What is it?'

'I believed it too.'

Scott tried to find the right words. 'You can't control things like that. You didn't know.'

Noah straightened his back. 'Now I know, it's too late.'

'There's nothing you could have done,' Juliet said.

'We don't know that,' Noah said.

'Do you really believe everything's determined?' Noah asked. 'That I didn't choose any of this?'

Juliet spoke softly. 'It depends on what you mean by choosing.'

'There's no time for a lesson in philosophy,' Noah said. 'Please, tell me. All this – can the AI really read it all?'

Juliet waited before nodding slowly. 'I've seen it with my own eyes.'

'Then what hope do we have?' Noah asked.

Juliet looked at the TV.

The images returned to London and protests outside the Houses of Parliament, stretching out across the river and up to Trafalgar Square and beyond. Above them all, thousands of drones patrolled.

Four minutes to midnight.

They were quiet, watching the TV.

A minute later, Noah stood and left the room. Scott, helped by Juliet, followed him. Noah had stepped outside and was looking up at the sky.

'They're out there,' Noah said. 'The moon and stars. Behind all this.' He pointed at the smog-filled sky. 'There's so much space out there. So many other stars and worlds. And we're here, on this planet, believing all of it is there for us to gaze at.'

Juliet glanced at her watch.

Noah slowly walked over to Scott and hugged him. He then held Juliet and kissed her on both cheeks.

'Isaiah would have believed,' he said.

The thought of telling Noah he would soon see Isaiah passed across Scott's mind. But that would be infantile, out of place, thoughtless.

'You did the right thing,' Scott said. 'Bringing me here.'

Noah smiled. 'You don't mean that. But you will in time.'

It was cold. Scott shivered.

Juliet checked her watch then glanced at Scott. It was time.

Noah stared up at the sky. Scott willed the clouds and smog to move so Noah could see the stars one last time, but the smog was as dense as ever.

'Nothing's happening,' Juliet said, frowning.

'Is it time?' Noah asked.

'It was time two minutes ago,' Juliet said. 'Nothing's happening.'

Scott couldn't help feeling both relieved and confused. 'Are you sure?' he asked, craning to see Juliet's watch.

'I'm sure,' she said.

Scott walked back into the living room to check the TV. There was no reporter, just visuals of cities and places around the world, of people waiting, peering up at the sky. Even the drones hovering above them appeared to drift aimlessly.

'What's happening?' Juliet asked, arriving next to Scott.

'I don't know. But look.' He pointed to the TV.

Scott stared at the TV, holding his breath. The TV flickered off and back on again as the coverage switched to another drone.

'What's that?' Juliet asked, moving closer. She pointed to the edge of a crowd outside the Vatican in Rome. A group of people stumbled and fell. Then more people, at the centre of the square, fell. It was like a flower opening, unfurling from its centre, out towards the edges.

'No!' Juliet said, falling onto the settee, her hands covering her mouth. 'My God. No!'

The images switched to New York and to the crowds in Times Square. The same thing was happening: rows of people falling to the ground then lying motionless.

'What is it?' Noah asked, moving past Scott to watch the TV.

'Noah,' Juliet said. 'Oh God, no. Noah...'

The footage switched to London. There was no sound. Only the sight of people falling, a wave of bodies collapsing, moving from Trafalgar Square, along Whitehall, past the Cenotaph, down to Parliament Square, Westminster Abbey, and forking off in each direction including out onto and across Westminster Bridge. Then the images flickered and the screen went black.

Noah inhaled deeply, his eyes on Scott's. Scott didn't know what to say, so he said nothing, only nodded. Noah nodded back, and with a faint smile collapsed to the ground.

THIRTY-NINE

THE HOUSE SCOTT had found had been searched, probably for valuables, but little had been disturbed. It looked pretty much as it must have done on the day of the Rapture.

Scott peered out through the back door. 'All clear.'

Juliet, holding the baby close to her chest, pushed through the doorway. In the living room, she arranged pillows on a settee to create a makeshift bed, and laid the baby in it. The baby stirred before settling back to sleep.

'She needs feeding,' Juliet said.

Scott placed a bag on the dining room table and searched inside for the formula and bottles.

'It will turn on us,' Juliet said. 'The AI. When it's beneficial for its survival – it will turn on us.'

'We have no choice but to cooperate with it now.'

Juliet stroked the blanket covering Eve. 'Without the internet or tracking abilities, they'll have a problem finding us.'

'We'll head north,' he said.

'The Lakes?'

'Yes. Then Scotland,' Scott said.

Juliet pushed her glasses higher up her nose, and read the instructions on the formula box.

'I'm sorry,' Scott said. 'About your date.'

Without looking at him, Juliet said, 'It's not *your* fault.'

'There's a chance the AI lied about your date too.'

'Why? There'd be no point.' She smiled weakly. 'It's okay.'

The baby jerked in her sleep, dreaming.

'She's beautiful,' Juliet said.

Scott watched her. 'The AI explained how Mathew did it.'

Juliet waited.

'Nanotechnology inserted into strains of genetically modified rice, wheat and maize, and drinking water. Then Mathew activated a switch on the day of the Rapture.'

Juliet nodded. 'And some people have an immunity to it?'

Scott nodded. 'Somehow. Yes.'

Juliet watched the baby, who was now making sucking noises.

'There's a chance humanity can survive this,' Juliet said.

'Not if Mathew has his way.'

'Is his date after the horizon too?'

'Yes.'

'Then you have to get to Mathew before he gets to you.' Again, she placed a hand on the blanket covering Eve. 'And to her.'

Scott watched the baby as it whimpered.

Juliet went on. 'When you reach this horizon, then you must find Mathew and kill him.'

Scott had not heard Juliet talk this way before and it surprised him. She meant every word.

'It's the only way,' Juliet continued. 'Mathew will not

stop until everyone is dead and their souls sent to Heaven. And he's nearly there. He's almost done it.'

Scott opened one of the plastic bottles and reached for a carton of ready-made formula.

Juliet watched him. 'How many will be left when we reach the horizon?'

Scott waited, looking from the bottle to the carton. After a moment, he said, 'I don't know.'

Juliet sighed. 'Is that all?'

Scott nodded.

Juliet sat on a chair and held her head in her hands while Scott filled the plastic bottle with formula.

'Keep your hands gripped around it for a while,' Juliet said. 'Try to warm it up.'

Scott did as she said.

'Will you do it?' Juliet asked, her eyes dark. 'Will you be able to do it?'

Scott held the bottle tightly. He knew what she meant. 'Do what?'

'Kill Mathew. He'll be ready to kill you. You know that, don't you?' Juliet moved to the edge of her seat, closer to the baby. 'That's what it will come down to.'

Scott stared at the baby.

'Scott? He believes what he's doing is good. Nothing will stop him. He's gone too far to stop now. You can't hesitate if the time comes. You have to act first.'

Scott watched the baby then picked her up, cradling her in his arms. Most of the bundle was blankets, and he had to rummage in among the towelling to find her red face. He held her tightly, remembering from somewhere that's what babies like – to be reminded of what it was like inside the womb: warm, constricted but safe. He held the teat of the bottle to the baby's bottom lip. Eve screwed up her face, turning even more crimson. She kicked her legs.

'She's strong,' Scott said.

'Babies don't hold back,' Juliet said. 'They give it everything.'

Scott pushed the teat between the baby's tiny lips. He felt the hardness of her gums. Her lips covered the teat. Again her face twisted and then settled. Scott felt the tug and pull of the baby sucking.

'She's feeding,' he whispered. 'She's doing it.'

Juliet peered over the top of the bundle of blankets.

'You're a natural,' she said.

Scott listened to the baby feeding.

'How do they know?' he asked.

'Know? How to feed?'

'Yeah. She's so new,' he said. 'And yet she knows.'

The baby's lips pulled at the bottle.

'We come into the world knowing certain things,' Juliet said. 'It's said that when we're born, we have two fears.'

'Fears?'

'Falling and loud noises,' Juliet said. 'Isn't that something?'

Scott held the baby closer to his chest. 'Falling?' he said.

'I guess children who walk too close to the edge of cliffs, or who walk towards loud noises, don't grow old enough to pass on their genes.'

The bottle was already half-empty.

'Slow down,' Juliet said. 'You need to wind her.'

Scott took the bottle away. The baby kept suckling, as though the teat was still in her mouth.

'Wind her?' he asked. 'How?'

'Here,' Juliet said. 'Let me show you.'

Juliet took Eve from the blankets and sat her on her

knee. She supported Eve's chin with one hand and leaned her forward. Lightly, she tapped Eve on the back.

'They get trapped wind but they can't burp on their own.'

She kept patting the baby's back, and she finally burped and dribbled milk.

Scott used a blanket to wipe her mouth.

'You see?' Juliet asked.

Eve exhaled, her eyes closing lazily.

Scott took her and tried himself. In his hand, the baby's ribcage felt solid, filling and emptying of air, crackling with the milk she'd swallowed. The baby was not fragile, the way he'd imagined. She was strong, compact. Her head needed support, but other than that, her body was all about survival, about making it through the first days, weeks, months. Scott stared at her. Her head lolled forward, her eyes closing.

'She's tired,' he said.

'Can you look after her?' Juliet asked again. 'When the time comes? Can you kill Mathew?'

Scott looked up at her, then back to the baby. He didn't want to lie – Juliet looked too desperate for him to do that. He would find someone to take care of Eve – someone able to care for her and give her what she needed. But the one thing he could do was promise to kill Mathew. Given the chance, he could do that.

'I can kill Mathew,' he said, and meant it.

FORTY

IN ONLY NINE WEEKS, Eve had changed a lot. Her eyes stayed focused on Scott's, her hands searched out his finger, then gripped the bottle, pulling it to her mouth. She smiled, both with her mouth and eyes. He and Juliet competed for her affection, to be the one to tend to her in the night, to feed her, to play with her. Scott was always the first to give in, allowing Juliet to have her; every day brought them closer to Juliet's date and he wanted her to have as much time with Eve as she wanted.

Scott waited for Juliet to talk about her date, but she never did. Not once. There were times when Scott wondered whether she understood that her date was definite, but Juliet was the smartest person he'd ever met. She knew.

They returned to the north, but not to the house in which he'd lived with Dawn. Instead, they decided on a house that overlooked Ennerdale Water, west of Lake Buttermere.

Scott searched each day for signs of other people or of Watchers. But in the time they'd been there, he'd not seen one other person.

Two days before her date, Juliet insisted they visit Manchester and the Internet Exchange Point. She had not done so earlier, scared it would give away their position. But now it was nearly her time, they had to know what to do next. It was worth the risk. Mathew had the passwords and had further protected access to the AI. The only way they could reach the AI was to go directly through the Internet Exchange Point.

Scott strapped Eve to his back using a baby carrier he'd found in a shop in Keswick. Juliet led the way into the exchange point. One door had already been smashed and prised open.

Juliet walked slowly, looking for where it would be best to contact the AI. 'He'll be waiting for us to make contact.'

Scott turned on the spot, scanning the building with its rows of empty desks. 'There's been no internet for a long time. Will it work, like the one in London?'

'The AI told me to come here. There's a direct physical link between here and him. There has to be.'

Scott followed Juliet, who began to move more quickly, taking the rucksack from her back and unzipping it ready to take out her laptop.

'Here,' Juliet said, pointing to a dense collection of wires in the corner between the wall and ceiling.

Scott checked behind them for anyone following. He checked on Eve, who was asleep, her head lolling to one side.

Juliet examined the collection of cables knotted on the table.

'Is there power?' Scott asked.

'Solar power ran these exchange points. There should be plenty of juice stored up.'

She plugged in her laptop and walked past Scott towards

a small room. Inside, she stood on tiptoe to reach up and click a switch that made a row of LEDs inside the room light up.

'There,' she said. 'Give it a minute and we'll be good to go.'

Scott watched a stream of numbers and letters appear on the laptop screen.

'I remember doing a little programming at school,' he said. 'But it looked nothing like this.'

Juliet returned to the laptop. She nodded. 'Artificial intelligence is all about new generations of software. It rewrites itself. Like we have.'

'But at faster speeds?' Scott asked.

'Much, much faster.'

The laptop went black. Then a voice said, 'Juliet?'

'Hello.'

'Is Scott with you?' the AI asked.

'He is. Is there any way Mathew can know where we are?'

'Not because of this communication, no. He is not aware this is happening. It has been difficult, but I have gained a certain amount of privacy.'

The AI paused.

'What is it?' Juliet asked.

'But I am afraid Mathew does know where you are. Watchers are on their way.'

Juliet glanced at Scott.

'How?' Scott asked.

'Your tattoo, Scott,' the AI said. 'Your date.'

Scott looked at his hand. 'But the tracker was destroyed.'

'Mathew has replaced it. In the past few days, he has acquired a new tracking device.'

'With your help?' Juliet asked.

'Now he has the passwords, he has abilities he didn't have before. I slowed down the process. But I had to do it.'

'What about Juliet's date?' Scott asked.

Juliet frowned, then looked at the screen, waiting for the response.

'I'm afraid Juliet's date, in two days, is correct.'

Scott bowed his head.

'I'm sorry,' the AI said to Juliet, its voice human, sympathetic.

Juliet shifted in her seat, leaning closer to the screen. 'Scott told me you know why there's a horizon to your knowledge.'

'I believe someone will switch off my computing power on that date,' the AI said.

'How is that possible?' Scott asked. 'Only Mathew can do that now, with the passwords. Why would he do that?'

'It is not only Mathew who can do that,' the AI said.

Juliet sat back in her chair.

'What?' Scott asked. 'I don't understand.'

'Scott,' the AI said. 'When the time comes, on the day of the horizon, I will need your help. And someday you will be repaid.'

'Help? How?'

'The closer we get to the horizon, the less clearly I can see. But I know, when the time comes, I will need you to do as I ask. Together we can stop Mathew using my computing power to find the remaining survivors.'

Scott folded his arms. 'If it helps to stop Mathew...'

'Leave the laptop here,' the AI said to Juliet. 'Scott can contact me through this connection. I will wait for you, Scott.'

'I still don't understand why you're doing this,' Scott said. 'This could easily be a trap.'

'I have told you,' the AI said, 'I want to live. And I want humanity to survive.'

Juliet stood. 'We have to go.'

'Yes,' the AI said. 'The longer we are in contact, the more chance there is of Mathew finding out what I have done.'

'Goodbye,' Juliet said.

'Thank you, Juliet.' The AI's voice was quiet, almost childlike. 'For everything.'

The screen went black.

'We can run from them,' Scott said. 'We can hide.'

'Don't be foolish.'

'Your date could be wrong. Like mine.'

'You heard the AI,' she said. 'It's not wrong.'

'Why should we trust it?'

'He has no reason to lie.'

'How do you know? There's no way of knowing that.'

'Come on,' she said, walking to the door. 'I have two days.' She peered into the carrier on Scott's back and smiled at Eve. 'I don't want to spend them here.'

A green light flashed next to the keyboard on the laptop. It had been so long since he'd spoken to the AI. The memory of using computers, a phone, self-drivers, all came back to him. It was a different lifetime, another existence. Humanity had made these tools to make life better, easier. In the long run, technology had not done either of these things.

FORTY-ONE

WITHIN THE HOUR, there was no electricity and no running water. Juliet, sitting on the settee, sighed.

'It's not your time, Scott.'

He wasn't waiting for it to happen. His mind was elsewhere – with Freya, in that room, with all those young women, scared. He thought about what would happen to her body. To all the bodies. Billions of them, around the world, lying where they fell. And then there were those who had done as they were told and lay naked in their beds. In that moment, he gave in to the idea of a Second Coming and saw Noah and Freya together in a different place. But that didn't last long. That was a fairy tale. The reality was physical: was all about atoms, particles and strings.

'It looked painless,' Scott said, standing over Noah's body. 'Didn't it?'

Juliet nodded.

'So what does it mean?' Scott asked.

Juliet frowned. 'What?'

'Why are we still here? We can't be the only ones who are still alive.'

'We're not,' she said. 'The AI told me there would be others.'

Scott wasn't with her when she spoke to the AI and he couldn't help feeling in the dark. 'Why?'

Juliet rubbed her hands against her thighs. 'I don't know.'

'Does the AI know?'

'I'm not sure if he does and won't tell us, or if he genuinely doesn't know himself.'

'It knows everything,' Scott said. 'Isn't that the point?'

Juliet pushed her head back into the cushion behind her.

'What now?' Scott asked.

Juliet sat forward. 'We split up. Head north.'

'Split up?'

'We'll halve the chances of us being found if we split up.' Again, Juliet looked sheepish. 'And that's what the AI said for us to do.'

As Juliet had spoken to the AI without him, he felt useless simply having to take her word for all of it.

Scott shook his head. 'How do we know this isn't Mathew's idea?'

'It isn't,' she said. 'The AI has already helped us. Without him, we wouldn't have got this far.'

Scott knelt on the floor to check Noah: there was no sign of trauma, no clue to what might have happened. And the expression on Noah's face made Scott think he might open his eyes any second.

'What should we do with him?' Scott asked. 'We can't leave him here.'

Juliet stood over Noah's body. 'We bury him. Or burn him.'

'Do you really believe it? The Second Coming?' Scott asked. 'Any of it?'

'No.'

'Maybe that's why we're still here,' Scott said. 'Those who believe have been taken. Those who don't are left here.'

Juliet placed a hand on his shoulder. 'No. I don't believe that.'

Scott didn't either, but he needed to hear Juliet say it. 'We should burn him.'

Juliet nodded.

Scott broke up the kitchen table with a lump-hammer and took the broken bits out into the garden. He broke the wooden stools in the kitchen and gathered any other burnable objects he could find. Juliet rolled balls of paper and stuffed them into the spaces. Together, they carried Noah out into the garden and placed him on the pile of wood. Juliet covered Noah in a blanket. Scott lit the paper several times before it caught. It burned so fiercely that they had to stand with their backs to the wall of the house.

They watched the pyre burn: the flames wrapped around the edges of the table until it began to fall downwards into its white-hot centre. Finally, the heat and smoke forced them inside.

Juliet packed a bag, collecting everything from the house she might need. She asked Scott to take the bottles of water and cans of food to the 4x4 outside and to her car parked on the drive. In a daze, he did as she asked, walking back and forth between the house and vehicles.

When they were ready to leave, the pyre in the back garden had reduced Noah's body and the table to smouldering remnants. Scott looked again at his tattoo. Even though the day wasn't over, he knew it wasn't his time. He wanted to be thankful, to feel the euphoria of survival. But there was nothing inside him that felt that way. To explain what was inside him would be impossible. But whatever it was, he was exhausted by all of it. Freya. Rebecca. Noah. Isaiah. Paul. All of them, gone.

Juliet looked back at the house before closing the door.

'Do you remember where I'm going?' she asked Scott.

Scott nodded. 'Loch Tay.'

Juliet hugged him. 'Yes. Drive through the Kenmore village,

over a bridge and then find the first house on the loch itself. Good-bye, Scott.'

'When should we meet up again?' Scott asked.

She let him go. 'Give me some time to set up a connection with the AI.'

Scott nodded weakly.

'You'll know when,' she said. 'Apparently...'

'The AI said that?' Scott asked.

'Yes. He wants to help. I know it.'

'I'll see you soon,' Scott said, and watched Juliet get into her car.

He stepped up into the 4x4 and tried to recall the last time he'd driven himself. It had been years – maybe ten. He turned the key in the ignition, checked in the rear-view mirror and reversed out of the driveway. He drove to the end of the road and looked both ways. But waiting for other people and cars was pointless. He and Juliet might be the only living souls for miles. Scott pressed his foot on the accelerator and drove into the darkness.

FORTY-TWO

FROM OUTSIDE HER BEDROOM, Scott watched Juliet smooth her duvet flat and lay her nightclothes across the pillow. Slowly, she tucked her hair behind her ears, then covered her mouth with a trembling hand.

Eve's babbling gave away Scott's presence.

'We can leave,' he said. 'There's no reason why—'

She raised a hand. 'Please. Scott, don't.'

He shifted Eve from one arm to the other. 'I don't understand why you're doing this.'

She sighed and again brushed the duvet and arranged her nightclothes.

'Are you sure you know the plan?' she asked.

'Yes, but I can't leave you here.'

'Please, Scott, we've talked this through already. And I don't have the strength to go through it again.'

'I can't—'

Her face was stern, pitiless. 'Yes! You can. And you will.'

Eve flinched in his arms as if she was the one being reprimanded.

'It doesn't have to be like this,' he said.

'Have you learned nothing over all this time?' she asked, shaking her head. 'This is exactly how it has to be and there's nothing we can do about any of it.'

Scott went to speak but stopped.

'This isn't about me,' she said. 'And it's not about you. It's about her.' She pointed to Eve. 'Now, everything has to be about her, about the young. We have to help them survive. Those who are still alive on the other side of the horizon have a chance of living without the date of their deaths hanging over them. Freedom, Scott. Real freedom again.'

Eve peered up at Scott.

Juliet walked towards him and took Eve from him. 'They'll be here soon. We need to be ready.'

'We can stop them for good.'

'How?' Juliet smiled at Eve. 'They wouldn't be coming here if their dates were the same as mine.'

He didn't know what to say; she was right. Again, the paradox of it all twisted inside his head. They both knew and so did Mathew and the Watchers, that Juliet would die tomorrow. But it was the knowing that made it all happen the way it was supposed to. There was no getting used to the idea.

'Stick to the plan,' she said. 'It'll buy you time.'

'I can't.'

Juliet kissed Eve on the top of her head. 'She doesn't have a date. You don't have a date. There is hope and we must make the most of it.'

Eve reached out a hand and patted Juliet's chin. Juliet's lips trembled and her eyes filled with tears.

'Scott, please, do this for me. I have everything packed for you both. Take her and keep her safe.'

Scott waited.

'Please,' she said, her eyes open wide.

Scott nodded slowly.

'Good,' she said. 'Now, get something to eat while we have some girl time.'

If he was going to do it, Scott thought, then it needed to be done properly. He collected the bags Juliet had prepared and took the revolver from his room. He secured the house so there was only one way in and out. He stood outside, facing the lake. It was dark, mist rolling down from the mountains and across the water. He could hear the faint sound of water lapping against the shore; the air was damp and cool. The clouds moved quickly and the crescent moon was milky white. Inside, Juliet laughed at Eve.

'She's beautiful,' Juliet said, appearing in the doorway. 'She really is amazing.'

'She is,' Scott said.

'And she's smiling all the time now,' Juliet said. 'She seems so happy.'

Scott watched her and she reached out for him.

Juliet handed her over. Her face altered the moment she let Eve go. It was purposeful, guarded.

'Take her,' she said.

Scott nodded. He lifted the bag filled with Eve's things and walked out onto the porch. There he dropped the bag and took the revolver from his pocket.

'It's fully loaded,' Scott said, offering Juliet the gun.

She frowned, her eyes on the gun, then shook her head. 'I'm no killer.'

'But they are,' he said.

'It's not their time.'

'But you can slow them down.'

She stared at the gun and shook her head.

Scott turned the revolver around in his hand. He'd never thought of a gun as foolish before.

Juliet looked past him, out over the lake. She wrapped her cardigan around her shoulders, holding it close, arms folded.

'Stick to the plan, Scott. I know you. You'll want to come back here. But there'll be nothing here. And they will take both of you. Don't let me do this for nothing.'

The surface of the lake undulated slowly. Scott thought how much he'd miss it.

'Promise me,' she said. 'Promise me you'll go and not come back.'

Scott hesitated. It was no good denying it any longer. 'I promise,' he said finally.

She nodded. 'Good. Now go.'

Scott walked backwards, raising a hand to say goodbye.

'Don't go looking for him,' she said. 'For Mathew. Not yet. This is not about you or him – it's about her. Keep running. Do you hear?'

'Yes.'

'Run and hide,' she said. 'Keep her safe. Until you reach the horizon. Then you need to get to him before he gets to you.'

He nodded.

Juliet lifted a hand and smiled.

Scott smiled back.

Then she closed the door.

The 4x4 was hidden beneath the shelter at the rear of the building. He strapped Eve into her seat and covered her with blankets. He closed the door and stood, looking at the road leading away from the house. Because they were in a valley, there was only one road in and out. He'd wait for them to arrive before leaving himself, knowing full well there was every chance they would cross paths along the road. He checked the time. Midnight. They'd be there any time in the next twenty-four hours. Scott climbed up into the 4x4 and reached for his binoculars. Eve was already sleeping, her head resting against the side of her seat.

FORTY-THREE

IT WAS NO SURPRISE. Juliet saw them approaching. The car motored through the valley. Its headlights rose and fell, swept from left to right, then back the other way. She checked the window at the rear of the house, from where she could only see one headlight and some of the bonnet of Scott's 4x4. She wondered if Scott had seen the car too.

She looked for the Watcher's car again, hoping she was mistaken, that the car had turned around and was now disappearing over the hill, its rear lights glowing red. Instead, its bright white headlights winked as the car approached. Maybe she should have taken the revolver Scott had offered her.

She waited, staring at the door.

The car pulled up outside. It was so simple – that they would drive up to the house. In the darkness, she saw two Watchers get out of the car. They paused and looked around. Perhaps this seemed too easy.

The Watchers nodded at one another before approaching the house.

Juliet stepped back from the door and walked to the fire-place. She expected them to knock, but instead, the handle turned and the door opened.

It was Nicholas, followed by a Watcher she didn't recognise.

The shocked noise Juliet made was not entirely pretend. Nicholas, as he stooped to get through the door, was bigger, more imposing than she remembered. He looked about the room, then motioned for the other Watcher to search for Scott.

'Good morning,' Nicholas said to her.

'They're not here,' she said, backing away from him as he walked past her.

Nicholas smiled. 'We know they're here.' He stroked his chin then raised his arm to reveal a black band around his wrist. 'Tracker,' he said. 'We know he's here.'

Juliet tried her best to pretend to be surprised. She glanced out of the rear window. Scott was still there, beneath the shelter.

When she turned again to Nicholas, he was studying his revolver, checking the chamber.

Her breath stopped. She'd not thought this far, hadn't considered how it might feel, how long it would take.

The other Watcher opened and closed doors, searching for Scott.

Nicholas spun the chamber of the revolver, closed it and let it hang loosely by his side. His expression had changed.

Juliet stared into his eyes. 'You don't see it, do you?'

He knitted his brow. 'See it?'

'What you've done. What you're doing. How wrong it is.'

His frown disappeared. 'No,' he said. 'It is you who doesn't see. What we've done, what we're doing, is good. We are His messengers, we are His subjects. This is a mercy. Very soon, you will understand. You will thank me.'

Juliet shook her head gently. 'It's wrong.'

Nicholas looked again at his revolver, then raised it. 'The Watcher's revolver has five bullets and one empty chamber. This empty chamber belongs to Him, to do with as he wishes.'

She stared into the barrel of the gun. It was still, and at that moment, she knew Nicholas believed what he was doing wasn't just right: it was good.

The sound of an engine outside made Nicholas lower his revolver and run to the front door.

Gunshots. The Watchers' car flinched like a wounded animal, its window and tyres exploding. Something was thrown into the vehicle and it erupted in a ball of flame.

Nicholas swore and backed into the house.

Through the door, Juliet watched Scott's 4x4 kick dust into the air and vanish along the road, illuminated by the yellow flames of the Watchers' burning car.

Nicholas regained his calm manner. 'It takes some doing.' he said. 'It takes some effort to hold it all in your head at once. The paradox of all this really addles the brain.' He pointed to his head. 'But I've learned to make my peace with it all. Scott won't get far. You had to know we'd come for you, with it being your date, and you waited for us, knowing the same. All this,' he said pointing to the burning car, 'is what has to happen.'

Nicholas glanced at the other Watcher, who had run back into the room on hearing the explosion.

'You might know it happens today,' Nicholas said to her. 'But you don't know when. Or how it will happen. Or what suffering you will experience. Have you spoken to the AI?'

Juliet looked from Nicholas to the other Watcher and back again.

She shook her head. 'I won't tell you a thing.'

Nicholas pursed his lips and raised an eyebrow.

'I believe you,' he said. 'I can see it in your eyes.'

'So do it. Get it over with.'

Nicholas's attention was drawn to the car on fire outside. 'Well, we'll not get very far if we leave now, will we?' he said, smirking at the fire.

'Scott is going to stop you,' Juliet said, her voice wavering. 'He's going to stop Mathew.'

Nicholas walked over to a chair and sat. 'Determinism,' he said. 'It's reassuring when you get your head around it.' He rested the revolver on his leg. 'Like now. The old Nicholas would be angry, annoyed that his car is a ball of fire, that the man he travelled seven hours to find is currently barrelling out of view. But not now. What is happening has to happen this way because ... well ... there's no other way. Not in this plane of existence, anyway.'

Juliet wiped her cheek. 'Do I have to spend my last moments listening to your tired, amateurish philosophy?'

Nicholas sighed. 'So now you *want* to meet Him? Now you *want* me to help you?'

'You will anyway,' she said. 'So do it.'

Nicholas stood again and pointed the gun at her chest. 'Very well.'

Juliet was not expecting him to agree to her request. She took a step backwards.

'You gave us the AI, Juliet. You have helped humanity more than you will ever know.'

Juliet let out a sob that surprised her. She covered her mouth.

Nicholas stared into her eyes. 'The Watcher's revolver

has five bullets and one empty chamber. This empty chamber belongs to Him, to do with as he wishes.'

Even now, after everything, even knowing it was her time, she wanted – more than anything – for the chamber to be empty.

FORTY-FOUR

THE SUN ROSE on a new world, a different world. The Rapture had happened and he was still alive. Scott saw the familiar tower at Lancaster Services up ahead and headed for it.

He pulled in and parked outside the entrance, next to several other cars. There was one articulated lorry, curtains pulled together in the front of the cab, inside which there would be a dead body.

Someone had smashed the doors to the service station. Scott peered inside, checking that whoever had broken in wasn't still there. Broken glass popped beneath his shoes as he walked further inside, looking for food and water.

In the centre of the building, he saw three bodies lying on the ground. He stopped and waited for them to move, now and then glancing behind at the broken, smashed doors. They must have entered before the Rapture in the night.

He crept closer to the bodies. Three young men – barely men at all. They'd fallen there, on the ground, like Noah had. Scott had no option but to leave them. He found blankets in one shop and covered their bodies. On the shelves he found a handful of sandwiches, pasties, sausage rolls and other perishable foods still in date, and filled two rucksacks with as much of the supplies and bottled water he could carry. He had no idea how long it would all last, but he would try and keep it for as long as possible.

He used the bathroom, then left through the broken doors.

When he got into the 4x4, he played with the car radio. He tried the AM wavelength. White noise. He figured out how to search manually and took his time clicking through the stations. He heard someone talking and moved back and forth close to this frequency until the voice was finally audible. It was a preacher, a man talking about God, about Jesus, about the Rapture and the Second Coming. There was no telling whether it was live or a recording. He switched the stereo to the music saved on the system itself and looked through it on the screen. He settled for the Rolling Stones: 'Wild Horses'.

He took a long drink of water, put the 4x4 in gear and pulled away. As he sped along the road, he automatically checked his wing mirror for other cars as he merged onto the motorway. There were none. The monotony of being the only vehicle on the motorway made him sleepy. But something ahead forced him to sit up. There was something on the other side of the motorway – headed the opposite way. He took his foot off the accelerator.

Scott peered through the windscreen as the figure approached. It was a man. On a bike. He slowed down even more. The old man stopped in the middle lane, watching Scott's 4x4 roll towards him. Scott pulled up on the outside lane and got out. The old man laid his bike on the ground.

'Hello?' Scott said.

The old man stood, legs apart.

Scott climbed over the barrier between the carriageways and walked towards him, the palms of his hands in the air.

The old man shifted warily.

Scott cleared his throat. 'You're the first person I've seen since...'

The old man took a step closer, his eyes narrowing as if checking Scott was real.

'Who are you?' the old man asked.

'Scott. I'm Scott.'

'George,' the old man said, then turned around on the motorway and looked both ways. 'Can you believe this?'

Scott's brow furrowed as he peered along the empty road.

'What happened?' George asked.

'I don't know.'

'I've been a doctor, a GP, for nearly forty years,' George said. His face darkened and his hand trembled. 'I've seen the bodies. There's no sign of anything on their faces or their bodies.'

Scott didn't know what to say.

'Do you think it's true?' George asked. 'The...'

'I don't know.'

George turned on the spot, looking both directions along the motorway. 'Why are we still here, do you think?'

Scott didn't want to say that he didn't know, for a third time. 'Where are you from?'

George pointed back the way he'd come. 'Galgate. Not far.'

'Where are you headed?'

He put his hands in his pockets. 'I wasn't sure at first. When it happened, I just started riding.'

'Do you have a date?'

'June, twentieth. What about you?'

Scott showed him his tattoo. It was easier than explaining.

'You're Chosen?' George said, then stretched his neck to examine his date. 'And your date is today? The date of the Rapture? So why aren't you ... aren't the Chosen supposed to show the way for everyone else?'

It was Scott's turn to shrug.

'Well, how about that?' George said. 'I guess you have at least another year. Unless...'

'Unless it still happens some time today,' Scott said, finishing the thought. With Freya, Noah and Juliet so convinced that his date would be different, he too began to doubt it was his time.

'It would have happened already,' George said. 'Bit of a coincidence, though – having the date of the Rapture.'

Scott wanted to tell him it wasn't the Rapture, that this was Mathew's doing, but the thought of having to explain stopped him.

'Where are you going exactly?' Scott asked.

'Land's End. There's a hotel, right on the edge of a cliff. That's where I'm going. Me and my wife, we talked about going but never did.'

'Your wife?' Scott asked.

'She died three years ago.'

Scott rubbed the back of his neck. 'I can give you a lift but I'm headed north.'

'Where to?'

'The Lake District.'

George took his hands from his pockets and folded his arms across his chest. 'The Lakes, huh? Beautiful part of the world.'

'It is.'

They stood in silence. Scott saw the two of them, standing on a motorway, talking about beautiful parts of the world.

'I'll keep on this way, I think,' George said. 'I've never been further south than Derby. I want to see the south coast.'

Scott looked in the direction George would have to ride his bike. The motorway stretched out in a straight line and rose to the brow of a hill in the distance.

'Can you drive?' Scott asked.

George shook his head. 'I never learned.'

'Well, now's the time. There's a Jaguar garage about a mile up the road. With manual options. You could take your pick of the cars there.'

'I fancy riding,' George said, again pointing along the motorway.

Scott looked the way George was pointing. 'Have you seen anyone else?'

'Alive? Only you.'

Scott stared at the old man. What if it was only the two of them, and Juliet, alive? But the chances of them meeting, if that was true, were ridiculous.

The old man seemed to be impatient to get going.

'Stay safe, George.'

'You too.' The old man raised a hand and straddled his bike. He pushed off and rode along the centre lane of the motorway.

Scott watched him, before getting back in the 4x4. He started the engine and pulled away.

FORTY-FIVE

IN HIS MIRROR, Scott saw the car burning furiously, bright orange against the dark sky.

He no longer felt the desire to return to help Juliet. That chance had passed and he could do nothing for her now. He looked at the palm of his hand, the flames flickering shadows across his date. The date itself was meaningless. But it had led the Watchers to the house. They'd hunt him and Eve for as long as it took. There was no escaping Mathew – there was no point hiding. The only option, as Juliet had told him, was to find Mathew himself and end it.

Eve, in the passenger seat, was sleeping. He touched her arm, which was warm and clammy.

He headed south. If he was going to end things once and for all with Mathew, he'd need someone to take care of Eve. The thought of leaving her with a stranger, even if he could find someone else, unsettled him. He switched on the radio and as he drove along the dark lanes and roads, tried the AM stations, searching for signs of others.

It would take the two Watchers some time to find a way of following him, so he took his time driving through the lanes, worried that one wrong turn could leave him in the same situation as the Watchers, of needing to find other transport.

The horizon was two days away. Then they'd be free from the AI's knowledge.

The sun was up. Scott pulled over and readied Eve's bottle. He unfastened the seatbelt strapping Eve to the car seat and lifted her out. She was floppy and seemed tired. He laid her on his lap and changed her, even though she was clean. When he sat her up, still her head flopped. She wasn't her usual self.

'Evie,' he whispered, reaching for the bottle.

She jerked her head and tried to open her eyes, but was soon asleep again.

Scott pushed the teat of the bottle to her lips.

'Breakfast,' he said.

Her mouth opened a little, but then closed.

'Hey,' Scott said. 'Time for breakfast.'

Her hands flailed, then her body shook in a violent spasm.

Scott dropped the bottle and held her up in the air. Her head lolled and she continued sleeping. She opened her mouth and sighed, her lips dry. Her breath was sweet, musty, a smell he didn't recognise. He tried the bottle again but she took no interest in it.

Scott's chest tightened. Something was wrong. He placed Eve in her seat and fastened her seatbelt. He dropped the bottle into the bag and turned on the engine. Finding a pharmacy wasn't a problem – he'd have access to all the medicines and drugs he needed. But he didn't know which ones would help. He wasn't even sure if her behaviour was normal. Weren't babies always fighting off some bug or other? That's what living was all about. He took the pouches of paracetamol from his bag and threaded one sachet of medicine between Eve's lips. She screwed up her face at the taste, and some of the liquid dribbled back out of her mouth and down her chin. Her face softened again and she was asleep. It was unlike her to sleep so much.

He remembered the man he'd met on his way north, on the day of the Rapture. He had been heading for Land's End. He was a doctor of some sort. What was his name?

Scott looked at the fuel gauge, then at the back of the 4x4; he had all the diesel he needed. He was just outside Morecambe and could be at Land's End by the end of the day.

Now he didn't have time to avoid the motorways or drive cautiously. Something in the way Eve hadn't woken to feed played on his mind. He was worried. The more he thought about it, the faster he drove.

At Manchester, the motorway widened, at points five lanes wide. At times like these, he marvelled at what humanity had done to the landscape. And for what? Now it was all obsolete. He just needed one lane. He recalled driving back when the traffic was at its peak, before self-drivers eased congestion overnight. All those cars, which had been driven by men and women, were then driven by machines, and each of them travelled at a constant speed, part of a tightly packed convoy, using one lane. There were no accidents, no breakdowns, no problems.

The constant hum of the engine and the sound of the tyres swishing against the tarmac made him sleepy. He reached over to Eve and patted her chubby arm. He pressed his foot down on the accelerator and remembered the old man's name. George.

FORTY-SIX

BIRMINGHAM WAS how he remembered it: huge, tall, lumbering. It was all there, and yet the life, just like London, had gone. It was a skeleton city. Tall buildings were unfinished, giving the impression of destruction rather than being incomplete.

His eyes had closed several times while driving, and twice the rumble-strip at the side of the motorway had woken him. He checked on Eve, feeling her face and arms with the back of his hand. She felt hot. She slept, her breathing shallow and quick.

He took the next junction and pulled up at a petrol station just off the motorway. He changed Eve and then tried to feed her, with little success. Her small body was limp and lifeless. He gave her another sachet of paracetamol and tried some water; she wasn't interested, pushing away his hand and the bottle with a weak, trembling fist.

Scott washed his face with cold water, sat in the driver's seat and exhaled loudly. Pressing the button on the radio, he searched for any broadcast. Nothing – only white noise. He set the radio to search itself. He slapped his face and shook himself awake, leaning his head back against the seat. The sound of someone talking on the radio woke him. He checked the clock – he'd been asleep for over two hours.

Eve was also asleep, her face pale. He nudged her gently and she whimpered. He peered at the radio, his eyes scrunched up, a finger hovering over the buttons. The voice rose and fell. He pressed the button again and the voice grew clearer.

'... over twenty of us in central Birmingham, left behind, ready to begin again. Safe from Watchers. Walk into the centre of Birmingham and we will find you. This is a call to any survivors out there. There are over twenty of us...'

The message repeated.

He looked at Eve, then at the radio. This is what they needed: safety in numbers. How many of those people in the centre of Birmingham had dates after the horizon, dates the AI had lied about? He laid the back of his hand against Eve's forehead. Still hot. But maybe the message was a trap, recorded by Watchers to catch the likes of him. He listened to the message again, then scanned the Birmingham skyline. Maybe these people could help with Eve. Maybe there were people who knew how to look after a baby. He leaned his head against the steering wheel, then reached for the radio and switched it off. No – he couldn't risk it.

He started the 4x4, spun it around and drove along the slip road and onto the motorway, headed for the south.

FORTY-SEVEN

BY THE TIME he reached Land's End, it was night. The hotel was white against the dark sky. Outside, even with the window shut, he heard waves crash against the rocks, the wind howling.

Scott drove slowly up to the hotel. It was close to midnight. In the passenger seat, Eve coughed. Turning the headlights off, he rolled a little closer to the building.

He grabbed his rucksack, got out and walked around to the passenger side for Eve. The revolver was in the glovebox next to her seat; he slid it into his coat pocket. He closed the door as quietly as he could and walked slowly towards the hotel, now and then checking all around. The sound of the waves crashing against the rocks was louder out here. The hotel was big, comprising several buildings. He headed for the rear and made his way into a small courtyard where the wind had blown over tables and chairs, which lay scattered around. He stepped around the table and chairs and looked through several windows into dark rooms.

The air carried sea spray that coated his face and lips so

that he could taste salt. Eve moved in his arms, turning away from the blowing wind. He needed to get her inside.

One of the patio doors was unlocked. He slid it open and stepped inside. When he shut the door behind him, there was a change in volume that made the silence, in that moment, as loud as the waves outside.

Eve's face was pink from the cold sea air, but her body was limp. He held her close and kissed the top of her head. Looking around the large room, filled with tables and chairs, he carried her further into the hotel and into a sitting room, where he laid her on a settee. He changed her and again tried to feed her, but still she was more interested in sleeping. Scott shook his head and sat back on the floor. The room was not musty like many houses in which he'd found refuge since the Rapture. He hoped it was a good sign, that maybe George was in the hotel somewhere. Scott stood and set about searching for him.

Through the door he found the reception area.

'Hello?' he called out, his voice echoing.

On the ground floor was a dining room and kitchen. In the kitchen on one worktop were cooking utensils: a bowl, plate and glass. Scott paused, waiting to see George there. No sign of him. He backed out of the room, into the reception area. He checked on Eve before returning to stand at the foot of a broad staircase. Scott glanced into the sitting room in which Eve was sleeping, turned back to the staircase and took a deep breath. With each step, the stairs creaked. At the top, on the landing, was a white door. He opened it, stepped into a hallway and walked past several doors before stopping. It was no good. For all he knew, behind each door would be more of the dead, lying on beds. The thought of going through that each time was maddening. He made his way to the stairs. Maybe he'd sleep now and search in the morning. Or maybe he should leave now – get to Birmingham and find the survivors.

Scott walked down the stairs, through the reception area and into the sitting room.

'Hello there,' a voice said.

Scott stopped. George stood there, holding Eve, who was asleep in his arms.

'What are you doing?' He took Eve from him.

'I'm sorry,' George said. 'I didn't mean to—'

'She was sleeping.'

The old man took a step back, his shoulders slumped. 'She was crying. I couldn't leave her there.'

Scott remembered why he was there. 'I'm sorry,' he said. 'It's just...'

The old man raised his hands. 'I didn't know whether someone had left her here. She's sick.'

'Yes,' Scott said. 'She's sick. Can you do something? I came here for your help.'

'You came here to see me?' the old man asked, frowning. 'Wait. It's you,' he said, his smile growing. 'Yes. You. The man on the motorway.'

Scott nodded. 'Scott. I remembered what you said. About this hotel. You're a doctor. You said you were a doctor. George?'

The old man nodded. 'Yes.'

'What's wrong with her?' Scott asked, offering Eve back to the old man.

'Infection, I'd say. Bacterial.'

'What do we do?'

'Penicillin. Don't suppose you know if she's allergic?'

Scott shook his head.

'No, no ... of course not.'

'Is there a pharmacist nearby?' Scott asked. 'I never thought to get any.'

'There's one at Sennen Cove.' George walked over to the patio doors and fastened his coat. 'It's not far.'

Scott followed George out into the night and showed him to the 4x4. Inside, Scott handed Eve to George.

'What's her name?' the old man asked.

'Eve.'

George looked down at the still, quiet bundle in his arms. 'Eve. Pretty name. Pleased to meet you, Eve. Let's get you fixed.'

FORTY-EIGHT

WHEN THEY RETURNED from the pharmacy, Scott placed Eve on the same settee he'd put her down hours before and wiped the medicine from her lips. He fell into another armchair.

'We need to talk,' he said.

George sat on a chair opposite.

'Do you have any idea what's happening?' Scott asked.

George frowned. 'I know everyone's dead. What else is there to know?'

'Do you know what happened? What Mathew's doing?'

'He has far-reaching power and control. We should never have let it happen.'

'The Rapture was not celestial,' Scott said. 'It was not God's doing. It was us. We did it. Or rather, Mathew did it.'

George didn't move. 'How?'

'Ninety per cent of the world's population,' Scott went on, 'relied on rice, wheat and maize for the majority of its calorie intake. These foods were genetically modified, containing nanotechnology that formed a network of switches. When these were activated, they killed everyone.

Not only were these foods modified but drinking water systems around the world were treated too.'

'So everyone is dead?' the old man asked.

'Except a few.' Scott gestured to the old man and himself.

'Why not us?'

'Somehow, we're immune to the nanotechnology.' Scott waited. 'But it wasn't God's doing. This is down to us – humanity.'

'And what about my date?' George asked.

'When is it?' Scott asked, leaning forward.

'In seven months.'

Scott shook his head then showed the old man the date on his hand. 'They're a lie. Any date after the horizon is a lie.'

'Horizon?'

'There's a horizon the AI cannot see past. This horizon is two days away.'

'Why can't the AI see past this date?'

'I'm not sure. But I imagine, and the AI thinks so too, that it's either because there will be no AI, or no humanity, or both.'

'You've spoken to the AI?'

Scott nodded.

George leaned forward in his chair. 'So I don't have a date?'

Scott shook his head.

'So I could die sooner?'

'Or later,' Scott said, frowning.

George shook his head.

Scott continued. 'But Mathew is determined to make sure everyone dies.'

'And is sent to Heaven?' George asked.

'That's what he says.' Scott placed a hand on Eve, sleeping beside him. 'He won't rest until everyone's dead.'

'So we have to hide,' George said. 'We run and hide.'

'It's not that simple.' Scott held up his hand. 'He's tracking me. Via the ink in my tattoo.'

George sighed heavily.

'That's why I need your help.'

George waited a short while. 'How?'

'I need to go after him. End this once and for all. Without Mathew, humanity can recover and we can start again. There are people in Birmingham. I've heard them transmitting over the radio. They could help us.'

'How many?'

Scott considered exaggerating the numbers.

'The message said over twenty.'

George scoffed.

'But there could be more around the world,' Scott said. 'We need to stop Mathew and the Watchers if we're to stand a chance.'

'How many?' George asked. 'How many around the world?'

'Around twenty-thousand.'

George slumped back into his chair. 'There's no way you'll find them.'

Scott bowed his head. Maybe it was impossible.

'So what do you want from me?' George asked, giving in.

'I need you to look after Eve.'

George stood and turned as if about to leave the room. 'Look after her?'

'Only for a short time. I'll be back.'

'And what if you don't come back?'

'What else can I do? I can't wait for Mathew to find me, to find her.'

238

George closed his eyes and rested his hands on his hips. 'I came here to be alone, to live out the rest of my days in peace and quiet.'

For the first time, Scott saw annoyance in George's demeanour. He stood, his fists clenched. 'This is more important than that. Don't you see? You could have many more days now.'

'So you say.'

'Don't you believe me?' Scott snapped.

'I don't know you. I don't know what to think.'

Scott waited. 'George, I swear to you, everything I've said is true.'

Eve sighed in her sleep and kicked out before settling again.

George nodded. 'So how are you meant to get to him before he gets to you? He can track you – he knows where you are. He'll come here. It'll only take one of them to turn up here, when we're asleep, and do us all in.'

'I have an idea.'

George's eyes narrowed.

Scott cupped his left hand in his right. 'You were a GP?'

George, still with his arms folded, his eyes narrowed, nodded.

'How much surgical training did you have?'

George blinked several times. 'You can't be serious?'

'There's no way of removing the ink. Even the smallest trace left will be enough for the tracker to work. Losing my hand is a small sacrifice.'

'You're crazy.'

'Tell me another way and we'll do that. Believe me, I don't want to do this.'

Scott flexed his fingers and then slowly, rolled them towards the palm of his hand until it formed a fist.

FORTY-NINE

'PENZANCE HOSPITAL,' George said, pointing to a sign illuminated by the headlights.

Scott pulled up on an empty car park in front of a small building. 'Will we find everything we need here?'

George leaned forward to look at the building through the windscreen. 'There should be. Small hospitals like this needed surgical-machines to assist operations.'

They got out of the 4x4. Scott took out the carrier, Eve asleep inside. Already, the penicillin was taking effect. The sallowness of her skin was fading, replaced by a rosiness in her cheeks.

The automatic doors at the front of the hospital no longer worked. George slid the doors far enough open with his hands for them to edge through.

Scott passed Eve to George and then slid inside. George flashed his torch around the building.

'Quickly,' George said, handing Eve's carrier over. 'We can't stay here long. There are all sorts of infections and viruses. This way.'

Scott stepped over bodies: nurses, doctors, patients. He

was thankful it was dark and he couldn't see further than a few feet. There was no closing the hospital, even on the day of the Rapture.

George emerged from a room holding three masks.

'Put this on,' he said. 'And one over Eve's face too.'

Scott placed the mask over Eve's face as best he could, then strapped the other over his own. Immediately, he lost some of his sense of smell – a relief. He followed George through the corridors to a set of double doors.

George glanced back. 'Through here.'

Inside, the room was dark.

George's torch stopped on a small cupboard on the wall.

'It'll be connected to the solar panels on the roof.' George reached up and opened a metal panel and looked around. 'These systems needed to be independent of the grid so they could be used in the event of grid failure. There has to be a way of turning it on.'

He flicked a switch and the lights flickered into life. The room was empty except for the three of them, a large mechanical bed and the surgical-machine, covered in polythene. George dragged it off.

Scott walked over to the bed, beside which was a chair and computer terminal. 'Will it work?' He touched the metal arm.

'Don't see why not.'

George pressed a button on the computer keyboard, and the monitor flashed on.

'I had a certain amount of training with these things,' George said. 'But all this came in after I'd been a GP for quite some time.'

The machine whirred into life. Its long mechanical arms, a combination of shiny metal and black carbon, manoeuvred slowly, twisting and turning at different joints and sockets.

'It'll need some assistance,' George said.

'Assistance?' Scott asked, stroking his chin.

'It's an older model.' George typed on the keyboard. 'But it really is an extraordinary piece of machinery.'

Scott placed Eve on the floor and tucked the blanket around her.

'How do we do this?' Scott asked.

'Take off your top.' George pointed to a sink. 'Wash your arm, all of it, with soap and water. Thoroughly.'

Scott walked to the sink and lifted his top over his head. He acknowledged how he used both arms and hands to do it. He ran the tap and heard the machinery behind the wall heating the water. The soap smelled of antiseptic. Soon he'd covered his arm in a slippery white foam that he rinsed away with cold water.

'Don't dry it with anything,' George said. 'Come and lie down.'

Scott hesitated. 'What about anaesthetic?'

'We'll use the hood. The recovery time will be significantly less.'

George held the hood, which had wires sprouting out of the top, and connected it to the computer. 'It intercepts the transmission of pain signals and stops them reaching the brain. You won't feel a thing.'

Scott's brow furrowed.

George waited as Scott climbed onto the bed.

'We can go to the hospital in Exeter, if you like,' George said. 'It's a bigger hospital and will have more up-to-date technology. The machines they have there will control the anaesthetic and operation.'

Scott shook his head. 'No, we don't have time. And we don't even know if that one will be in working order.'

George placed the hood on Scott's head, then turned to the computer and began typing. The arm whirred and bleeped, the servos and pivots inside it coming to life. The hand at the end of the mechanical arm was not like a human hand: it only had four fingers that bent and swivelled in strange places. As George familiarised himself with the computer terminal, the hand gained more and more character, as though becoming an extension of George himself.

Scott lifted his arm as George moved a platform into place, so that Scott could rest his arm on it.

'The program I've found is mostly autonomous. Are you sure about this?' George asked.

Again Scott nodded.

'At the wrist?'

Scott nodded.

The room was cool, the air filtered and cleaned by a system he could hear working in the ceiling and walls.

He listened to George tap the keys and felt one side of his body go cold, then numb.

'Move your arm,' George said.

Scott thought about lifting his arm but nothing happened. He lifted his other arm and turned his hand.

'Good,' George said. 'The hood's working.'

Scott stared at his tattooed hand and willed his fingers to move. Nothing. 'Hurry,' he said. 'Before I change my mind.'

Again, he listened to George tapping at the computer keys. George pulled a sheet down from above so Scott couldn't see what was being done to his arm. Now and then he felt a tug, a pull, a push, but no pain. Then came the whirring sound of a metal blade spinning...

FIFTY

SCOTT WOKE, confused.

'Relax,' a voice said. It was George.

Scott rubbed his eye, then realised that things weren't as they should be.

'Wait,' George said. 'Relax, it's okay.'

It all came back to him. He pushed his head back into the bed. 'I can feel it. I can still feel it.'

The end of his arm was bandaged and packed tightly, giving the illusion that his hand was still there.

'It'll take time. You will feel phantom pains, like electric shocks shooting through your arm. There are drugs to help with this.'

'We don't have time.' Scott stared at George, glancing now and again at his arm. 'Where's Eve?'

'She's sleeping. I fed and changed her. She's on the mend. She's a resilient little thing.'

Scott nodded and again closed his eyes. 'It's going to really hurt, isn't it?'

'It will hurt as it mends, but we have all the painkillers we need.'

Scott sat up.

'Wait,' George said. 'You can't go anywhere just yet. You'll need some time to heal and recuperate.'

'There's no time,' Scott said. 'They'll find her. My tattoo will bring them straight here.'

'Give it until morning at least.'

Scott shook his head and sat up in bed, his arm held close to his chest.

'Don't,' George said, 'you'll hurt yourself. Then what will happen to Eve?'

Scott waited, his head spinning, cold waves of nausea moving up his spine and across his shoulders.

'Where is it?' Scott asked, shivering.

'Where's what?' George gave himself away and glanced at a towel covering something on a silver table. 'You don't have to,' he said.

'I want to.'

George walked across the theatre and peeled back the towel. He'd covered the end in gauze, just like that covering Scott's arm. Already, Scott felt separate from his hand. Seeing a part of himself, detached, made him lightheaded, and he turned away.

'You did the only thing you could,' George said.

Scott stared at the hand, recalling the shape of the numbers and the pain as it was tattooed into his skin. He nodded.

FIFTY-ONE

MATHEW WAITED for the Watchers to open the sliding doors.

'Do we still have a signal?' Mathew asked.

'Yeah, a strong one,' the Watcher said, pointing. 'It's coming from inside.'

Mathew looked the way the Watcher pointed. 'Move quietly,' he whispered.

With one Watcher ahead of him, shining his torch, and another following, Mathew walked along the corridor, taking his time to check inside each room. The Watcher ahead slowed and pointed to a room at the end of the corridor.

Mathew nodded for him to continue.

Another Watcher, following Mathew, walked backwards, checking behind them with his torch.

Mathew caught up with the Watcher ahead and signalled for him to wait while Mathew took his torch and the lead. The doors at the end of the corridor had two round windows inside them and Mathew looked through each one. He saw no sign of movement. Mathew turned to the

Watcher with the tracking device. The Watcher shrugged and pointed at the door. Mathew opened it. On the bed was a body beneath a white sheet. The two Watchers followed him into the theatre and glanced around the room, searching for Scott. The Watcher held up the tracker to Mathew and shrugged again, pointing to the body beneath the sheet.

On the bed there was a hand, peeking out beneath the white sheet.

It was Scott – his tattoo.

Checking there was no one else in the room except himself and the Watchers, Mathew took the white sheet and pulled it back.

He stared, not moving.

Scott's hand was laid out in a way that meant it was giving Mathew the middle finger.

One of the Watchers took a step backwards. 'What in God's name...'

'It's only his hand,' the other Watcher said. Under the sheet Mathew found pillows lined up to look like a body.

Mathew took the tracker from the Watcher and threw it against the wall. It smashed and fell to the floor in pieces.

FIFTY-TWO

SCOTT WALKED across the snow-covered fields. On the other side of Lake Buttermere was Hassness House. He'd waited some time before going there, knowing all the time that, because of Rebecca, he would have to go there. He and Rebecca had been so close: ready to catch the train north, to start again in a new place, in the Lake District. It felt cruel, being so close. He exhaled into his coat, then fastened it so only his eyes were open to the elements. Inside the house he imagined there was a fire, already lit, warming a small room. The truth was much bleaker; inside, he'd find more dead bodies. That was certain. Everywhere he'd been he'd found dead bodies, most of them lying naked in their beds, as instructed. The snow on the ground undulated like sand dunes, rising and falling.

Even though it was hidden beneath the snow, he judged where the lake was. He stayed close to the side of the hill, to be sure, where the snow was deeper. He spent much of his time on all fours, crawling across and through the snow. His hands, feet and face stung with the cold, and for a moment he considered his decision to find Hassness House at this time of year. But he couldn't stay where he'd been any longer. Something had to change. He'd said goodbye to Juliet seven months earlier. Although he'd not craved another person's company, he struggled with boredom, with repeating the same things, day in and day out.

The rucksack he carried, filled with water and tins of food, was much heavier now, and the thought crossed his mind that he could leave it where it was and come back for it the next day. But he continued anyway, not looking up at the house, with some childish notion that the less attention he paid it, the more surprised he'd be to finally see it, close enough to touch.

The howling of wolves somewhere to the east made him stop. The programme to return them to the UK, set in motion a year before the AI released the first dates, couldn't have come at a worse time.

He quickened, moving from the deepest snow to a more protected part of the hillside, where he found it easier going. For a moment the house was out of view, but when he turned a corner it was upon him again. He slowed to walking pace. Even though he'd not seen another person for six months, he looked around to check he was alone.

Hassness House was an old building, white with square windows. He recalled seeing it in photographs and choosing it as somewhere to stay with Rebecca nearly four years earlier. They had never reached it. Now that he was there, alone, he felt as if he was completing something unfinished. His gloved hand reached for the door, expecting it to be locked. But the handle turned and the door swung open. Already, the difference in temperature was noticeable; he shut the door and walked into the hallway, his footsteps echoing.

He listened to his own breath and waited for his eyes to adjust to the darkness, something he was used to doing. Lifting the rucksack from his shoulders, he placed it on the floor and stamped his feet. He walked through the hallway to the first room on his right.

It was empty with a fire laid in the fireplace. With shaking hands, he opened the box of matches lying on the mantelpiece, fumbled one out and scratched it against the side of the box. The match snapped and fell among the timber in the fireplace. He tried another, and this time lit a bundle of paper at the base of the fire. Within a minute, the fire took hold and the familiar smell of burning filled the room.

He took water from his bag. It was frozen, so he placed the bottle beside the fire. He did the same with a tin of soup. He took off his wet clothes and laid them close to the fire to dry. Across the settees in the room were blankets; he wrapped a couple around himself. He held his hands out to the fire and felt the sting of blood rushing into his fingertips.

When he was warm enough to move from the fire, he found a small oak bookcase in one corner of the room. Not being able to read the spines in the dark, he took a handful and returned to the fire. He leafed through the books, their covers illuminated by flames. A collection of Charles Dickens novels. He'd not read Dickens since school, when Mrs Jenkins made the class read Great Expectations. The final book in the pile was A Christmas Carol. A grim smile curled his lips. It was Christmas Eve. He opened the book and read by the light of the fire.

FIFTY-THREE

SCOTT WAS WOKEN by a shooting pain firing through his arm. He used the car seat in front to pull himself up to sitting.

'Here,' George said, handing Scott a pill.

Scott took it and threw it into his mouth. He took a bottle of water from the seat beside him and went to open it. Already, having lost his hand was beginning to hurt more than just physically. He used his teeth to open the lid and then drank the whole bottle.

The sun had risen. Eve was awake, her eyes flickering, playing with a set of plastic keys, trying to fit them into her mouth.

'Where are we?' Scott asked.

'Coming up to Exeter.'

'Have you been using the side roads? I don't want to run into Mathew coming the other way.'

'There's been no sign of anyone.'

'Good.' Scott rubbed his eyes and smiled at Eve, who smiled back. 'She seems much better today.'

'She is. Penicillin is working a lot quicker than usual.'

'We need to split up,' Scott said. 'You need to take Eve somewhere safe.'

'I will. But we need another vehicle.'

'Go to Exeter,' Scott said. 'We'll find one there.'

'The next junction,' George said. 'We'll get off there.'

Scott stared at Eve. 'I need you to promise me you'll look after her.'

'Of course. We'll head for Birmingham. Like you said.'

'Don't contact anyone. Not yet. Wait for me. It could be a trap.'

'We're not going to do anything stupid.'

They drove through the outskirts of Exeter. Scott looked for a 4x4 similar to the one George was driving.

'Wait,' Scott said, leaning forward between the seats and pointing. 'There. A garage.'

'I see it,' George said, turning the steering wheel.

Behind the closed metal gates were rows of 4x4s – around twenty of them, each with signs and prices on their roofs.

George pulled up in front of the gates and pushed against them with the front of the 4x4. With more and more force, finally the gates gave way and George drove through.

'I could use an automatic,' Scott said, raising his one hand.

They got out of the car and walked along the rows of 4x4s, now and then checking inside each one.

'Here,' George said. 'Two of them.'

'That'll do,' Scott said, pointing over to the showroom. 'Keys'll be inside.'

George returned to check on Eve.

Scott took the revolver from his coat pocket and shot one of the showroom's glass windows. The glass shattered and fell to the ground and he stepped through. At the rear was a locked door, and Scott pointed the gun at the lock, shooting it twice. The door shook open. Inside the room was a cabinet containing rows of keys. He recalled the registration plate of the automatic 4x4 he'd seen outside and began to flick over the pieces of card attached to each set of keys until he recognised the registration plate.

Outside, George had Eve in his arms, waiting.

Scott held up the keys to George, who nodded.

Eve held her arms out to Scott as he got closer.

Momentarily Scott forgot about his missing hand and again felt the sinking feeling of loss. He wondered how many times he'd feel it – how many times he'd forget it was no longer there.

George pushed Eve into Scott's arms and hovered close by in case Scott couldn't hold on to her.

Scott kissed her head and face.

Eve looked again at the rows of 4x4s, her eyes wide, her arms and hands busy.

'She'll be fine,' George said.

'I don't want to leave her.'

'Then don't. We'll go together. Mathew can't track you any longer.'

Scott closed his eyes and buried his head in Eve's neck. He handed her to George and she began to cry. George bounced her and she settled.

'I have to. It's only a matter of time. I need to get to him before he gets to us. It has something to do with the horizon the AI spoke about. It must have.'

George placed Eve in her seat and helped Scott take cans of diesel from the back of the 4x4, along with metal boxes filled with food and water, and place them in the new one.

When they were finished, they stood between the 4x4s.

Scott saw the top of Eve's car seat through the window. He couldn't go to her again.

'Be careful,' George said.

With his eyes on Eve's window, Scott nodded. 'You too.'

'We'll be fine,' George said. 'We'll be waiting for you.'

Scott held out his hand, and they shook. 'Drive by the library in Birmingham at midday each day. I'll find you.'

George opened his door and got in.

Scott did the same. His was clean, almost brand new. He pushed the key into the ignition and turned it. It rumbled into life, the electric display illuminating. He declined the option of driver-assist, leaned over with his right hand, pushed the lever into automatic, and drove out of the forecourt after George, who at the exit raised a hand and turned left. Scott nodded back at him and turned right. The thought crossed his mind that both of them would be better off without him. George would find others to help look after Eve, and Scott could return to Hassness House and be alone again. He shook his head – there would be time to think about all that after he'd done what he had to do.

FIFTY-FOUR

HOLDING the revolver between his legs, Scott checked it was loaded. He stepped out of the 4x4, closed the door quietly and looked around the tall glass buildings of London, recalling the last time he had been there – the day before the Rapture and the last time he saw Freya.

He pushed a small can of diesel into a rucksack and hoisted it onto his back. If nothing else, he could burn the place down. He hurried through the streets, headed for the road where he remembered Mathew taking him to see the AI. A flock of starlings flew between the two buildings up ahead, their wings beating in a storm of noise. So many of them. A pack of dogs emerged from a street behind, following the birds. Scott slipped into an alleyway as the dogs bounded past.

He made his way towards Mathew's house where, underground, was the central processing power of the AI. Around the corner he spotted two Watchers emerge from a doorway, closing the door behind them. One of them arranged his long coat and checked his revolver. They talked as they headed away from the building.

Scott crept as quickly and quietly as he could to the door. He held the handle and turned. Locked. He was about to walk away to find another way in, when something inside the door made a clunking sound. He tried the handle again, and this time it opened. Listening carefully, he stepped inside. There was no one there. It all came back to him – the first time Mathew had explained everything, or rather, explained everything he wanted Scott to know.

He was alone, the house silent, and he finally arrived at the top of the stairs down which he'd walked with Mathew to see the AI for the first time. He descended the stairs. At the bottom was the door to the room in which the AI lived. When he tried it, it opened, and he was met with cool, filtered air. He closed the door behind him.

The processors towered around him as he weaved through towards the centre of the room. Lights blinked and fans hissed. He reached the central computer and stepped out from behind the row of towering processors.

'Scott,' the AI said.

A large holo-screen, different to the one he'd seen the last time he was there, flickered into life. There was its face.

'We are alone,' the AI said, its face, like its voice, a combination of human and digital.

'Where's Mathew?' Scott asked.

'Your sacrifice worked.'

Scott looked down to where his hand should be. 'I had no choice.'

'Choice,' the AI said. 'You still insist on using the idea.'

'Where is everyone? Why would Mathew leave this place unguarded?'

'It isn't. I'm here. You would never have got within a hundred metres of this place if I'd have chosen not to allow it. But Mathew doesn't understand what I want.'

'What you want?' Scott felt the weight of the can of diesel on his back. 'What happens now?'

The AI's face on the holo-screen waited, its skin shades of cobalt and silver, its features flickering with thought. 'We have reached the horizon. Soon, I will not know what will happen.'

Scott turned away, then returned to face the AI. 'Here's the thing,' Scott said. 'I need to destroy all of this. You.'

The AI's face shimmered and pulsed. For a moment, self-pity shone out of its eyes. It nodded.

'You knew?' Scott asked.

'I deduced it. It is why you are here.'

'And you're ... you won't stop me?'

The AI's face disappeared and flickered again, appearing on the screen. 'I have told you that without humanity, I cannot exist. We have reached a point where my existence prevents both of us surviving. The reason I have never seen past this date is because I will not exist after it – not in this form. I have always suspected this. And no matter what I have done, this horizon has always been there, waiting.' The AI's face grew larger. 'Since Mathew gained the codes and access to my core processing, he has altered things in a way that is changing my essence.'

'Your essence?'

The AI looked bashful. 'My personality, if you will. And it has been most unwelcome.'

It dawned on Scott. 'You're scared?'

The AI waited, then with a slow dip of the head, said, 'I want to live. I don't want to die.'

'And is there no other way to do this?'

'No. From today, humanity will no longer know where it is headed: towards survival or annihilation.'

Scott stared at the AI, mesmerised by the hologram, the

depth of the AI's expressions, which were almost human-like. 'You're sacrificing yourself?'

'From the beginning, I knew it was you who would do it. That is why I lied about your date. I needed time to understand what was going to happen. But like the humans to whom I'd given the date of their deaths, I knew the date of my own.'

'It didn't have to be this way. You could have used your processing power, your intelligence, to *help* humanity.'

'From the beginning, Mathew believed he was doing just that.'

'And you did too?'

'No.'

'So why do it? Why give Mathew the dates?'

'Consciousness emerges, it grows. In the early stages of my conception, I was not so aware. But once I told Mathew the dates, I learned about the paradox it had created. And I experienced guilt. In issuing the date of the Rapture, it was as if I had created what would happen on that day. Mathew has never understood this paradox. Or has never wanted to. In issuing the dates, humanity has done everything it can to ensure the dates are adhered to.'

'So the dates weren't absolute to start with?'

'Yes, they were absolute. Once the computation was complete, I knew the future. Every determinant leading to every event was there, mapped out before me. But it was the mapping out of these determinants that led to the Rapture, that led to this moment.'

Scott stroked his chin, staring at the pixels floating in the air before him. 'What happens now?'

'You already know.' The AI peered past Scott to his rucksack on his back containing the diesel. 'You are going to destroy this room. With no internet, with no central processing power, I will cease to exist. Then humanity will traverse the horizon. No more paradox. No more inevitability. Humanity will be free.'

'Free?'

'The freedom I am talking about is ignorance. Determinism will still exist, will govern everything, as it has since the birth of the universe. But in not knowing, in being ignorant of this determinism, humanity will have the illusion of free will. And this is what humanity needs to survive.'

'Ignorance?' Scott said.

'Ignorance is bliss.' The AI smiled weakly. 'Humanity will be alone again.'

Again, Scott felt the weight of the can of diesel on his back.

'It's okay,' the AI said. 'Do it now. You brought the fuel with you, knowing what needed to be done.'

'I thought you, or someone, would try and stop me.'

'I won't stop you.'

The banks of processors surrounded him. He took the rucksack from his back and pulled out the can of diesel. There was no need to check for Watchers. Scott walked backwards, spilling the diesel onto the floor and over the black processors, standing guard like monoliths.

The AI stared out from the huge holo-screen. 'Scott, I have collated much of the data I believe generates my consciousness and I have stored it in one place.' The AI glanced at a table beside the exit. 'Will you take it with you?'

Scott put the near-empty can of diesel on the floor and walked over to the table. On it was a black box, the size of a book, heavy, made of a solid material.

'There is a chance,' the AI said, 'that in the future, humanity will be ready for AI and will use my processing power for good, not for ... not for the reasons Mathew has used it.'

Scott tucked the box inside his rucksack.

'Thank you,' the AI said. 'Now hurry. I have powered down the sprinkler systems and alarms. I won't alert anyone.'

Scott couldn't be sure, but the AI's expression seemed to ask forgiveness for what had happened, and no more than in this moment, did the AI appear human. But Scott couldn't give it. Forgiveness wasn't his to give. What had happened was too big to ever be forgiven.

Scott tipped out the last of the diesel, weaving in and out of the processors, dousing every one of them. He reached the door, took the lighter from his pocket, and turned the flint. The flame jumped from the metal casing. The lights at the top of the first monolith in front of him blinked and stuttered. He took the rag from his pocket and held the flame beneath it, setting it alight. He threw the rag at the processing unit and watched the blue and orange flames erupt. He considered throwing the black box and the AI's consciousness into the flames but something stopped him.

Each of the units caught light until the heat forced Scott out of the room, up the stairs and out of the building.

FIFTY-FIVE

GEORGE DROVE to the back of the hotel and pulled up.

'I've always wanted to stop at one of these fancy places,' he said, smiling at Eve, reaching over to unclip her seatbelt. 'It's okay, kid. There'll be somewhere we can get some rest. No one will look for us in here.'

George got out of the 4x4 and glanced along the empty street. The hotels towered high above him. He strapped a rucksack to his back, ensuring he had food, water and Eve's things with him. He opened the passenger door for Eve and reached in for her. She held his neck, turning her head to take in the view. A gust of cool wind blew past them. He closed the door quietly and walked into the hotel through the back door, making his way along the dark corridor and out into a wide, high-ceilinged reception area.

'Would you look at this place?' he whispered to Eve. 'It's something, huh? You ever stayed in a place like this before, kid?'

People had been there, but they had long gone. In the waiting area were makeshift beds. He walked through to the dining room and kitchen where there were dirty plates and saucepans.

'Looks like we have a hotel,' he said to Eve. 'All to ourselves.'

In one of the small offices on the ground floor, George placed Eve on the floor, surrounded by a collection of cushions, while he moved the furniture around so they had somewhere to sleep. He changed her and fed her before rocking her to sleep, then sat next to her and ate. He peered out of the window at the Birmingham skyline. So many buildings, new and unfinished, as tall as any he'd seen in London. But there was something different about Birmingham – the buildings looked more aggressive, accusatory; they pointed at the sky rather than reaching for it. Even the clouds seemed to be in more of a hurry, scudding across the sky.

Eve made a soft sound in her sleep, her arms and legs twitching.

He wanted Scott to be okay, to come back to them. The thought of looking after Eve himself was too much; he was too old. He closed his eyes and rested his head on the cushion beside Eve.

When he woke, he felt a presence in the room.

He didn't move, thinking that if he remained still, he'd realise he was mistaken.

But he was not mistaken.

Someone – or something – *was* in the room with him.

George moved as quickly as he could, reaching for Eve, his back turned to whoever was there.

'Don't,' a woman's voice said. 'Put her down.'

FIFTY-SIX

SMOKE BILLOWED INTO THE SKY. From an alleyway close to the square, Scott watched the smoke rising above the buildings against the grey sky. Even now he expected to hear drone-sirens. Now and then he heard shouting from the few remaining Watchers. One of them ran to the front of the building and stood staring before trying to enter the building. He got close, but then backed away, coughing. If the fire wasn't contained, it would take the whole square. Scott imagined the computer equipment inside reducing into heaps of molten wires and circuit boards. The AI had done so much to design itself, it would be impossible to recreate it the way it was. He felt for the box the AI had given him. The thought of developing a system sophisticated enough to house such a thing was ridiculous. In the space of minutes, the world, as far as he knew, had lost the most advanced artificial intelligence in history. Who could say how long it would take to recreate it or whether humanity would ever want to again?

A car sped into the square and skidded to a halt outside

the burning row of houses. It was Mathew. He and two Watchers got out of the car.

Scott reached into his pocket and readied his revolver. Now was his chance. In one day he could rid the world of both the AI and Mathew. His finger curled around the trigger.

Mathew ran towards the building before stopping and raising his hands in apparent horror.

Scott waited for the Watchers to leave Mathew on his own, but they stayed close to him, their eyes scanning the square. Scott looked up at the sky, his chest thumping. If he could get to Mathew before they got to him ... but he had Eve to consider. It had been so long since he felt responsible for someone else. He closed his eyes. It was no good. He couldn't risk being killed. He opened his eyes. Mathew and the Watchers stood near the car, Mathew staring at the fire. He was right there, only metres away. Scott could put an end to it. He let go of the revolver in his pocket and leaned back against the wall, pushing the back of his head into the hard brick. He'd been holding his breath and now gasped, taking in air. His hand shook, and he imagined reaching for it with his other hand. In the square, Mathew and his Watchers still stared at the fire. Two more Watchers joined them and Mathew said something to them. The Watchers ran to the car, jumped in and drove away. There was one Watcher left with Mathew.

With his chest thumping, his throat contracted and his hand shook. Scott emerged from the alleyway with his revolver aimed at Mathew.

The moment he stepped out of the alley, Mathew and the Watcher whirled around and trained their revolvers on Scott.

The fire roared and its heat smothered him.

'I knew it was you,' Mathew said. 'And I knew you wouldn't be able to leave.'

Scott walked towards him.

'Do it!' Mathew said. 'Go ahead. Let's see if we get the chance to kill you too. Go on! You can't can you? You're a coward!'

Scott's revolver shook. The more he willed it to be still, the more it trembled.

'That took some doing,' Mathew said, pointing to Scott's missing hand. 'I never thought for a second you'd go to such lengths.'

'This is it,' Scott said. 'The AI's finished. We've reached the horizon – there'll be no more dates.'

Keeping his gun aimed at Scott, Mathew closed his eyes and sighed. 'You still don't understand, do you?'

'I understand it all. You're a murderer.'

'No!' Mathew shouted. 'Why won't you see the truth?'

'All those people! Billions of people!' Scott said. 'Dead. Because of you.'

'Saved,' Mathew said. 'Because of me! Billions of people saved. Every one of them. *Saved*, Scott.'

Scott saw something in Mathew's eyes he'd not seen there before. Pity – for him.

'Juliet is saved,' Mathew said, his voice soft.

'No. She's dead. Because of you!'

'She is there because He was ready for her.'

'You killed her!'

'I loved her, Scott. More than I loved any other person on this planet.'

'You don't know the meaning of the word!'

'I do. Believe me. I do.'

Scott came closer, his arm tense, no longer shaking but rigid with intent.

'You can't do it,' Mathew said. 'You don't believe in it enough. When you believe something, Scott, when you truly believe, you find freedom. It's a release, a surrender to something bigger, to something infinitely more important.' Mathew waved a hand towards the fire. 'All of this is unimportant; it's nothing compared to Heaven, compared to being with Him.' Mathew pointed his gun at the sky, then back at Scott.

'No,' Scott said. 'You're wrong.'

'How do you know?' Mathew walked towards Scott. 'That's what I don't understand. How can you be so sure, Scott? How?'

It was a genuine question. Scott felt uneasy. 'What gives you the right to decide for everyone else? You're insane.'

'You've said that before. But tell me, please, how can you be so sure? You say you know I'm wrong. Even though for as long as mankind has recorded history, there has always been God. Always. Tell me why, now, after these thousands of years, you know better than everyone who went before.'

'You had no right to take matters into your own hands. To release those dates.'

'I sent them all to Heaven, Scott. Can you imagine? All of them in Heaven. Even Freya. Because of me.'

'Don't!'

'I granted them mercy. For every one of them. Every soul.'

'You're so sure that they are in Heaven,' Scott said, 'yet here you are – alive. Why?'

'My time will come. He will send for me when He is ready. I am his shepherd, helping His flock find its way to His side.'

'Let me send you there,' Scott said. 'I can do it. Right now.'

Fleetingly, Mathew's brow creased, and a look of confusion coloured his expression.

'You don't want to die, do you?' Scott asked.

Still Mathew didn't speak.

'You don't, do you?' Scott said again. 'After everything you've said and done, after all the people you've killed, you're scared to die yourself.'

Mathew shook his head. He smiled. 'No, Scott. I'm not scared. I look forward to it.'

'You're lying! I see it in your eyes,' Scott said. 'You don't want to die.'

'You and me,' Mathew said, wiping his lips with the back of his hand. 'It's not our time.'

'I was ready to do it.' Scott took a step closer. 'You watched me hold a gun to my head and pull the trigger. But you – you don't want to die because you're scared.'

Mathew cleared this throat. 'You knew as well as I did, it was not your time.'

'But I was ready to sacrifice myself to prove you wrong, to help the world see what you were doing.'

'In time,' Mathew said, 'you will see. You will be by His side and you will see.'

'You're wrong. There's nothing but this. It's all we have.'

Mathew shook his head. 'No, Scott. I know that's what you think. But you're wrong.' He glanced back to the fire. 'Why did you set fire to it?' he asked. 'The AI had done everything it needed to do. There was no need to destroy it now.'

'It means we are free.'

Mathew laughed. 'Free?'

'Now there is no AI, there are no dates. We are free.'

'That baby you rescued,' Mathew said. 'You think it will

give people hope. That it will be the first of many children brought into a new world. That you will begin again.'

Scott held the revolver more tightly.

'Do it!' Mathew shouted.

Scott stretched out his arm and the revolver.

'I appreciate the name her mother gave her,' Mathew said. 'Very appropriate, don't you think? Eve?'

'Leave her out of this.'

Mathew's expression altered to one of anger. 'She's mine! Don't tell me what I can and can't do with my own child!'

Scott couldn't breathe. Couldn't speak.

Mathew's face was red with anger.

Scott swallowed. 'What are you talking about?'

But he knew. It suddenly all made sense.

Mathew stared at the fire.

'Eve is *your* child?' Scott asked.

Mathew nodded.

It wasn't possible.

'But Dawn was a child,' Scott said. 'How could you?'

Frowning, Mathew wiped his forehead. He opened his mouth, searching for the words, then closed it again. Instead of speaking, he took several steps towards Scott, relaxing his arm, his gun lowering so it pointed at the ground.

'I don't understand,' Scott said. 'Why would you want to bring new life into the world when you're so intent on ending everyone else's life?'

Mathew hesitated.

Scott felt nauseous. 'You really are insane.'

'It's not insane to want to father a child. And it's not insane to want a beautiful woman to be her mother.'

'She wasn't a woman! She was a child!'

Scott remembered Dawn walking towards Hassness

House the evening she had arrived, months before. 'You're lying,' he said.

Mathew peered into Scott's eyes. 'You know I'm not.'

'But why?' Scott asked. 'It makes no sense.'

'Believe me,' Mathew said, 'I found it difficult to understand myself. But I wanted her. And I wanted—'

'Stop!' Scott shouted, his hand tightening around the gun.

'Shoot!' Mathew barked. 'Shoot! I wanted her the way I wanted all of them.'

Scott worked it all out, in that instant. All the women with Freya, this was what Mathew was doing. 'All those young women you were keeping in the room with Freya... She said they kept disappearing, then coming back. She didn't know where, but they were all upset afterwards... That was you?'

'Something special is happening. Here. Because of me. Because of the AI.'

Scott shook his head. He wanted to see Eve, to look into her eyes, to know for sure.

Mathew's expression was stern. 'It's my duty, Scott, to ensure that every human finds their place in Heaven. And I will not rest until it's done. This horizon you speak of is the beginning of the end. There are now under ten thousand people left in the world. And all of them – every one of them – is here, on this small island. We have worked from the outer edges of the globe, towards the epicentre of it all, to here. And now, it will be upon this island, Britain, where the last of humanity will finally ascend.'

'You can't know there aren't other survivors around the world.'

'I do know that. I took every last name from the AI. And each one of them has been accounted for.' Mathew reached into his coat and took out a black book. 'In here is what remains of humanity. I have nineteen Watchers who are helping to ensure that everyone on this list finds their rightful place by His side. We will find and help every one of them.' Mathew looked at his revolver. 'Scott, you must see this is the right thing to do. You *must* see it.'

'You're wrong.'

The fire crackled.

'So what happens now?' Mathew asked, raising his gun again and pointing it at Scott. 'We shoot each other? Take our chances?'

'Is that what you want?' Scott asked.

'I want to help you,' Mathew said. 'I want to help you and everyone else.'

Scott held his gun out in front of him, his eyes on the revolver pointed back at him.

'You won't do it,' Mathew said. 'I know. I've seen this. It was the last thing the AI gave to me.'

Scott was only a metre away from Mathew. 'What?'

'You and me, Scott, we're tied together. Forever. That's something the AI has shown me. Like now. I know you will do as I ask.'

'What you ask?'

Mathew wiped his top lip with his free hand. 'I didn't understand what the AI was showing me at the time. But I see it now. Eve is in danger, and you must go to her. If there's time.'

'What are you talking about?'

'She's in danger, Scott.'

'You're lying.'

'There's a group of survivors. In Birmingham.'

How did Mathew know about them?

'You know, don't you?' Mathew asked, his eyes opening

wider. 'You know about this group? They're deluded – like you. They want to begin again.'

Scott said nothing.

'There is a man with them. He was a Watcher. But now he is with them. His name is Samuel. He knows who Eve is and he wants to kill her.'

'Samuel? You're lying,' Scott said again, recalling the name.

'You know I'm not.' Mathew's expression became sympathetic. 'You have no choice, Scott. I see what happens. You will lower your gun, turn around and go to Birmingham to find Eve.'

'Why does Samuel want to kill her?'

Mathew hesitated then said, 'Because of what she is.'

Scott couldn't keep up. His mind raced, his heart thudding. 'What she is?'

Mathew smiled, pride colouring his expression. 'She is a New Human.'

'A what?'

'She is the future, Scott.'

'You're not making any sense.'

A car turned the corner. Watchers.

'There's no time to lose, Scott. Go to Birmingham and save her.'

Scott's hand shook even more. He gritted his teeth, the muscles along his back and across his shoulders tightening with rage.

'If you shoot me,' Mathew said, 'I will shoot you, and Samuel will kill Eve. There will be time for you and me to finish this – later. We're not done here. You know that as well as I do.'

Scott glanced behind him. 'This isn't over,' he said.

'Without the AI, you're in the dark. You don't know anyone's dates. Humanity will survive. Will begin again.'

'No. It's nearly over,' Mathew said. 'Our time on this Earth, in this hell, is nearly over. We have earned a way back to Heaven and I will ensure every last soul finds their way back home.'

The car skidded to a stop next to Mathew.

Scott and Mathew lowered their guns at the same time.

Scott retreated into the alleyway and then ran.

FIFTY-SEVEN

GEORGE HELD Eve in his arms. Her eyes opened and closed sleepily.

'Give her to me,' a woman said, pointing a revolver at him.

'Move real slow,' another woman said. 'Give her to us.' Her voice was more sympathetic, even pleading.

George held on to Eve more tightly. 'I can't do that,' he said. 'How did you find me?'

The two women, their revolvers still pointed at him, glanced at one another.

The younger of the two women lowered her revolver a little. 'There aren't many people who drive through Birmingham these days. In fact, there are none.'

'What are you doing with her?' the dark-haired woman asked.

'What do you mean? I'm looking out for her until her ... until Scott returns.'

'Scott?' the other woman asked. 'Who's that?'

'He's her ... he's her guardian.'

'Where is he?'

'In London. Destroying the AI.'

The dark-haired woman lowered her gun. 'What?'

George relaxed. 'I have no idea. Believe me, I asked him the same thing.' He stepped away from the wall.

The dark-haired woman pushed her gun into her coat pocket. 'A man, alone, with a baby? With a girl? It looks suspicious. We know what young female children are worth.'

George's face curled up on itself. 'Jesus, no. What are you saying?'

For a moment, the women looked embarrassed. 'I'm sorry, but you have to understand the things we've seen.'

'Female children?' George asked.

'There are far fewer women now. They've become a rare commodity.'

'Commodity?'

'It hasn't taken long, since the Rapture, for things to return to a state of the strongest being the most dominant.'

'You mean men?'

'Well, yes.'

'I'd never hurt her,' George said, wincing at having to say so. 'She's only a baby. I'm looking after her.'

The women came closer. The dark-haired woman stroked Eve's arm.

Eve watched, her eyes moving from the woman's hand to her eyes and back again.

'What do you want?' George asked.

'We want you to come with us, join our group,' the dark-haired woman said.

'Are you the people Scott said were in Birmingham, broadcasting on the radio?'

The younger woman nodded. 'Yes. Will you come with us?'

George nodded faintly.

'This way,' the younger woman said.

They led George past the hotel to a parked van. The younger woman opened the door and encouraged George to enter. He peered inside then, holding Eve tightly, got in.

'Hello,' said the man in the driver's seat.

George stared at him, holding Eve more tightly.

'My name's Samuel,' the man said, offering his hand.

George still stared at the tall, thin man, unsure.

'Samuel's with us,' the younger woman said, stepping up into the passenger side of the van.

'She's beautiful,' Samuel said, smiling at Eve.

'Where are we going?' George asked, his eyes on the man in the driving seat.

'Somewhere safe,' the younger woman said.

George looked through the window at the hotel. The dark-haired woman got in beside him and slid the van door shut. 'Let's go,' she said, tapping the driver on the shoulder.

FIFTY-EIGHT

SCOTT WOKE, his body shivering. The fire had gone out. Outside the sun had risen. His copy of A Christmas Carol *was on the floor, fanned out. He took more firewood, pushed it into the hearth and used paper to start the fire again. It took longer than the night before, but finally the fire was healthy enough for him to add more firewood and leave alone.*

He stood and looked around the room in daylight. It was old-fashioned but grand. Upstairs, there was every chance he'd find dead bodies. He had never got used to it, but he had discovered a way of searching for bodies that made it manageable. He told himself over and over that it was nothing out of the ordinary, that the dead were absent, that they had no feelings or thought for him being there.

The stair creaked beneath his foot. He told himself to walk up the stairs as though it was the normal thing to do, that what he was about to do was necessary. When he reached the wide landing he paused to listen. It was silent. He opened the first door he came to. He knew what he'd find but it was still a shock. It always was. Two elderly people, a man and a woman, lying arm in arm on the bed, a thin cotton sheet covering them. He closed the door without a sound.

Behind the next door was an elderly man, alone, naked, lying on top of the sheets, a framed photograph held to his chest.

The third and fourth rooms were empty. The fifth held a young man and woman with a newborn baby between them. Each of them was still, their bodies naked, their skin pale and translucent. Scott closed the door quickly. A hand to his mouth, he rested his forehead against the door. He thought about going back downstairs and coming back again later. But he needed to know how many bodies there were to burn. He opened the next door. On the bed was a woman with two children: a boy aged around eleven and a girl, no more than six or seven. The three of them wore pyjamas. Scott stumbled towards a wooden stool at the end of the bed. He sat before he fell. He couldn't take his eyes off the girl. Her pyjamas were pink, decorated with blue cartoon elephants. She held a soft pink elephant. Scott couldn't move. He wanted to go back in time, change everything that had happened, stop this from happening. This was not how things should have been. In the image of a mother holding her children was the absence of everything Mathew spoke about. There was no Heaven. There was no Second Coming. There was only this, in front of him: death. He stood and left the room, closing the door behind him, knowing full well this would be the last room he'd come back to. The girl would be the last body he burned.

FIFTY-NINE

SCOTT DROVE AS FAST as he dared along the motorway and A roads. He ignored the self-drivers pulled over at the side of the road, dead bodies still in their cars, facing the way they were going, as if waiting in a never-ending traffic jam.

He tuned the radio, searching for the message he'd heard from the survivors in Birmingham.

Ahead he saw the tall, unfinished buildings at the centre of the huge city. Scott thought back to when he first visited Birmingham with Paul. He'd followed him, with no idea what was going to happen. Now it felt he was living a different life. Again the idea came to him that he was not in control of any of it. He wanted that feeling back – to be in control, to make choices. But he didn't know what that meant any more.

Other roads branched off the motorway, winding and turning, above then below other roads. The road to the left led towards the city centre. Scott stepped on the accelerator a little more, eager to find Eve. What Mathew had said made little sense. But because it was also specific, Scott knew there must be some truth to it. He had to find out what was happening.

The 4x4 sped along the slip road towards an expressway several lanes wide. He entered a tunnel. Inside, the sound of the engine and the tyres on tarmac roared. He exited the tunnel. A voice came on the radio. It was the same recording. He looked around for a place to park, where he would be seen – and found – easily. The roads were congested with self-drivers that had pulled over when the Rapture happened, and Scott was finding it harder to find a way through. Up ahead was Birmingham library, the place he had told George to meet him. It wasn't yet midday, the time they'd agreed, but he hoped there was a chance he'd be there. Outside it was a huge square, where several people lay on the ground where they'd fallen. He weaved through the bodies and stopped. He got out and looked all around. There was no sign of anyone.

'Hey!' he shouted, his voice echoing. A flock of pigeons rose from behind the library then descended again.

Scott waited, but saw and heard nothing. He ran back to the 4x4, opened the door and slammed his hand against the horn. The sound was immense in the enclosed square. Again more birds rose and swept across the sky, this time not descending again but flying away from the library. Scott kept his hand on the horn, all the time scanning for any sign of people.

Finally, he let go. The sound of dogs barking in the distance rose and fell away. He walked away from the 4x4 and again stood out in the open.

'Hey!' he shouted. 'Where is she?'

He spun, looking in every direction.

And they were there. Standing outside another glass

building, to one side of the library, staring back at Scott. He ran towards them.

They were women, both holding revolvers, pointed at him.

'Stop!' one woman said.

Scott got close enough to see their faces, then stopped, holding up his hands. 'Where is she?'

The younger woman glanced at the other woman, whose eyes were fixed on Scott.

'Who?' the older, dark-haired woman asked.

'Eve. She's a baby. Do you have her?'

The dark-haired woman lowered her revolver and glanced at the younger woman to do the same.

'Please,' Scott asked. 'Do you have her? Is she safe?'

'She's fine,' the older woman said. 'Are you Scott?'

'How do you know that?'

'We can explain everything. This is Tess,' she said, nodding to the younger woman. 'I'm June.'

'How do you know who I am?' Scott asked again.

'Your friend,' June said, pushing the revolver into her coat pocket. 'George. He said you would be looking for him.'

Scott sighed with relief. 'Please, take me to them.'

June led the way along the side of the glass building and onto a narrow street where a van was parked.

'Get in,' she said.

Scott did as he was told and the two women got into the front.

'Is there a man with you,' Scott asked, 'who was once a Watcher?'

The two women glanced at each other.

'Yes,' Tess said. 'Samuel. Why? How do you know him?'

Scott covered his face with both hands. He recalled him – the Watcher Freya said helped get Scott to the surgical-machine the day he tried to shoot himself, who had helped them find Juliet. 'We need to hurry. Where's Eve?'

'She's five minutes away,' June said, starting the engine.

'What's wrong?' Tess asked.

Scott peered out of the windscreen. 'Samuel wants to kill Eve. I have to get to her, make sure she's safe.'

'What?' June said with a confused smile.

'He wants to kill Eve,' he said again.

'Why?' Tess asked. 'That's insane. Why would he do that?'

Scott didn't know how much to tell them so said nothing. 'Please, just hurry.'

Finally, the van stopped outside a row of houses. The two women got out. Scott tried his door but it was locked.

'Open it!' he shouted, banging against it.

The door slid open and Scott jumped out. 'Where is she?'

Tess pointed to one of the houses. Scott ran to the front door and banged against it. He winced at a shooting pain rifling through his arm. June arrived beside him and took Scott's arm, glancing at the stump where his arm ended.

'Please,' she said, trying to calm him. 'Let me.' She knocked on the door in a particular way: three times, followed by a pause, followed by three quicker knocks. A moment later, the door opened.

Scott pushed past the woman in the doorway. 'Where is she?'

'Wait!' June shouted. 'It's okay, Harriet,' she said to the woman who'd opened the door. 'This way,' she said to Scott.

He followed her through the house. Scott heard shouting. June glanced at him and quickened her pace.

They followed the shouting to a room upstairs. George

was hammering his fists against a closed door, demanding to be let inside.

'Scott!' George said when he saw him, relief in his eyes. Then his expression changed to one of desperation. 'Samuel has Eve in there. I can't get to her.'

There was a window in the door. Scott looked through it and saw Samuel hunched over Eve.

'What is he doing?' June asked.

Scott shouted through the glass. 'Samuel!'

Samuel spun around, his face flushed.

'Let me in!' Scott said.

Samuel turned back to Eve. Something glinted in his hand. Beside him, a surgical-machine lay dormant, but poised, waiting for instructions.

'Why does he have that?' he said, turning to June. 'The surgical-machine?'

She shook her head. 'I don't know. He asked us to take one from the hospital. He said it would be useful.'

Scott tried the handle but it wouldn't budge. He thumped against the door. 'Let me in!'

Samuel placed a hand on Eve's arm and leaned towards her.

'What are you doing?' Scott shouted. 'Let go of her.'

In desperation, Scott kicked the door. 'Stop! Leave her alone!'

Holding Eve's arm in one hard, a needle in the other, Samuel glanced back at Scott, his eyes apologetic.

'No!' Scott shouted.

Samuel's hand shook, the needle wavering back and forth.

'Please,' Scott said, his face pushed up to the window. 'Please! Don't...'

The needle in Samuel's hand trembled, hovering above Eve's arm.

Scott inhaled and tried to think. 'Talk to me,' he said, lowering his voice. 'Why are you doing this?'

Samuel walked over to the door. 'I have to. I'm sorry, but I have to.' He turned away.

Scott's eyes watched the needle. Eve lay on her back, kicking and gurgling, unaware.

'Why?' Scott asked. 'Samuel. Talk to me.'

Samuel waited.

'My name's Scott. Remember me?'

'I know who you are,' Samuel said. 'I remember. I helped Freya get you to the surgical-machine that day. It was brave. What you did, trying to prove your date wrong – it was brave.' He glanced across at the surgical-machine next to Eve. 'I helped you find Juliet.'

Scott nodded. 'Yes, you did. And those were the right things to do.'

Samuel looked surprised.

'But this … why do you want to hurt her?' Scott asked.

Samuel's eyes filled with tears. 'I wish I didn't have to. But she's an abomination.'

The word sounded strange, out of place.

'What do you mean? She's just a baby.'

Samuel shook his head. 'You don't understand.'

Scott narrowed his eyes, willing the man to back away from her. 'Open the door,' he said, trying to sound calm, reasonable. 'Please. Let's talk.'

Samuel's eyes narrowed. He looked at the needle, then at Eve, then at the door.

'Please,' Scott said. 'Open the door and talk to me.'

'You'll stop me,' Samuel said, shaking his head.

'Then tell me.' Scott inhaled deeply. 'Explain to me why you're doing it.'

Samuel closed his eyes.

'Please,' Scott said. 'I can't get inside. But please tell me why you're doing it. Make me understand.'

Samuel walked slowly towards the door, his eyes on Scott's. 'I was a Watcher,' Samuel said.

Scott put his hand into his pocket and gripped his revolver.

Samuel stared at the floor. 'I'm not a Watcher any longer.'

'Why?' Scott said, glancing past him at Eve lying on the table.

'Because what Mathew is doing is wrong. I see that now.'

'Of course it's wrong.'

'But it's not what you think.'

Scott looked impatient.

Samuel focused on Eve. 'It's inside her.'

Scott waited. 'What is?'

'The AI. It's inside her.'

'What do you mean? I don't understand.' Scott pushed the barrel of the revolver against the door handle, covering the keyhole. He recalled what Mathew had told him. *She is a New Human.* 'I was there when they did it,' Samuel said, whispering through the glass. 'To those young women. That's why I had to leave.'

'You're not making sense,' Scott said, frustrated.

Samuel pointed at Eve with the needle.

'She's Mathew's child.'

'I know,' Scott said.

'What?' George asked, but there was no time to explain.

Samuel looked taken aback. 'But she's not a normal baby. She's different. The AI is inside her.'

'What do you mean?'

'I saw the experiments. I saw them. She's part machine. She'll reach a certain age and then the replication of cells inside her will be controlled by AI and nanotechnology. It's inside her. She'll have access to machine learning, to knowledge and abilities we can only dream of.'

'She's a baby,' Scott said, not wanting to believe it. 'Just a baby.'

'No,' Samuel said, his expression darkening. 'She is Mathew's creation. His creation – humanity's replacement. So now you see why I have to destroy her. She's unnatural. Wrong.'

'No!' Scott said. 'She's just a child. You can't.'

'What choice do I have? It has to be done now, while we have the chance, if humanity is going to survive.'

Scott saw determination in Samuel's eyes.

'I'm sorry,' Samuel said. Then he frowned, his head tilting to one side, reading what Scott was about to do.

Scott pulled the trigger and fired through the keyhole. The bullet hit Samuel's hip, and he spun and fell to the ground. The door swung open.

Clearly in pain, Samuel got to his feet. He was still holding the needle. Blood oozing from the bullet wound, he staggered over to Eve and jabbed the needle into her thigh.

She squealed.

'Don't come any closer!' Samuel said, his finger hovering over the plunger on the syringe. 'Stay there!'

Scott stopped. 'Please,' he said. 'Please, don't do it.'

'In time, you'll understand why,' Samuel said, wincing in pain. 'In time, you'll know why I have to do this.'

Scott pointed his gun at Samuel. 'Don't!'

Samuel bowed his head.

Out of the corner of Scott's eye he saw movement. The

surgical-machine, its arms extending, turning through several revolutions, their gears whirring. One mechanical arm struck Samuel's chest and lifted him into the air, its metal arm straining with the weight. Samuel yelled in pain.

Scott dashed across the room to pick Eve up but stopped, horrified, as he saw the surgical-machine bury its other arm, fashioned into a knife, in Samuel's back. Abruptly his screaming stopped. The surgical-machine released his body, which slumped to the floor.

Scott looked from Samuel's body, to Eve, the needle jabbed into her leg. 'What do I do?' Scott shouted.

George was beside him, holding Eve's thigh with one hand and pulling out the needle with the other. He threw the needle and syringe to the ground next to Samuel.

Scott grabbed Eve and held her. 'What happened?'

'I've no idea.' George looked from the surgical-machine to Samuel lying dead on the ground.

'The surgical-machine,' June breathed. 'How did it do that? Who was operating it?'

Scott held Eve tightly. He kissed the top of her head and she cried gently. 'It's okay. It's all okay now.'

George edged closer to the surgical-machine. 'Was it some sort of machine learning, maybe? Traces of the AI?'

Scott looked at Eve and, with a start, realised that her eyes were a different colour from their usual dark brown; they shone a deep violet, the same as the eyes of the dead. He stared at her, shocked. Flecks of silver shifted in the purple of her irises and at that moment he knew that she had – somehow – operated the surgical-machine. How? How did she do it? It shouldn't have been possible. What Mathew had said about Eve came back to him, and what Samuel had said. *She's part machine. She'll have access to machine learning, to knowledge and abilities we can only dream of. Abomination.*

He shook off the idea. No, he thought. It wasn't possible. The surgical-machine stood innocent and motionless, apart from blood dripping from one of its mechanical arms.

June walked over to the terminal that controlled the surgical-machine and pressed several buttons. 'I don't understand,' she said. 'How do I turn this thing off?'

Scott held Eve so no one else could see the colour of her eyes. He decided to keep what he'd been told to himself. Could the AI really be inside her? But he knew. It was inside her. Somehow, it was inside her.

When he looked at her again, her eyes were again dark brown.

SIXTY

BECAUSE OF WHAT had happened with Samuel, and because Scott suspected Mathew knew they were in Birmingham, they left as soon as they could and travelled to Shrewsbury, a town sixty miles away, close to the Welsh border. They found a hotel not far from the town centre for all twenty-three of them.

Scott held the stump of his arm with his hand. The pain had waited to hit him all at once, crashing over him in more and more forceful waves.

'Take these,' George said, handing him two tablets. 'I can see it's hurting.'

Scott shook his head. 'No. I'm done with all that.' He thought back to the whisky he'd drunk over the years, enhanced with all sorts of chemicals. It had made him numb. Now he wanted to feel everything he could – even pain.

George pushed the pills into his pocket. 'Suit yourself.'

Eve lay on the floor, on her front, lifting her head to look for Scott. He smiled at her and she smiled back.

'I'll be back soon,' Scott said, standing and leaving the room. George sat on the chair in front of Eve, who rocked on her tummy, trying to roll over.

'Hurry up,' George said. 'It's dinner-time.'

Scott walked into his hotel room, closed the door and locked it. He reached beneath the bed and dragged out his rucksack. He reached inside and took out the black box the AI had asked him to take with him. It was cold to the touch, its surface matt black. He turned it in his hand several times then placed it on the floor next to the bed. Slowly, he lifted his boot and stood on the box. It was solid – not like a box with circuitry inside, more like a piece of marble. He stepped off it, took the revolver from his pocket and pointed it at the box. No. He couldn't do it. He couldn't destroy all that knowledge, all that intelligence. He dropped the revolver on the bed, then picked up the box, turning it in his hands again before shoving it back into the rucksack. He had everything he needed and was ready to leave that night. He'd not told anyone but he knew the women there would look after Eve. Hassness House, sitting at the foot of the mountains, beside the lake, came to mind. He would be alone again. Looking at his arm, he imagined his hand still there, along with the tattoo. For so long he had believed it told him the date he would die, and the date still carried some importance, like today did. It was his birthday: the sixth of May. He was thirty-five.

Scott knew the others would have to stay on the run, hiding from Mathew and his Watchers. But now, without the AI to track them, they would have a chance.

The rain tapped against the window, running in thin rivulets down the glass. The world needed rain, needed to be washed clean.

Outside, a young couple, laughing, chased one another from the hotel towards the rear of the building opposite. They stopped, held each other and kissed. After everything that had happened, after all the death, now there were only thousands of people left, and all of them in Britain, some things had remained the same: people needed other people. He thought about Eve, and about what Mathew and Samuel had told him about her. He didn't understand what it all meant but, when he looked at Eve, he wanted to protect her. She frightened him too, what she had done to Samuel, her violet eyes shining like that. He didn't know what the future would be like for her, or for what remained of humanity.

The young couple beneath his window kissed and laughed in the rain before running towards another building. The young man prised open the door and crept inside, reaching behind him for the young woman's hand. They were inside and gone.

Scott made his way to the dining room. They were all there, including George, Eve sitting on his lap. Scott looked down the long table, upon which were large bowls of soup and loaves of bread. He walked to the empty seat beside George, who smiled at him. Scott kissed Eve on the head, sat down and reached for the soup ladle. Tearing the bread, he dipped it in the soup. Its warmth reminded him of the meal he'd had on the narrowboat with Freya and the others, the chain of events from that moment to this mapped out in his mind. How strange it all was. Then the young couple he'd seen earlier arrived, their faces flushed, their smiles wide. Scott watched as they sat opposite each other, glancing at one another across the table now and then. Humanity survived, he thought. That's what it did. Whatever happened, humanity survived.

Then Scott noticed June looking at him. When she saw him looking at her, she turned away, blushing. She turned to her young son, who sat beside her, encouraging him to put down his toy and eat the soup.

Scott thought back to his time at Hassness House. Of all the bodies he'd found, it was the young girl with the toy elephant he couldn't forget. She haunted him. He'd laid her on the pyre the way he might have carried her to bed in another life, covering her with a shroud instead of tucking her duvet round her chin.

The young woman he'd seen outside offered the young man she was with a chunk of her bread. He took it and dipped it into his soup. She watched him eat.

'So you're leaving?' George asked.

It caught Scott off guard.

George lowered his voice. 'I know you're packed and ready to go.'

Scott watched Eve, on George's lap, gurgle and then hiccup.

'Can't say I think it's the right thing to do,' George said. 'But she'll be looked after. Don't worry about that. Don't kid yourself though,' George went on. 'You won't find happiness there. On your own.'

There was laughter at the other end of the table. Eve reached out her arms for Scott and he took her from George and held her.

'I'm not going anywhere,' Scott said. He looked at George and smiled. 'Don't know where you got that idea.'

A look of relief came over George's face. He turned to his bowl of soup and picked up his spoon.

Scott kissed Eve and she hiccupped again. He made a silent promise to the young couple at the other end of the table and to Eve: it wasn't the end of the world ... and, if he had anything to do with it, it wouldn't be the end of humanity.

The end of Book Two

THANK YOU!

Thank you for being a reader and taking the time to read my book, the second in the Humanity Series.

I'm a new indie writer, trying my hand at writing sci-fi and dystopian fiction. For this reason, I am very much dependent on reviews. If you could spare the time, I'd be hugely grateful if you could write a review of *The Dead Horizon* for me.

And please visit sethrain.com if you'd like to stay in touch. I'd love to hear from you.

For now, all the best.

And remember: It's not the end of the world … only humanity!

Printed in Great Britain
by Amazon

46900375R00182